Praise for

Death at the Door

"Engaging . . . Understated local color and a charming cast of supporting characters will keep Annie's fans glued to the page."
—*Publishers Weekly*

"Great characters and an enjoyable story . . . After reading *Death at the Door* . . . you'll want to go back and read more of Carolyn Hart's books."
—*Fresh Fiction*

"This long-running series continues to produce strong story lines and wonderful characterization . . . The mystery's careful construction will draw in readers."
—*RT Book Reviews*

Praise for

Dead, White, and Blue

"Annie and Max . . . tackle multiple suspects and clues reminiscent of the classic mysteries offered at their bookstore. Their fans will enjoy rooting among the suspects in preparation for a denouement straight out of Agatha Christie."
—*Kirkus Reviews*

"*Dead, White, and Blue* is the perfect fiftieth book by a master of mysteries. It doesn't matter if you haven't read previous Death on Demand books. If you love mysteries, you'll want to add this latest Carolyn Hart treat to a collection of satisfying mysteries in which justice prevails."
—*Lesa's Book Critiques*

"A highly satisfying read that builds to a stunning climax."
—*Mystery Scene*

continued . . .

Death
at the
Door

CAROLYN HART

BERKLEY PRIME CRIME, NEW YORK

THE BERKLEY PUBLISHING GROUP
Published by the Penguin Group
Penguin Group (USA) LLC
375 Hudson Street, New York, New York 10014

USA • Canada • UK • Ireland • Australia • New Zealand • India • South Africa • China

penguin.com

A Penguin Random House Company

DEATH AT THE DOOR

A Berkley Prime Crime Book / published by arrangement with the author

Berkley Prime Crime Books are published by The Berkley Publishing Group.
BERKLEY® PRIME CRIME and the PRIME CRIME logo are trademarks of
Penguin Group (USA) LLC.

For information, address: The Berkley Publishing Group,
a division of Penguin Group (USA) LLC,
375 Hudson Street, New York, New York 10014.

ISBN: 978-0-425-26618-2

PUBLISHING HISTORY
Berkley Prime Crime hardcover edition / May 2014
Berkley Prime Crime mass-market edition / May 2015

PRINTED IN THE UNITED STATES OF AMERICA

10 9 8 7 6 5 4 3

Cover design by Jason Gill.
Interior text design by Laura K. Corless.

To Barbara Peters,
a grand champion of the mystery

1

Everything was set. She should be dead next week. Only one person threatened success of a carefully planned murder with a ready-made suspect. Something tipped Paul off that night at the open house. Some action forewarned him. A movement? A look? Had there been a flash of unguarded hatred when she unveiled the painting? The relish of knowing that she was enjoying her last week on earth? Fury flickered. Paul knew. There had been knowledge in his gaze, knowledge and a hardening of features. He'd always been smart.

It might turn out he was too smart to live.

Jane Corley rarely second-guessed any decision. She'd chosen to ignore the odd sensations she'd felt recently. That someone was watching her. That something was wrong.

That danger was near. Once again, firmly, she pushed away a ripple of uneasiness and concentrated on the ball. Head down. Smooth swing. Her drive was lovely, straight, and true down the fairway. She waited in the shade of a live oak as Irene swung her club.

Irene's ball scudded and jumped, landed in the rough a few yards from Jane. Irene gave a puff of disappointment. She pointed her club at the rough and the heavy silver bracelets jangled on her wrist. "Not my lucky day. Looks like I landed in the rye and you got a perfect lie. Oh well, I'll only be two strokes down."

Irene's white-and-green-plaid skirt, the latest from Golf-tini, emphasized her extraordinary legs. Blond statuesque Irene was always expensively and beautifully dressed. Her face had the aura of a woman with perhaps a few too many life experiences, but she was self-possessed and confident. She moved easily in an affluent society, though she had little to say about her background. She was also an excellent golfer though not quite up to Jane's level.

"I wouldn't count chickens," Jane murmured. She glanced at Irene's face—a shade too much makeup—but no one could deny she was dramatically attractive. Quite a coup for somewhat boring Kevin Hubbard to snare her. However, Kevin was smoothly handsome, dressed well, and belonged to the country club, a perk from his employment at Corley Enterprises. Irene lived to play golf and shop.

Jane enjoyed playing with Irene, who was ebullient and good enough to make the match interesting. Was there a tense undercurrent today? Had Kevin told her his salary was being cut? Probably not. But Irene had to know he was worried.

Jane's shoulders moved a little under her polo, a disdainful shrug. Too bad. Kevin should have done a better job. Some of the numbers for the marina shops didn't ring true. The tourist trade had picked up this past year, and that increase in shopping should be reflected in the income. Maybe Kevin had been diverting income into a fake account. Maybe she'd call in an independent accountant for an audit.

Jane stood by her bag, estimated the distance to the green. She pulled out a five iron. Tomorrow she'd float the idea of an audit. If he was skimming off the top, he'd be spooked and then she'd know what to do. She assumed her stance, waggled the club, swung through, and felt a spurt of satisfaction as the ball landed about ten feet from the hole.

She waited in the cart for Irene. Her pleasure in the afternoon was again marred by an eerie sense of something wrong. Was she disturbed by Kevin's possible dishonesty? Or the tension she felt in Irene? Or was her uneasiness caused by David's debts? He'd be livid if he knew Madeleine had come to her. Or was she disgusted by Sherry's weak will when it came to that brooding hulk of a husband? Or was Tom's roving eye bothering her? Tom would have to choose. Did that pretty young girl matter more to him than his chance to star in galleries? Did Tom really want to be a starving artist in a seedy motel, give up a studio with the finest supplies and lighting that money—her money—could buy?

Jane was rarely introspective. She despised self-absorbed people. Life was too full of color and action to waste time thinking about those who easily took offense or indulged themselves in agonies of worry. She didn't tolerate fools. She expected those around her to maintain a decent front of good humor. As she'd told more than one person, nobody gives a damn about your feelings. Everyone around her knew that any drama queen—or king—would elicit a brusque *Come off it*.

What excuse did she have? She'd never let anyone run roughshod over her and she never would, so to hell with all of them. Her expressive mouth quirked in exasperation: *Come off it, Jane.*

The wry self-admonition had no effect.

Like a horse scenting a rattlesnake, she sensed that something around her was wrong. Some event in the last few days had jarred her. Had it been the expression on someone's face? The tone of a voice? She'd been uneasy ever since the night of the open house, a preview of the exhibition of Tom's paintings at an Atlanta gallery.

Something was wrong . . .

Frankie Ford smiled as she completed the sale, murmured thank you, and held the door as Mrs. Wilkins carried out her purchase. Frankie looked after her with a slight smile, marveling at how even the most expensive fall casual wear did nothing for a dumpy figure. But Mrs. Wilkins was good-humored and a very much appreciated customer at Wyler Art Gallery. Very appreciated. Last year Mrs. Wilkins had casually spent more than a quarter million for a Georges Braque painting. Today she'd spent a mere four thousand for six watercolors by up-and-coming Pennsylvania artist Andy Smith.

Someday Tom's paintings would sell just like Andy Smith's. The thought was a little explosion of happiness.

Like most explosions, the burst of color and sound quickly faded to nothing.

Tom . . .

Frankie walked slowly toward the back of the shop. She needed to crate a collection of Lowcountry art to ship to a villa near Florence. A nice twist on art traffic. She was always careful and methodical in her work. Paintings she crated would arrive intact. Maybe she could focus her mind, push away thoughts of Tom.

Angrily she reached up and wiped away hot tears. That's all she did these days, think about Tom and try not to cry and wonder how in the world she had ever come to this point. How could love that should be so right be so wrong?

Tom Edmonds's long graceful fingers held the handle of the mallet firmly, struck the point chisel with precisely modulated force. He liked beginning a new sculpture, pitching off portions of marble, working toward the rough image in his mind. He paused, glanced at a watercolor on an easel to his right. One of his best. Sunlight glancing off the water almost drew the eye away from the figure standing on the pier.

But not quite.

Nothing overshadowed Jane's face, not in a painting, not in life. She stood at the end of a pier, one hand resting on a weathered railing, and gazed toward a distant sailboat, a dark-haired woman in summer white. He'd captured her essence, sharp humor, blunt candor, imperious certainty, vivacity that almost translated to beauty despite the strength of a too-square jaw. A transcendent personality was evident in intelligent green eyes, a compelling face.

Jane . . .

His wife.

Tom stared at the block of marble. He knew suddenly that greatness awaited him. This sculpture would be the best he'd ever done. The face—that's what he would carve. Jane's incredibly vibrant, alive, unmistakable presence would inhabit the marble, turn it from stone to a masterpiece. He'd need to have Jane come, stand there—his eyes moved to a sunlit space just past the worktable—and he would feed off her vitality, transform the marble.

His shoulders slumped. He looked around the studio, his beautiful, perfect, magnificent studio. The studio and its contents belonged to Jane. The work was his, but he didn't have the money to pay for the tools or the just-begun sculpture on a block of the finest Italian marble.

Frankie wanted him to leave, walk out, leave everything behind. He didn't have a portrait of Frankie. He wanted to paint her. Her heart-shaped face. Blue eyes deeper in color than sapphires. Chestnut hair bright as burnished copper. He couldn't live without Frankie.

His eyes rested on the marble. He had to create the sculpture of Jane.

David Corley looked up from the deck of his sailboat. He knew before he turned that the quick clip of high heels on the ramp to the dock meant trouble. He watched his wife hurry down the incline. She looked like somebody running from the zombies in a disaster movie and she was carrying that stupid dog. Something was up, that was for sure. In a raspberry linen dress and matching heels she wasn't dressed for a marina. And no hat. Madeleine avoided hot sunlight, always wore summery hats to protect her magnolia white skin. She was bareheaded.

He winced as she came aboard in those stupid heels. Not good for the deck, but the look on her face kept him silent. Was she going to start in on him again about having kids? Maybe someday. Not now. Now was the time to have fun, go places, do things. He'd looked into a safari in Kenya. Maybe that would divert her.

She was breathing fast, face drawn and pale, eyes huge.

When they met, he'd gone after Madeleine with his usual determination, been his most charming. He wanted to possess her, know she was his for the taking, her swirling ebony hair and lovely body his to touch. He felt a quiver of shock as he realized what Madeleine would look like when she was old. The aquiline face that had drawn him like a moth to flame was haggard. Even her elusive grace was absent, her movements stiff and halting. The words came out in bursts, her voice anguished.

As she spoke, his stomach knotted. Yeah, she was upset for sure. He stared at the wriggling, snuffling little dog, Madeleine's fingers clamped in Millie's silky fur. He felt a hot flicker of anger. Madeleine cared more about Millie than she did about him. Didn't she have any idea what could happen if he didn't come up with the money?

S herry Gillette slipped through the darkened room. A soft splash from the waterfall in the den masked her steps. Her throat was dry. If Jane found out, there would be hell to pay. But she had to see Roger. He'd been furious at the idea of meeting on the beach in the middle of the night, insisted she tell Jane to leave them alone, demanded Sherry come home. She had to make Roger understand. Jane never made idle threats.

She felt a flutter of panic. What could Roger do? Still, she had to warn him. She knew—the little scarlet threat of truth burned inside—that she'd created this mess. Now Jane didn't believe her when she told her the truth. Oh Lord, what was she going to do?

Paul Martin closed the study door behind him. His withdrawal again from the usual evening spent in the den watching a movie or reading would add to Lucy's concern. She knew he was worried. No surprise. Sisters knew your bare bones. He'd never been able to fool her. Not that he tried. Lucy was a woman in a thousand, recognizing boundaries, never presuming. She wouldn't ask. She'd fix his favorite meals and encourage him to take off time to sail and watch him when she thought he wasn't noticing. Lucy had come to help him when Valerie was so sick, all the chemo and radiation. Lucy loved her sister-in-law and she was a rock for Paul to lean on after Valerie died. Damn, he missed Valerie, missed her laughter, the way she always sang as she did the dishes. He knew Lucy missed her, too, and it was almost like having Valerie there as they talked of her. When he got the situation resolved, he'd take Lucy on a trip to New York, see some plays. They'd spend a sunny day in Central Park, visit the water lily pool in the Conservatory Garden.

He sipped his scotch and soda, remembering the placid peace of the pool. A face intruded into the idyllic picture, familiar features twisting for an instant into hatred. Even more chilling was the movement of lips gloating in triumph. The image had lasted for only an instant, but Paul knew what he had seen, knew what it meant. The object of that hatred was doomed. He had looked into the face of Death.

Paul put his drink on the coffee table. If he were a big-city doctor, he wouldn't know his patients as neighbors and friends, people he'd shared time with as he'd grown up, packing away into corners of his mind this fact and that about people and their histories, hidden secrets, alcoholism, abuse, instability. Perhaps what disturbed him the most was the realization that the threat didn't surprise him. He'd looked across the room and reckoned that the seeds of evil had always been there and perhaps he'd always been on alert for a moment such as this.

His partner hadn't grown up on the island. Sam would tell him he needed to take a break, that he was getting to be like an old woman who hunts for the burglar under her bed at night, that things like that didn't happen.

But they did.

Paul retrieved a nine-by-twelve sketch pad of cream-colored paper and returned to the couch. He flipped the cover and held a soft-leaded pencil above the empty page. As a matter of habit, he marked the date in the upper left-hand corner. He wanted to make a plan. He grinned a little. His dad had always asked, "What's the program?" He'd still been asking when he was in hospice in his nineties. So, what was the program?

He stared down at the sheet and the pencil began to move.

He loved creating an image on paper, making something out of nothing. His dad had thought Paul might be an artist. Dad always encouraged him. Paul had known he was good, but not good enough. Instead, sketching offered comfort when pain and caring weighed on him. The pencil moved with no particular aim, his thoughts racing, his mind willing the pencil without conscious direction. When he looked at what he'd drawn, he felt a chill. Interesting. His thought was clinical. Definitely his subconscious was at work. Not a bad likeness. Except for the lips drawn back over the teeth. His pencil had turned a symbol of grace and welcome into a harbinger of danger.

He had a choice. Contact the police or warn Death away.

He had to decide which approach to take, contact Billy Cameron or confront the threat. He'd taken a couple of days to think and was glad. At the open house when their gazes had met and locked, both had understood. Now Death was waiting to see what he would do.

The island police chief had been his patient since he was a little boy, a stocky, sandy-haired kid who grew up and joined the island police force as a rookie cop, eventually became chief. Billy, in his late thirties now, was a good man, an honest cop. He would listen and believe. What could he do? Very little. A restraining order, maybe. Possibly not even that. There was no evidence, only Paul's memory of a face.

That was not enough.

Paul realized he'd made his decision. Billy might try but there was little he could do. Paul accepted the truth. It was up to him to forestall Death, as he had so often in his life. He felt a sense of peace. He would draw the line tomorrow night. *Stop. You can't succeed. I know.*

On the pad, he sketched three witches dancing around a boiling cauldron and wrote on the pad in his slanting backhand: *Evil in a look. I saw it. I'll deal with it.* He added a stark admonition to himself, underlined the words twice, tore the sheet free.

Annie Darling leaned forward and moved one book just a fraction in the front-window display area. That should make the arrangement even, but she'd better take a look from the boardwalk to be sure. Hurrying to the front door of Death on Demand, she stepped outside.

She pretended she was just a tourist walking by, stopped and looked. Cool, baby, cool, if she said so herself. On either side of a small European village were posters of *Vogue* covers and brochures featuring Johannesburg, Venice, and Singapore. Travelers needed lots of new books to read. She sold plenty of paperbacks, but now there were links to Death on Demand for e-books as well, so she could enjoy the best of both print and digital publishing. Books with their covers out were lined up beneath the posters. The titles offered fascinating destinations: *Assassins of Athens* by Jeffrey Siger, *Death at La Fenice* by Donna Leon, *Suddenly at Singapore* by Gavin Black, *Gorky Park* by Martin Cruz Smith, and *The Shanghai Union of Industrial Mystics* by Nury Vittachi. A miniature train wound past the village with another raft of books in front of the tracks. She especially liked—

Ingrid Webb stepped outside, glasses pushed high on her thin nose, and joined Annie to peer through the plate glass. "Nice." She cleared her throat. "Why the poster?"

"Ladies who jet around the world love the latest fashions."

"Oh." Ingrid straightened the collar of a plain white cotton blouse. "Actually, I think most readers are a lot more interested in stories than outfits."

Annie played devil's advocate. "How about the books by Dorothy Howell and Ellen Byerrum? The best of both worlds."

Ingrid surrendered. "We can't keep *Death on Heels* in stock." Her head swiveled toward the door. "The phone. I'll catch it." She whirled to rush inside.

Annie followed. As she started down the broad central corridor, she took pleasure, as she always did, in the best mystery bookstore north of Murder on the Beach in Delray Beach, Florida. Hundreds and hundreds of books in honey-colored gumwood bookcases, an American Cozy retreat with comfortable old chairs and Whitmani ferns in blue pottery pots, a raffish stuffed raven to remind of Edgar Allan Poe's immortal verse, a coffee bar featuring mugs inscribed with the names of famous mysteries, welcoming tables and chairs, a fireplace where flames crackled merrily in the winter. And, of course, the regal presence of the bookstore's gorgeous, imperious feline, Agatha.

Annie paused at a side table where Agatha stretched on a silk cushion and smoothed silky black fur. "World's finest cat."

A soft purr indicated agreement.

It would be fun to add a handful of fashion mysteries to the display. Should she gather up the books, return to her task? Hey, all work and no play was not the island way. She turned toward the coffee bar. Ingrid had already brewed a pot of the finest Kona coffee. Annie filled a mug to the brim, noted the book title and author inscribed in red: *Home Sweet Homicide* by Craig Rice. Annie decided it was time to reread the book, one of her all-time favorites.

She paused for a moment in the center of the coffee bar area to admire the watercolors hung above the fireplace. Maybe this month someone other than Henny Brawley or Emma Clyde would be the first to identify each painting by title and author to win a free month of coffee and a new book.

In the first painting, a slender young woman in a crisp white shirt and black slacks paused on her Segway to survey a side hall of a shopping mall. On one side was a manicure salon, a reptile store, a teen shop, and a sporting goods store. On the other, a little kid stuff-your-own-animal store, a dress boutique, a sunglasses emporium, and a toy store. Reddish-brown hair framed an intelligent, expressive face. She had an air of authority.

In the second painting, lightning flashed against heavy clouds in the night sky. Mist almost obscured dim light from lampposts at the periphery of a car lot and the woman bending to look closely at the grille of a large black sedan. Her body was tensed, her concentration absolute.

In the third painting, smoke coiled in the evening sky above a white frame house. Fire trucks blocked access. A lean man in a blue shirt, string tie, and black trousers hurried as fast as he could across the ground, obviously favoring one leg. His face mirrored despair. A big woman, red hair all loose, face smudged with soot, Astros T-shirt grimed by smoke, moved toward him.

In the fourth painting, a woman grasping a flashlight

splashed through a foot of water toward a woman tightly bound to an overturned chair and desperately struggling to keep her head above rising water in an unlighted room.

In the fifth painting, a slender blonde behind the wheel of a sporty Mazda stared in shock at the bruised and battered face of a fortyish man wearing a Stetson and sunglasses as he slid into the passenger seat.

Annie nodded approval and returned up the central aisle. At the traditional mystery section, she carefully placed the mug atop the bookcase and gathered titles by Laura Bradley, Dixie Cash, and Nancy J. Cohen as well as Dorothy Howell and Ellen Byerrum. The colorful covers would make a great addition to the display.

She plucked *Shear Murder* from the shelf—

"Annie." Ingrid's voice held sadness.

Annie turned to look toward the cash desk.

Ingrid held up the phone. "Henny couldn't get you on your cell."

The cell was in her purse in the storeroom.

"Terrible news. Paul Martin's dead." Ingrid's eyes were wide with shock. "Annie, they think he shot himself."

A nnie waited in the alley behind Death on Demand. She wasn't dressed to go to a house of mourning. This morning she'd chosen a pale blue blouse with an embroidered flower hem, beige linen slacks, and sandals, comfortable and perfect for a fall afternoon among books, happy clothes for a happy day. Instead, the day was somber, framed by darkness.

You never knew what a day would bring. Some days were

pleasant, memorable only in that her life was good and she often smiled. Some days were blessed by a quick elusive thrill of sheer happiness, the beauty of water shimmering in sunlight, the sound of her husband's voice, the ineffable grace of a hummingbird. Some days were hard, the rough reality of death disrupting the daily spin of ordinary life. When everyday tasks no longer mattered, the precious nature and fragility of the commonplace became apparent.

Lucy Ransome, a widow, had arrived on the island three years earlier to help her brother Paul take care of his dying wife. Annie had worked on church rummage sales with Lucy. She was much older, nearing seventy, but she added a spark to any group, good-humored, outgoing, kind. She'd been a statistician for diabetes research. She had a careful, quick mind and spoke precisely. She and Henny Brawley, Death on Demand's most enthusiastic customer, loved to talk about mysteries as they ironed linens for the Altar Guild.

Annie heard a familiar rumble as Henny's old black Dodge turned into the alley. Henny kept the car in good repair. The motor was loud but steady. Annie hurried down the steps from the loading dock and climbed into the passenger seat.

Henny, too, was in fall casual wear, a white-and-blue cotton pullover and navy slacks. "I was at the church, putting fresh candles in the chapel. Father Jim told me." Henny's narrow face was grave, her dark eyes somber.

Annie took a quick breath. "Suicide?" Her tone was doubtful.

The Dodge chugged out of the alley. "That's what Billy thinks." Henny sounded weary.

Annie's forlorn hope that Henny's source was wrong

wilted. Island Police Chief Billy Cameron gathered evidence before he spoke. Billy knew his island and the people on it. He was a native of Broward's Rock and it was very likely he'd been a patient of Paul Martin's. Paul's practice drew most of the old island families.

Annie sighed. "I can't imagine Paul doing something like that."

Henny drove for a moment in silence. She turned onto Sand Dollar Road. They drove beneath a canopy of intertwined live oak branches. Finally, she spoke. "We don't know what is going on in someone's life."

"He was a wonderful doctor." Annie spoke with a catch in her voice. She looked at the magnificent pines that bordered the road. Sunlight slanted through the canopy above, dappling the road. Paul Martin would have driven this way many times. He liked to fish and had kept a boat in the marina overlooked by the shops. Annie had waved to him just last week. He'd looked like what he was, an island man, used to boats and water, billed cap, cotton shirt rolled to his elbows, faded khakis, scuffed Docksides. He'd looked happy and carefree and had given her a thumbs-up before he started down the ramp.

"The last time I saw him, he looked great. Maybe a little tired." He wasn't young. Midsixties. "He was happy."

"That was then," Henny said quietly.

Annie struggled with the concept. One week a man heads out to fish in the Sound, the next week . . . "How did it happen?"

"Muzzle to the temple, pulled the trigger."

Annie blocked the image that came to mind. She wanted to remember Paul Martin as he started down the ramp to his boat, his lean, somewhat ascetic face relaxed, lines of care and worry smoothed out, moving with the ease of a man who knew his way around a dock, a little slump-shouldered from years at a desk but still lithe, agile. Alive.

"He loved being a doctor." They drove in silence. It wasn't far now to the residential area near downtown. They passed antebellum homes, an occasional modern brick ranch, wooden cabins, the variety that was part of the charm of the older streets. A few more blocks and they'd leave sunlight behind, step into a stricken house. Dead.

By his own hand . . .

Annie clenched her hands. "It must be true if Billy thinks so, but—" She twisted in her seat to look at Henny. "Do you remember when Gail Barnett took that overdose?" Annie didn't wait for an answer. Of course Henny remembered. Gail had been in her fifties and her husband dumped her for his secretary and cleaned out their bank account, leaving her in debt and facing treatment for leukemia. "Pamela Potts was at the hospital that night. She said Paul wouldn't give up. He worked and worked and all the while he kept saying, 'Dammit, don't throw away life because of a jerk. Life's precious. Come on, Gail. Live, dammit, live!'" Gail lived. Several years later she met a retired accountant and they married and the last they'd heard they were somewhere in the Caribbean on a sloop. "Henny, he wouldn't."

Henny gave her a look full of sorrow and sadness as they drove past the gates, said again, "We don't know what's going on in someone's life. For now, we need to be there for Lucy."

She made another turn and they pulled into Calhoun Street, a shaded curving street that should have been quiet on an October afternoon. Halfway up the block, Henny stopped behind a row of cars. A woman carrying a casserole dish was entering a two-story white frame house that was a living monument to the Lowcountry's past, when island roads were unpaved, summer meant wide-open windows to catch the prevailing southwesterly breezes, and houses sat high on tabby foundations, the better to survive storm surges. Built in the early 1800s, double verandahs gave the house a jaunty air. A half-dozen cars filled a narrow front drive. Several more were parked in the street.

Annie recognized the rector's modest beige Toyota. Priests came in times of joy and in times of mourning. Father Jim was balding, plump, affable, and a rock for his parishioners.

Henny moved briskly, Annie hurrying to keep up. They didn't knock or push the bell. Times such as these didn't require formality. Henny opened the door, heard the sound of muted voices.

Pamela Potts, always a stalwart figure in times of crisis, greeted them softly, blue eyes lighting when she saw them. Blond hair drawn back into a chignon, she was a sturdy figure of calm in a white ruffled blouse and scallop-hemmed violet skirt. "Lucy's in the living room."

Henny and Annie stepped through an archway into a living room with easy chairs, a well-worn sofa, and mahogany end tables dotted with frames holding family pictures, photos through the years of Paul and his wife, Valerie, and their kids, Ellen and Pete. The kids—long grown now—would be coming. Ellen taught biology in Grand Rapids. Her husband, Jay, had an insurance agency. They had three children. Pete was a surgeon in Philadelphia, a huge Phillies fan, and he and his wife, Sue Lee, had seven boys who all played baseball.

The room was homey and comforting with turquoise drapes and pale gray walls. The drapes were open for sunlight to spill inside. A French Empire clock and matching Dresden figures sat on the Adam mantel above the fireplace. Traces of water glistened on the potted ferns that sat on either side of the hearth. Pamela Potts would have seen to everything, including watering the plants.

They nodded at familiar faces and walked across the room to the couch where Lucy sat, a small figure slumped in sadness. Lucy managed a smile as Henny reached down and gave her a hug. Annie touched her arm. "I'm sorry, Lucy."

"Thank you for coming." She gestured toward several Chippendale straight chairs. "Come and join us. Pamela brought in some chairs from the dining room. I was telling everyone what happened . . ." Her voice was steady, but her blue eyes held enormous sorrow and shock.

As Lucy talked, Annie and Henny slipped into two of the chairs. Annie knew that no matter how painful it was for Lucy to describe Paul's last evening, the telling helped. When loved ones face final, irrevocable separation, words that speak of the end are the beginnings of a path to acceptance. What is, is.

". . . something was bothering him this week. He went to his office every night after dinner instead of relaxing in the den. Last night when we got home from a party, I was very tired. He said he'd be up in a little while. That was the last time I saw him. But I thought as we drove home from the party"—her voice was plaintive—"that he seemed better than he'd been for a while, more at peace."

Janet Bristow nodded decidedly. Tall, broad-shouldered, strong-jawed, she was a decided kind of woman, president of a half-dozen clubs, blunt, offering opinions whether welcome or not. "Mark my words, he'd made up his mind. Nothing you could do, Lucy. It wouldn't have mattered if you'd stayed downstairs." Her pugnacious expression dared anyone to disagree.

"I didn't know he had a gun." Lucy's gaze moved toward the hall. "Of course, I'd never looked in his desk drawers. But the bottom right-hand drawer was pulled out and there was a half-full box of cartridges. The police said the gun couldn't be traced. It was old, some kind of Army .38 Special. I suppose he'd had it since he was in the service."

She massaged one temple. "Anyway, I went upstairs and took a shower. Maybe that's when . . . I don't know. I went to bed and fell asleep. I didn't hear anything. This morning I went down and fixed breakfast but when I didn't hear Paul stirring around, I went back upstairs and his bed hadn't been slept in. That's when I started to look. I couldn't imagine where he could be. His study door was closed and he always left it open when he wasn't using it. I found him. He had fallen face-forward on his desk. There was blood . . . I came around the desk and the gun was lying on the floor by his hand."

The church was filled to overflowing, folding chairs set up in the narthex. Annie and Max sat on the Epistle side midway to the front. They knelt, heads bowed as Father Jim read from the burial service: "'The Lord shall preserve thee from all evil; yea, it is even he that shall keep thy soul.

The Lord shall preserve thy going out, and thy coming in, from this time forth for evermore . . .'"

She felt a sting of tears. There was always sadness at funerals, even those where family and friends celebrated completion of lives fully and well lived. She had a feeling that those gathered now were bewildered, some of them resentful, and among the family there could only be emptiness, despair that they had not seen or understood or helped.

Paul Martin had left them of his own volition. Not in the goodness of time.

Paul, why?

2

Annie retrieved the newspaper from a perilous perch on a granite bench near the goldfish pond in the front yard. The delivery woman seemed to have unerring aim, but Annie was always amazed the *Gazette* wasn't frolicking with goldfish. She was late getting home—a book club from Beaufort came for the afternoon—so she trotted around to the back porch and hurried up the broad steps. Lights shone in the kitchen. She opened the door and was greeted by a delectable scent. She paused. "Mmm, something smells wonderful."

"Flank steak simmering with onion and bay leaf, soon to be Cuban shredded beef seasoned with sauterne and Burgundy." Max emptied the contents of a bowl into the skillet, adjusted the flame.

"Wonderful." Every bite would be delicious. She dropped her purse on the wooden table by the door. "Sorry I'm late.

You wouldn't believe how many books the Beaufort ladies bought." Book clubs were a bookstore's best friend. "Ran out of copies of Hank Phillippi Ryan's new suspense novel."

Max looked over his shoulder. "The rice should almost be done."

To her continued delight, Max was, in her estimation, not only the best-looking dude on the island, tall, blond, blue-eyed, broad shouldered, and muscular, he was a wonderful chef. Moreover, she admired his willingness, despite an inherent predilection toward play rather than work, to create a truly unusual business. Confidential Commissions definitely was not a private detective agency, but Max was always willing to help people solve problems, whether it was a search for a long-missing uncle, a Civil War photograph in an archive, or the best present for a stymied husband to give the wife who had everything. The last request had resulted in a bushel of quahogs direct from Cape Cod for the client's New England–born wife.

Annie slid onto a seat at the marble counter on the center island. She opened the *Gazette*, intending to take a quick look. The main story was usually about a zoning disagreement or a controversy on the city council.

Her eyes widened. "Max."

He turned from the stove, caught by her tone.

She read the headline. "'Island Socialite Battered to Death.' Marian wrote the story." The *Gazette*'s ace reporter, Marian Kenyon, was an old friend. Annie read the story aloud.

"'Jane Jessop Corley, thirty-four, island native and member of a longtime island family, was battered to death in the family room of her home at One Corley Lane sometime

Monday afternoon, Police Chief Billy Cameron revealed in a news conference this morning.'"

Annie lifted her eyes from the page. "We saw Jane yesterday morning at Paul's funeral. Someone killed her that afternoon." Her voice held disbelief.

Max joined her at the counter.

Annie remembered Jane in the receiving line in the parish hall, vividly alive, visibly sad. Annie had heard a few words of her condolences to Paul's son. "Paul was part of our lives. Dad always turned to him when things went wrong. He was our doctor but so much more than that . . ."

Annie took a breath. "'Chief Cameron said the weapon appeared to be a sculptor's mallet belonging to Jane Corley's husband, Tom Edmonds, twenty-nine. Edmonds told police he wasn't sure when he last saw the mallet. Edmonds said he hadn't been working on a sculpture this week. Edmonds told police he could not explain the mallet's presence in the house.

"'A 911 call from the Corley home was received by the police dispatcher at four forty-nine P.M. Monday. When police arrived, Edmonds led them to the scene of the crime. According to Chief Cameron, Edmonds said he discovered his wife's body shortly before five. The body was lying on the floor of the family room near a pool table.'"

"The Corley house is pretty remote, surrounded by acres of woods. You have to know where it is to find it," Max said.

Annie understood. No one would simply wander by the house. The next sentence confirmed his thought. "'Chief Cameron said there was no indication of a break-in at the home nor was there evidence of a struggle. He also said the victim's purse was found on a side table in the main entrance hallway and its contents appeared undisturbed. An autopsy is planned, but the initial report from the office of the medical examiner indicates death as a result of blunt trauma to the back of her head.'"

Max stepped to the stove, checking the rice. "That explains why she didn't call for help. If she was hit from behind, she didn't know she was in danger."

Annie nodded. "'Edmonds told police he had not seen his wife since lunch. He said that he went to his studio in the garden and was framing a canvas. He finished about four-thirty but had a drink by the pool before entering the house. Police said there is a wet bar in the poolside cabana. Edmonds told police his wife was in good spirits at lunch, but that he had not seen her since that time. Edmonds told police he heard no sounds from the house.

"'Chief Cameron said also present in the house that afternoon were Kate Murray, Ms. Corley's personal assistant, and Sherry Gillette, a houseguest. Both were upstairs and were unaware of the crime when the body was found. Gertrude Anniston, the cook, spent part of the afternoon grocery shopping. She was otherwise occupied in the kitchen and did not leave the kitchen.

"'Ms. Corley's first husband was the golf pro Baldwin McCrae. They were divorced in 2011. Ms. Corley married Edmonds in 2012. She retained her maiden name after both of her marriages and was the daughter of the late Bolton Corley and Sherrybeth Jessop Corley . . .'"

Annie stopped quoting. "Lots of family stuff. It all boils down to Old South and rich. Her great-grandfather married an Eastern railroad heiress." Annie shook her head. "Jane was so hugely alive. Bigger than life." Annie's voice was small. "Everybody else faded when they were near her. She had a strong personality, but why would anyone kill her? And it doesn't seem likely a stranger attacked her." It wasn't only the remoteness of the house that argued against a stranger. The island had never been host to dangerous vagrants. Broward's Rock was far enough offshore and accessible only by a ferry, so people came for a purpose, to live or vacation.

Max moved back to the counter and eased the flank steak onto a cutting board, used two forks to shred the hot meat. "That sounds bad for Tom. Only he or someone familiar with his studio would be able to get that mallet." He gestured toward the skillet with a fork. "Will you check? It's on simmer."

Annie folded the paper and popped down from her seat. She gently stirred the onions, green pepper, and chopped garlic. "The story's definite that his mallet was the weapon."

Max was crisp. "Not only is the house remote, the studio is definitely off the main track. You have to have been there to even know it exists. That narrows down the number of people who could have taken the mallet to Tom or maybe a handful of others."

Annie set the table, admiring the vase with a gorgeous marigold arrangement. She'd picked the flowers early that morning. She took a deep sniff. She loved the woody, pungent scent, but this evening the smell reminded her of the fall garden tour and Jane Corley's magnificent garden with roses that ranged from ghost white to ruby red and every shade in between and beds of riotous marigolds. "I wonder if Tom locks his studio. Probably not. The Corley garden is almost on a scale with Magnolia Plantation, tons of trees and shrubs and ponds and lots of separate areas. One of the ponds has huge cypresses. In the spring when the azaleas bloom, they are reflected in the water. It's gorgeous. His studio is about halfway between the house and the cypress pond."

Max carried the shredded beef to the skillet. "Somebody took the mallet to the house. You don't sculpt in a den."

Annie slipped into her chair as Max carried the steaming bowl to the table. "I hope it's not Tom." She liked Tom. He reminded her of old daguerreotypes of Stephen Foster, dark hair brushed back smoothly, deep-set eyes beneath a high forehead, a long nose, nice mouth, a sensitive, intelligent face with an aura of dreamy remoteness. He receded into a shadowy background when Jane was around. Annie had thought them an unlikely couple, though Tom had a definite appeal. He was not only an artist and a good one, he was handsome and, when encouraged, charming though diffident in conversation.

Max reached over and took her hand. "I hope not. But Billy will do the right thing."

Emma Clyde's deep voice was brusque. "As Marigold often points out to Inspector Houlihan, wisdom is rarely conventional and conventional wisdom is rarely wise." The island mystery author's spiky hair was an improbable hydrangea red this morning, almost a match for the splash of crimson in one of the mystery watercolors above the fireplace.

Death on Demand hadn't opened yet. In the fall and winter, the bookstore opened at ten. Annie had arrived early, hoping to get off some book orders to get ahead of the Christmas rush, but it was only a few minutes after nine when the island's famous mystery author arrived, along with mystery authority Henny Brawley and Max's mother. The trio didn't worry about the locked front door, Laurel using the key Annie had never managed to retrieve from her. They'd marched straight to the coffee bar and settled around a table. It would have been churlish to remain in the storeroom, so Annie fixed mugs filled with strong Colombian. She carried the mugs to a table near the fireplace and smiled a welcome as she joined the Intrepid Trio, as Max had dubbed them.

Emma, pleased with her comment, looked from Laurel Roethke, Annie's always unpredictable mother-in-law, to Henny, whose dark eyebrows registered annoyance, though her expression remained pleasant.

Emma concluded grandly, "Tom Edmonds. Pshaw."

Annie had never heard anyone utter *pshaw*. How Emmaesque.

Henny said mildly, "There's good reason why the spouse is always considered first in a murder case."

Emma became her most didactic. "As an author who has had a bit of success—" She paused, waited.

Emma awaited accolades. They were the breath of life to the writer. Annie knew her duty. "Emma, you are hugely successful." Emphasis on the adverb. Annie loathed Emma's protagonist Marigold Rembrandt, a redhead Annie found snippy and insufferable. "How many millions of books have sold now?"

Gratified, Emma took a moment to trumpet the sales figures.

A savvy bookseller, Annie wanted to murmur that of course the huge number was for books shipped, not actually sold, but life was too short to aggravate Emma. Besides, Emma's sell-through was well above 80 percent. Marigold was beloved across the nation, so what did Annie know? Besides, Emma had a trenchant mind, a devotion to her friends, and a curmudgeonly charm. Sometimes.

"Perhaps I do have a modest understanding of motivations and character. Therefore, I can categorically state that Tom Edmonds is not the stuff of which villains are made."

Laurel smoothed a tendril of silver blond hair away from her classically lovely face and looked pensive. "I hope that is true."

Annie's gaze sharpened. Laurel's tone indicated a personal concern. Why should Laurel have more than a passing interest in the fate of Tom Edmonds? Of course, almost everyone on the island was talking about the murder of Jane Corley. More than a week had passed. There had been no arrests. However, yesterday afternoon's *Gazette*, with its usual above-the-fold follow-up, made clear the direction of the investigation.

Henny tapped the newspaper. "Billy Cameron named Tom Edmonds 'a person of interest.' The circuit solicitor announced an arrest is imminent."

Laurel's husky voice dropped. "Those dear young people must be terribly frightened." A mournful sigh.

Three sets of eyes turned to her.

Henny broke the sudden silence. "'Dear young people?'"

Laurel made a slightly deprecatory gesture with one graceful hand. "Not that I countenance infidelity. I always found it a better practice to be divorced first."

Annie was never quite straight on Laurel's list of husbands, which she'd buried and which she'd divorced. As for lovers . . . Some conjectures about one's mother-in-law were better avoided. At this very moment, Annie focused on maintaining a bright expression of interest without a hint of skepticism.

Laurel's vivid blue eyes briefly touched on Annie. Her quite perfect lips quivered for an instant in amusement.

Annie felt her face turn bright pink. Was it her imagination or did one perfect eyelid drop for the tiniest moment in a wink before Laurel continued?

"However, I have a sense—mind you, I know it is very unlikely in today's world—but I think the sweet young things hadn't quite reached that point. Very nineteen-fiftyish, if you know what I mean." Laurel's perfectly arched eyebrows rose in amazement. "Simply soulful looks and secret trysts to talk and hold hands, two souls irresistibly drawn together yet mindful of the barrier between them."

Emma's stubby fingers tightened on her coffee mug. "What are you talking about?"

Laurel's eyes widened. "I assumed all of you knew. Tom Edmonds and Frankie Ford, of course. Frankie's in my yoga class. Such a sad face in recent times. And one day I saw Tom Edmonds going into the gallery. His expression had nothing to do with art. I am not privy to their private encounters, but," she spoke with quiet authority, "I know everything about love."

From anyone else the sweeping statement would seem absurd. Annie considered the source, decided Tom and Frankie definitely were an item.

Laurel nodded toward Emma. "Emma's understanding of character is beyond parallel. I quite agree. Tom Edmonds committing a brutal murder seems quite inconceivable to me."

Emma frowned, the dowager queen of crime apprised of previously unknown information. "Humph." It was an acknowledgment that facts alter cases. "Have to say, if there's suspicion of adultery, that recasts my thinking." She slid an unhappy sidelong glance at Henny.

Henny was too graceful to crow. Her tone was conciliatory. "Certainly your insights into character are profound, Emma, but I rather had an inkling. I saw Tom's and Frankie's cars parked in the lot for the forest preserve behind the library."

Annie popped up to retrieve the coffee hottle. Life on an island had its charms but was rather similar to inhabiting a fish tank. It was hard to find a private spot. She had recently visited the gallery and bought some ink drawings of cats for their den. Annie remembered Frankie's sweet face above a white piqué blouse embroidered with daisies. How dreadful if Frankie was caught up in the darkness of murder.

A s the service for Jane Corley ended, Max shot a questioning look at Annie. She whispered, "I think we should." They followed the mourners walking toward the parish hall. The order of service program had invited everyone to join the family there.

Annie wasn't surprised at the size of the crowd. Jane Corley was from a well-known island family. Less charitably, Annie imagined some of those present wouldn't pass up a moment to have a word with Tom Edmonds. Annie knew her own motive was mixed. Yes, she'd known Jane Corley, liked her. But she couldn't forget Laurel's concern about Tom Edmonds and Frankie Ford. Perhaps in a way Annie wanted to banish the thought of Tom Edmonds with the sensitive face and gifted hands as a man who might have committed murder.

The receiving line moved slowly. Annie and Max were within sight of the family. Tom Edmonds's long face held a mixture of discomfort and restiveness. Next to him was Jane's sister-in-law, Madeleine, and brother, David. Madeleine's austere beauty was softened by reddened eyes and trembling lips. David looked stiff and uncomfortable in a black suit and crisp white shirt, a definite change from his usual island casual wear. Next to David was Kate Murray, a stern-appearing woman with short white hair. Annie had met her a few times. She was not only some sort of family connection, she served as Jane's personal assistant. Last in the receiving line were a dark-haired young woman, a little too heavy, talking a little too fast, and a tall, heavyset man, likely her husband. His suit was noticeably more shabby and ill fitting than Tom's or David's. Annie's gaze moved back to Tom. She felt a tinge of shame. Was she like all the other vultures, there to pick apart appearances? Did he look shifty? Was he under stress? His head bent toward a gray-haired middle-aged woman who looked at him imploringly, hands twisting together. Tom tugged at his shirt collar, looked uncomfortable. He shot a look at David, turned his hand as if to point the woman toward him.

Annie was struck by the woman's obvious distress. But she didn't have the appearance of grief. Instead, she appeared despairing, desperate. She turned a little and Annie saw her more clearly, a broad, worn face that might once have been pretty but was now drawn and tight. She started to speak, stopped, pressed her lips together, scuttled to David, began again in a rush.

David listened for a moment then, with a frown, said something brusque and turned to the next in line. Kate Murray gave her a dismissive look and turned to speak to the dark-haired young woman, effectively preventing any conversation.

The woman's face drooped. She turned away and Annie had a picture of a closet filled with worn, shabby clothes. She moved out of the line, head down. As she walked toward the hall door, there was defeat in every line of her body.

A few moments more, she and Max reached the family, murmuring condolences.

Tom looked down at her. "Good of you to come." They'd met before but he gazed at her blankly. She shook his hand and the moment was past.

Annie carried with her a memory of Tom's long face with its deep-set eyes and chiseled features. There was no indication of anguish, but his eyes held a look of shock and disbelief. She agreed with Emma. Tom was not the stuff of which villains were made.

Max was already at their favorite booth at Parotti's Bar and Grill. They often lunched at the island's down-home eatery but had a standing date for dinner on Mondays. As Annie often said, the week went better when it began with dinner at Parotti's. Since gnomelike Ben Parotti had married Miss Jolene, the owner of a mainland tea shop, and brought her to his island, he had opted for polos and slacks instead of bib overalls. The café had been tweaked as well, vases with flowers on the wooden tables, quiche and sorbet in addition to the best fried oysters in the world and grits to die for, new menus unspotted by years of grease and sticky fingers. Unchanged was the sawdust-laden floor of the attached bait shop with its coolers of squid, snapper, grouper, black bass, and chicken necks.

Max slid out of the booth and reached out to touch her arm. "What's wrong?"

His words were as reassuring as the warmth of his touch. He always knew when something had disturbed her. She held up the *Gazette*. "Have you seen the paper?"

His grin was small-boy mischievous. "Kind of slow at the office today. I went out to the practice tee."

Annie was glad that he'd been out in the sun, free to swing a golf club, laugh or sigh at the result. She loved to work. Max was equable about work, but much more interested in enjoying the moment, whatever it was. He was glad to help those who came to his unusual business but happier to focus on her, on a great painting, on an absorbing book, on sitting with their white cat, Dorothy L, on his lap. In her mind, she heard Max's voice, "Gooood cat," and wished she could focus on happy thoughts like Max and Dorothy L and not on the distressing news she brought.

She slid into the booth. "Marian brought me a copy. Hot off the press. Sad picture of Tom Edmonds." She pushed the newspaper across the tabletop. "Marian said the circuit solicitor continues to be the world's biggest ass. They've arrested Tom and are holding him on suspicion of murder. He's going to be arraigned tomorrow. The circuit solicitor tipped the *Gazette* they were going to pick him up, so Marian was out in the street with her Leica. Marian said Tom looked about as murderous as the straw man in Oz. She said she'd taken pics of lots of perps and they looked defiant, cool, hostile, smooth, sometimes vacant or nuts or high, but not like the straw man."

Parotti came up to the booth, spiffy in a Tommy Bahama shirt and tan slacks, and pointed a gnarled finger at the newspaper. "They got him in a cell. Have to say I never thought a stranger wandered in and bashed her, but I don't see an artist as a wife killer." His gravelly voice was just this side of dismissive. "Course, I hear they only found his fingerprints on the hammer. Mallet, they call it. Fancy name for a tool, seems to me. Claims he doesn't remember the last time he saw the hammer. Said he quit working on the marble a week or so ago. And he never locked his studio. But still, you'd have to know the layout over there to even know there was a studio. Not exactly a thoroughfare." He leaned forward. "Any truth to the rumor he had a girlfriend?"

Annie pictured fish swarming in a bowl, there for everyone to see. She wasn't sure why she felt sad. She and Max knew Jane Corley as they knew so many on the island. They were friendly, but not close. But they knew her and had welcomed her new husband into the fabric of the island social scene, exchanging greetings at civic events, attending open houses at Wyler Art Gallery, nodding across the dining room at the country club. Was sadness caused by remembering a light-hearted, laughing Frankie Ford at a picnic last summer? Or was it the horror of trying to fit sensitive Tom Edmonds with his long artistic hands into the image of a man bringing down a mallet on his wife's skull?

A nnie took an extra moment on the boardwalk to look over the marina. It was a perfect October morning. Fluffy white clouds dotted a pale blue sky above placid water. A big yacht from Maine had pulled in last week, stopping over for the owner and guests to play a few rounds of golf before continuing a leisurely cruise to the Bahamas. At least that was the gossip Annie had heard from Ingrid, whose husband, Duane, had gone out deep-sea fishing with a friend whose boat was in the next slip. Annie studied the three-deck, 121-foot yacht, *Come On Along*, with interest, but not envy. She loved imagining how the lives of others played out, a musician in a symphony orchestra, a master carpenter, a wildlife photographer, a translator fluent in Arabic. For each she might have an inkling of their daily lives but she simply couldn't envision the lives of those who wandered the world in incredible splendor. Of course, with the miracle of satellites they could have e-books . . .

She laughed aloud. Life without books to her would be no life at all, but who knew how these travelers whiled away their days. In fact on a yacht that size, there would be room for a paneled library with deep easy chairs. She was still pondering endless days at sea and stacks of books to read when she pushed inside Death on Demand and flicked the switches to turn on the lights. Her silky black feline, Agatha, raced up the aisle, leaped to the counter of the cash desk, and crouched.

Annie knew the drill. She walked to the cash desk, pulled a sheet from a white notepad, skillfully avoiding a swat from one black paw. She crumpled the sheet into a ball and threw the enticing wad down the center aisle.

Agatha launched herself, landed lightly, and raced after the paper. Soon she was knocking the paper ball down the aisle and into the coffee area.

Annie took a deep breath of books and gave a thumbs-up to the molty raven perched atop the entrance to the children's retreat. She was ready to begin the day, placing orders, making calls, unpacking books.

A knock sounded behind her. It was fifteen minutes until opening time, but hey, the lights were on. If a deprived reader needed books, the welcome mat was always out. She opened the door with a smile.

Lucy Ransome looked apologetic. Her curly white hair looked unaccustomedly shaggy, as if she'd only managed a hurried swipe or two with her brush. Her white cotton shirt was misbuttoned. "I know you aren't open yet, but Max said he was sure you wouldn't mind—"

"Come right in." Annie sensed a burning intensity that Lucy was trying to keep leashed. This was obviously not a casual visit.

Lucy brushed back a tangle of curls. "Thank you. I have to tell someone. And you're always so capable . . ." Her voice trailed away.

Annie hoped she could help. But if it was something to do with Paul's estate, Max would be a better choice. She gave Lucy a quick smile. "I'll do my best. Let's have some coffee."

Lucy followed her down the center aisle, murmuring, "I don't really know what to do. I didn't even take time for breakfast."

"I have some great cake doughnuts. Max's secretary, Barb, loves to make them. I'll pop a couple in the microwave to go with coffee."

They settled at a table near the coffee bar with fresh Colombian and a doughnut apiece. Annie drew in a scent of cinnamon and hot doughnut, took a bite. Barb should be a pastry cook, not a secretary.

Lucy's expression held a note of defiance. "The police won't listen to me. I have to do something." The last words came in a rush and her face squeezed in determination. Anger tinged her tone.

Annie was startled by the intensity of Lucy's taut words. This was something far different than grief. "What's wrong?"

Lucy's blue eyes held a look of hope. "Maybe you can tell me what I can do. You and Henny saved Jeremiah Young when there was that dreadful crime at Better Tomorrow." Police had sought Jeremiah, the handyman at the island thrift shop, when a volunteer was murdered. "And now poor Tom Edmonds. The police have arrested him. I know he wasn't there."

Annie was puzzled. How could Lucy possibly know where Tom Edmonds had been when his wife was murdered?

Lucy brushed a hand through her silvered hair. "You are looking at me just like that police chief did. He thinks I'm unbalanced. I suppose I didn't sound rational to him, talking about Paul's desk and the party and saying I don't believe there was a gun."

Annie schooled her face, trying to appear receptive though her thoughts whirled. Jane hadn't been shot. What did Paul's desk have to do with Tom Edmonds and a sculptor's mallet? What party?

Lucy lifted her purse from the floor and drew out a folded sheet of thick, cream-colored paper. She closed her eyes briefly, opened them. "Early this morning"—she had difficulty forcing the words—"I started clearing out Paul's desk. I needed to find some papers for the kids, but mostly I wanted to start packing away his things. Some of them I can donate. Some I'll send to the children . . . But that doesn't matter. I'd scarcely been in the room since I found him there."

Lucy stared past Annie, her eyes full of pain. "Everything had been cleaned up, but it was terribly hard. Like I told the police when they asked about the gun, I never had any occasion to look in his desk. I didn't know anything about a gun. Paul never spoke of owning a gun." Her lips compressed for a moment. "Once he said there were too many guns, that it was sick to have a country where anybody could get a gun if they wanted it. He said people found them stored away in attics, kept them, gave them away, that some gun shows and shops didn't worry about checking anybody. They sold old guns without asking any questions. He was angry. There'd been one of those awful shootings. They seem to happen now more than ever. Now I don't think"—her voice was firm—"he ever had a gun in his desk."

"But, Lucy, there was a gun." That's what Lucy had told them, Paul slumped in death on his desk, the gun lying on the floor by his dangling dead hand.

"Oh yes." Her voice trembled. "There was a gun and that gun killed Paul. But I don't believe there was ever a gun in Paul's desk. There weren't any rags or stuff to clean a gun. My husband had a gun. He kept it in his desk along with an oil spray and some silicone cloths and brushes and picks. I looked in the drawer that was pulled out, where they found the half-empty box of cartridges. I didn't look closely that morning. Then I just saw that the drawer was open and there were cartridges. But today I looked carefully. The police took away the gun and the box with the bullets. I asked them this morning and they said that was all they took. So, why wasn't there any cleaning material? And there were other things in the drawer, nothing to do with a gun. There were some folders on the bottom and that's all. Life insurance. Bank slips. I think someone came with a gun and shot him. What if someone came that night and walked around the desk, maybe saying 'I want to show you something,' and then, real quick, put the gun to his temple? When Paul"—her voice wavered—"fell forward, why couldn't someone have taken his hand and placed the fingers around the stock and on the trigger? That policeman said they did a test and found gunshot residue on Paul's hand. He said Paul's fingerprints, from both hands, were on the cartridge box. I don't care. Maybe the murderer wiped the hand that held the gun on Paul's hand to leave traces of gunshot residue. Someone could have picked up his hands and touched all over the box." Her glare was defiant, her small chin resolute.

Annie had felt instinctively that Paul Martin wouldn't have killed himself. But the evidence seemed clear despite Lucy's misgivings now. "You said yourself"—her voice was gentle—"that he was upset that week." She heard her own words, knew they meant she'd come to terms with his death. His self-inflicted death.

Lucy nodded in vigorous agreement. "He was worried. Now I know why." She unfolded the heavy sheet of creamy paper and carefully laid it on the table. "This is what I found in his desk. See, there's a date. He always put a date on a sketch. There it is: 10/8."

Annie looked. Lucy seemed to see great significance in the date. October 8 was the night before Paul was shot. Annie glanced from the date to the pencil sketch, stone walls on either side of pillars with shrubs beyond, a rearing horse

41

to the right of the pillars. Annie knew the source of the drawing, a ten-foot-tall bronze statue that stood outside the entrance to the sprawling acres of Jane Corley's estate.

There was one stark difference between the sketch and the statue. The upflung head of the statue depicted a horse pleased at its display of power, commanding, imperious. In the drawing, the horse's teeth were bared in fury, signaling danger.

Below the sketch of the pillars and horse was another drawing, this one more attenuated but readily deciphered, Shakespeare's three witches dancing around a boiling cauldron.

Annie felt a chill as she read words written in a slanting backhand: *An open house, a hard heart. Evil in a look. I saw it. I'll deal with it at the party.*

Lucy tapped the sheet emphatically. "That's Paul's handwriting, and look there."

A final sentence was underlined twice: *Protect Jane.*

Lucy's words tumbled, fast as a plunging mountain stream. "He drew this Tuesday night. Wednesday night we went to David Corley's house. Madeleine had a party for his birthday. Don't you see?"

Annie tried to sort out the meanings but there was too much, Paul's preoccupation, his sketch with its bald statement, *Protect Jane*, the snarling horse, gunshot residue on Paul's hand, Lucy claiming there never had been a gun, Paul planning to confront evil at a party. David Corley's birthday party? Jane would have been there.

Lucy leaned forward. "I told everyone Paul was upset, but I supposed he was worried about a patient. I never believed he was depressed or thinking about shooting himself and, the more I think about it, I don't think there ever was a gun in his desk—"

Annie held to a central fact. On the sketch Paul underlined his determination to protect Jane. But Paul died. Then Jane was murdered.

"—and now that I've seen the sketch, I'm sure Paul saw something at the art gallery open house, the Sunday night before we went to the birthday party. Paul says he saw evil in a look. It was after the open house that he was preoccupied and worried. Now I know why. He saw something at the open house that told him Jane Corley was in danger. Paul's drawing indicates he intended to deal with that at a party. He had to be talking about David Corley's birthday party because we came home from David's party and that's the night he was shot. He talked to someone, told them nothing better happen to Jane. That's why he was relaxed when we got home. If only I'd noticed which guests he talked to. But I loved sitting there watching the young people have fun. Some of David's old fraternity brothers came from Atlanta. I talked about quilt patterns with Kate Murray. I spoke to Frankie Ford but she didn't have much to say and I thought it was sad that she seemed so alone at the party. I wasn't watching Paul. All I know for certain is that when we were driving home, he wasn't upset any longer. It's not"—the negative was as emphatic as a clenched fist—"because he'd decided to shoot himself."

Lucy's hypothesis was as flimsy as a house made of paper until Annie looked at the sketch and the double-underlined words: *Protect Jane.* If Jane Corley were alive, the sketch didn't matter, but Jane had been battered to death in her home on the Monday after Paul was shot.

"They've arrested Tom. And that's wrong." Lucy sounded indignant and despairing all at the same time.

Annie's face creased in thought. Why was Tom's arrest wrong? Maybe Paul saw danger in Tom Edmonds's face. Maybe Paul talked to Tom at David's party. Like Henny said, there was a reason police looked at a spouse first. Unbidden came an image of Tom Edmonds with his sensitive artist face and cute but no longer perky Frankie Ford.

Lucy clapped her hands together. "You look just like Billy Cameron, patient and nice and thinking I don't understand about Tom and Frankie and anyway who had a better motive? I don't know who had any kind of motive, but I know Paul didn't kill himself. That means someone came to Paul's study that night. I told you that Paul seemed more himself after David Corley's party. He talked to someone there. That's why I know Tom Edmonds is innocent. Tom missed the party. He wasn't on the island that night. He was in Atlanta."

3

"Maybe there's a unicorn over the next sand dune." Billy Cameron's voice was genial, which softened the words, but his blue eyes clearly held a skeptical gleam. His desk was neat, three closed folders. His computer screen showed Outlook Express. Blue skies and placid waters were postcard perfect through the window that overlooked the bay. There were no clouds on the police chief's horizon today.

Annie knew her concern had been tipped overboard like a too-small fish tossed back into the water. "Lucy brought you the sketch."

Billy leaned back in his chair, comfortable, at ease. "Yep." His broad face was sympathetic. "Look, Annie, you got a heart as big as Texas, but this time you don't have a dog in the hunt. Paul's scribbles are just that. Nobody followed him home from a birthday party with all the stuff that was needed to make his death look like a suicide. His sister admits he'd been upset. FYI, we didn't release it to reporters because you can't prove something from nothing, there was a blank sheet of paper on the desk and a pen next to it. Looked like he was going to write a note, didn't, got on with it."

Annie perched on the edge of the hard wooden straight chair in front of his desk.

"Lucy said you agreed somebody could have smeared gunshot residue on Paul's hand."

"Like I said, nobody can prove there aren't unicorns, even though nobody's ever seen one. Sure, some clever devil could have held a gun with a hand sheathed in a plastic glove, caught Paul right on the temple, shot him, stayed calm enough to strip off the glove, use the glove to swipe Paul's right thumb, palm, and part of his fingers. Of course"—now Billy leaned back and folded his arms—"that also presupposes somebody showed up ready to kill him with a gun that couldn't be traced and a half-full box of cartridges. Lots of requisites there. Not only did somebody come in the den planning to kill him, but, once he was dead, the dude was smart enough to use both of Paul's hands to put fingerprints on the cartridge box, then smeared residue on his right hand. No residue on the cartridge box. Got to keep it in order. The box had to be touched up before the residue was transferred to his right hand. Lots of planning there. Plus, we have that blank sheet of paper. Lucy probably never saw it because he fell forward and it was pretty much covered with blood. Sorry. I don't think so."

Annie ignored Billy's dismissive tone. "He could have had the paper out for another reason." Her words sounded empty

46

to her. She hurried on. "The paper doesn't count. If he was going to write a suicide note, he would have. Anyway, maybe somebody plans real carefully. Paul was afraid for Jane. There's no way you can dismiss that. He knew someone planned to harm her. Billy, she's dead."

Billy shrugged. "The dog barks and you stub your toe on a rock. Cause and effect? I don't think so. Face it, Annie, she had a two-timing husband whose fingerprints are all over the hammer that killed her." Billy's face creased in exasperation. "No matter how much Lucy Ransome wants to change what happened, Paul Martin shot himself. There's no proof anyone came to his door, no proof the gun didn't belong to him, no proof anyone other than Tom Edmonds murdered his wife. I'm sorry Paul shot himself. He was a great guy. A good doctor. I don't know what the hell was wrong in his life. But that sketch could mean a lot of things. When people doodle, their thoughts may be scattered all over the place. Maybe Paul was thinking of a horse who needed a good dentist. Maybe Jane Corley needed to take better care of herself. Maybe he drew the witches because he was thinking about *Macbeth* and that's the evil in a glance. Maybe a lot of things. But I don't believe anyone followed Paul home from a birthday party and blew his brains out and had the balls to set up a suicide scene."

Annie looked at Billy's square, strong, confident face. He obviously hadn't picked up a crime vibe from Paul's death. Billy never hesitated to follow a hunch. This time he didn't have a hunch and he had a man in jail whose hammer had been used to kill his wife. What happened after David Corley's birthday party had no relevance for him.

A hunch . . . Billy wasn't going to be enticed into looking further at Paul Martin's death. Billy had always said when anything occurred in a murder investigation that seemed off-kilter, pay attention, your subconscious often saw more than you realized. But maybe she thought of it now, at this moment, because the incident had seemed so wrong. She asked abruptly, "Billy, were you at Jane Corley's funeral?" She hadn't seen him, but she was certain he would have attended.

He blinked a little at the sudden transition, then nodded. "Sure."

"Did you see the older woman who went through the line and she was upset, but I could tell it wasn't about Jane. She asked Tom something and he gestured toward David and then David wasn't nice about it, whatever it was. The woman dropped out of the line and walked out of the parish hall."

"Can't say I did. And . . . ?"

"Billy, there was something wrong about it. I think she'd come from off island. I don't know everybody but I know a lot of people. I'd never seen her before. Who was she? Why did she come to Jane's funeral?"

He waited.

Annie turned her hands up. "I know it doesn't sound like much. But the woman appeared to be under enormous pressure. I don't think she wanted to ask whatever she asked but she forced herself and then she was rebuffed. She looked devastated as she walked away."

"What do you want me to do?"

"Find her. Ask what was wrong."

He drew a small pad closer. "Description?"

Annie pictured that moment in the parish hall. "Gray haired. Maybe fifty, maybe a little older. Sturdy. Long arms and legs, short torso. About five-five, maybe a hundred and fifty pounds. Wide face. Brown eyes. Dark shadows under her eyes. A droopy mouth. Rounded chin. Scarcely any makeup. Wore a navy suit but it was old, really old. The skirt was too long. It had that shiny look when fabric's been cleaned too often."

"I'll see what I can find out." He squared the tablet on his desk, and Annie knew he was signaling an end to the interview. And likely to his patience.

At the door, she paused with her hand on the knob. "If Lucy's right, if the person who killed Jane also shot Paul, then Tom Edmonds is innocent. Lucy said Tom was off island the night Paul died. Would you check and see if Tom was off island?"

Billy shook his head. "I'm interested in Tom Edmonds the afternoon his wife was killed. If you want to know what he was doing some other night, check it out."

"Hey, Annie." Barb's voice was lifted in a greeting. "Come on in. I just made pound cake."

It was only half past nine in the morning but the scent of freshly baked cake was unmistakable.

"Three sticks of butter. And caramel-flavored whipped cream." When Barb cooked, which was often, Max and Confidential Commissions were in a lull between clients, to phrase a lack of activity gracefully.

Barb tilted her bouffant hairdo in the direction of Max's

closed office door. "He's talking to that sweet girl who works at Wyler's gallery. She has a broken heart pasted all over her face." Barb lifted expressive eyebrows. "Honestly, divorce is so much simpler than murder. Some guys never get it right. He probably didn't have the cojones to tell Jane sayonara. Or"—a cynical moue—"he didn't want to lose out on all that money. Anyway, let me get you a slice and I'll poke the light on Max's intercom—dot and dash for an *A*—and he'll know you're here."

Morse code? Annie decided time must indeed have been hanging heavy at Confidential Commissions. Max loved Morse code, dots were light and quick, a dash heavier and longer. Barb was probably the only secretary on the island proficient in Morse. Max also loved the Green Hornet. Was the next best thing going to be a Confidential Commissions' Superpower Ring? But now wasn't the time for lighthearted nostalgia or pound cake. She held up a hand. "Let's wait on the pound cake. I think I know why Frankie's here. I can help."

Annie knocked lightly on the door, turned the knob.

Frankie Ford huddled in a webbed chrome chair facing Max's desk. The face she turned toward the doorway was tear-streaked and hopeless, a sad contrast to shining chestnut hair and bright-and-fresh short-sleeve white blouse and long blue chambray skirt.

Max had the aura of a man trying to be kind, but wishing he could draw the interlude to a close. He saw Annie and his eyes lighted, grateful for her interruption. He started to rise.

Annie waved him to his seat with one hand, shut the door with the other, and rushed across the room to look down at

Frankie. "Where was Tom the Wednesday night before Jane was killed?"

Frankie looked at her in surprise.

"The night of David Corley's birthday party. Was Tom at the party?" Perhaps Lucy missed seeing Tom. Frankie would know. As David's brother-in-law, Tom would have been invited.

Frankie brushed back a lock of hair that had fallen across one damp cheek. "Tom wasn't there." She was clearly uncomfortable and her gaze slid away from Annie. "It was an awful evening. Jane didn't like me." She looked miserable. "I had to be there because of the gallery. Toby always finagled any invitation he could to the Corleys' because of Tom's work."

Frankie was totally focused on how she'd spent an uncomfortable evening, apparently unaware Tom's whereabouts that night might be important. "Did Tom come late? Did he leave early?"

Frankie was bewildered. "I don't know why you care, but Tom was off island that night. He was in Atlanta."

"Atlanta?" Annie was glad for the confirmation of Lucy's claim. "When did he go?"

"That morning." Her voice was empty. To her, the answer didn't matter.

"When did he leave?" Could his departure be proved?

Frankie gave an impatient shrug. "The ten o'clock ferry. He drove to Atlanta to take some paintings to a gallery. He didn't come home until the next day. At David's, Jane was talking about how she had an in with the gallery owner. You'd think the paintings were chosen because of her. But the owner said Tom had a golden future. He wanted to put on a really big show." Her face twisted in despair. "Not now, of course. Everything's over now." Her voice quivered. "Tom was so excited. He stayed with the gallery owner. He called me about midnight. He was sorry to call so late. The owner's one of those people who likes to drink and Tom waited until the host called it a night."

Max looked puzzled, likely wondering why Tom Edmonds's whereabouts on the night of October 9 mattered.

Annie didn't care about the phone call. People can call anywhere on a cell and say they are somewhere else. But if Tom Edmonds was having drinks with his host until late that night, he was not on the island during David Corley's party. Or moving later in darkness to slip unseen through Paul Martin's side yard to knock softly on the door to the study.

Max could check with the gallery owner. If Frankie's story was confirmed, there was no way Tom Edmonds could have returned to the island later that night. In October, the last ferry came into the harbor at ten thirty P.M. There wasn't another ferry until morning.

Annie grinned and turned up her thumbs. In her heart, she thought Lucy Ransome had it right. Paul was killed by the person who bludgeoned Jane. "Maybe there is a kindly Providence. Maybe Tom had an angel perched on his shoulder. Here's what happened." She described the drawing Lucy Ransome found in her brother's desk. When she finished, she was struck by the sharp contrast in how her information was received.

Max's face crinkled in thought, but he didn't look convinced.

Frankie Ford came to her feet with a squeal and hugged

Annie. "Tom's innocent. I knew he was innocent—" Frankie's eyes were wide, her voice shaky.

Annie felt a tiny inward lurch as she realized Frankie had been afraid, terribly afraid, and not solely because Tom Edmonds was in jail.

"—even though—" She clapped a hand over her mouth. Her head swiveled toward Max, back to Annie. She gulped. "I mean, things looked bad."

Annie looked into blue eyes that harbored knowledge. Frankie knew something else, something that had made her fearful that Tom was guilty.

Max studied Frankie with narrowed eyes, then turned toward Annie. "Did Lucy Ransome take the sketch to Billy Cameron?"

Annie lifted her chin. "Yes."

"And he said?" Max quirked a blond brow.

Annie took her time answering. "He admitted someone could have come with a gun, maybe worn a latex glove on one hand, walked behind Paul's desk, caught him by surprise, jammed the barrel to his temple, shot him, and set everything up to look like suicide, putting Paul's fingerprints on the cartridge box, wiping the gunshot residue on Paul's right thumb and index finger and palm. Billy didn't believe a word of it. You know how people are. Somebody claims someone else was behind an elaborate frame and everybody says that's not realistic. Billy dismissed the idea of somebody being 'a clever devil.' He was sardonic about somebody doing 'a lot of planning.'"

Max's face stilled. His blue eyes darkened with memories.

She wished she could bite back the words.

His gaze dropped to his desk. She knew he didn't see the magnificent red of the mahogany refectory table that served as his desk. He saw a dusty road dappled by moonlight and heard the baying of hounds. Finally, he looked up. The memory of that hot August night when he'd been taken into custody with blood—not his own—on his shirt was there in the bleakness of his gaze. "Yeah. People can make plans, snare somebody innocent. But"—his gaze at her was level—"there's a damn big difference between me and Tom. I was set up from start to finish. I had no reason to kill that woman." He looked at Frankie, shook his head. "I'd be lying if I said I thought I could help Tom."

Her face turned white. Slowly she pushed up from the chair, walked blindly toward the door.

Annie hurried after her, caught her arm. "Wait, Frankie, please." Annie turned toward Max. "If we send Frankie away, she doesn't have any hope. Maybe you're right"—Annie heard Frankie's indrawn breath—"maybe Tom's guilty. He's got a reason to want Jane dead."

She saw certainty in Max's eyes and realized he was basing his opinion on something she didn't know, something he didn't want to mention in front of Frankie. For an instant, she doubted her conviction. But Lucy knew her brother well. She knew he'd been worried. She knew that worry was gone when they came home from David's party. She'd never heard him speak of a gun. More than that, Annie remembered how Paul Martin fought to save a woman who wanted to discard life.

Life mattered to Paul, that of his family, his wife, his patients. Himself. Now in his grave, he bore the burden of having taken his own life. If that was a lie, Paul deserved better.

"Maybe we need to remember that Tom's innocent until proven guilty." She gazed steadily at Max. "Let's find out the truth. If Tom's guilty, nothing we discover will make a difference for him. If he's innocent, we save his life."

Max's face softened. His blue eyes told her he loved her, admired her, thought she was stubborn and wrong, but he was on her team. He stood and came around the desk. He looked down at Frankie, his face regretful. "Tom looks guilty to me. But my wife"—a tilt of his head toward Annie—"sometimes sees a reality not apparent to anyone else." He shot Annie a wry look. "Maybe this is one of those times. We'll do what we can."

Annie wanted to throw her arms around him and give him a huge hug. He had no faith that Tom was innocent, but he would help look for the truth of Jane's murder. She turned to Frankie. "Come on, we've got work to do."

Max leaned back in his comfortable red leather chair, arms behind his head, feet crossed, and studied the photograph of Annie on the corner of his desk. Flyaway dusty blond hair, serious gray eyes, lips slightly curved in a smile. "Sweetie," he addressed the picture mildly, "have I ever told you that you have a talent for strays, you are a sucker for sob stories, and you always see sunshine behind a cloud big enough to blot out the sky? There's no happy ending to this one."

After Frankie and Annie left, he'd texted Annie what he

overheard in the men's grill at the country club. David Corley was lunching with a friend who loudly groused about an upcoming family reunion and a cousin who always had something unpleasant to say to everyone. David responded he should count himself lucky, at least he was dealing with a cousin and not a sister who could double as a vampire. Max remembered David's exasperated words, "It's my birthday, for God's sake, and Jane is busy sharpening a stake for the heart of this cute kid who had to be there to show off some of Tom's paintings. Sure, I've heard the gossip. Tom has the hots for her but, still, couldn't Jane have picked a different time?" And, Max pointed out in his text, that conversation occurred after the birthday party and before Jane was murdered. He knew Annie would scan her phone before she and Frankie settled down to talk. Annie should know the word was out on the island that there was more between Frankie and Tom than interest in his art.

He spoke firmly to the smiling picture. "That cute kid with the gorgeous hair had a motive as well as Tom if the rumors David heard are true. I know," he answered her imagined response, "Tom was in Atlanta the night Paul Martin died." Max was thoughtful. He agreed that Paul Martin blowing out his brains for his sister to find didn't sound like the man and doctor he'd known. "Okay, Annie. I'll root around like a hungry hog. But I'm checking out everybody, including the lovebirds."

He turned to his computer. Everything had a beginning. If Lucy Ransome was right, the beginning of the end for Paul Martin started at the October 6 open house at Wyler Art Gallery. He began to type.

RUN-UP TO MURDER

Sunday, October 6—Dr. Paul Martin and sister Lucy Ransome attended an open house in honor of Tom Edmonds at Wyler Art Gallery.

Tuesday, October 8—Paul sketched the horse at the entrance to Jane Corley's estate. *Protect Jane* underlined twice. Also, *An open house, a hard heart. Evil in a look. I saw it. I'll deal with it at the party.*

Wednesday, October 9—Paul and Lucy attended a birthday party for David Corley, Jane's brother, at David and Madeleine's home.

Wednesday, October 9—Lucy said good night to Paul, leaving him in his study.

Thursday, October 10—Lucy found Paul at his desk in his study, dead of a gunshot wound to the head. Circumstances compatible with suicide. Lucy had no knowledge that he possessed a gun.

Monday, October 14—Jane Corley bludgeoned to death at her home during the afternoon. Weapon a sculptor's mallet belonging to her husband. Tom Edmonds discovered her body and called police at approximately a quarter to five.

Monday, October 21—Tom Edmonds taken into custody.

Tuesday, October 22—Lucy Ransome finds sketch.

Max tapped the first paragraph. He and Annie had attended the open house at Wyler Art Gallery. Guests wandered from the wide entry hall where wine and hors d'oeuvres were served into the long gallery to stroll through a display of Tom's paintings. Max methodically re-created his own movements that night, recalling glimpses of particular faces.

Jane Corley dominated the evening. She greeted guests with a flourish of her champagne flute. In an off-shoulder ruby dress, she'd appeared glamorous despite her too-strong features. Her ebullient laughter could be heard in every corner. She'd led the way into the gallery, sweeping guests before her like so many obedient children, and it was she who pulled the cord to unveil the central painting. She'd presented her usual commanding aura that evening.

Another memory slid into his mind. As he'd turned away from the unveiling—Annie was across the room talking to Henny Brawley—he'd noticed Paul Martin a few feet away from the oil painting of Jane standing at the end of a pier. Paul wasn't looking at the painting. He stared into the distance. He stood, a little stooped, holding a glass of wine, but his face was not that of a man enjoying his evening or judging art. The muscles of his face were slightly slack, drooping, a man who'd seen or thought something unexpected, something disturbing.

Max considered the possibilities. Lucy insisted Paul hadn't been the same since the open house. Maybe he indeed saw something that evening that led him to fear for Jane's life. It was equally possible he had a sudden touch of vertigo or his mind dredged up something ominous from a patient's symptoms that hadn't occurred to him or he was plunged into dark despairing thoughts about his own life.

It wasn't helpful to imagine what-ifs. Max knew he needed to focus on verifiable facts. Most important, who among those attending might have had reason to want Jane to cease to live. He knew the best place to start. He glanced at his watch, made a quick call. "You going to be in the newsroom for a while?"

Marian Kenyon was brisk. "Just finishing up the story about Tom Edmonds's arraignment. Nothing else exciting on the news front. You got something for me?"

Frankie Ford looked hopefully across the worktable in the Death on Demand storeroom-cum-office. Her tone was excited. "What can you do?" Although her face was still splotchy, the tears had stopped.

Annie felt the burden of Frankie's eagerness and hoped that she could do something to help. "Mostly talk to people"—she saw Frankie droop—"who were close to Jane. This crime was planned by someone familiar with the house and with Tom's studio. No stranger dropped by Tom's studio and filched that mallet. The studio is too remote for an outsider to find."

Frankie's eyes widened. Perhaps for the first time, she focused on who might have killed Jane rather than her fear for Tom. Overwhelmed by the threat to Tom, Frankie apparently hadn't thought about the crime and how it was committed.

"Do you think someone wanted Tom to be blamed?" Frankie's voice was faint.

"If he's innocent, then the mallet was deliberately used to implicate him. Let's consider the people who lived in the house or who were in the house that Monday." Annie held a pen above a pad.

Frankie brushed back a tangle of chestnut curls. "Sherry Gillette's been there for several weeks. She left a few days after Jane died. Tom never paid much attention to anything, but he said Jane didn't like Sherry's husband. He said Jane wanted Sherry to dump him."

"Is Sherry a cousin of some sort?"

"Tom said she was the daughter of an old friend of Jane's mother and he didn't see why Jane cared what Sherry did but Jane always had ideas about everybody's life."

Annie wondered if Tom's attitude was affected by his own relationship with Jane, though he may have had a good point if Sherry wasn't even related to Jane. "Where do Sherry and her husband live?"

Frankie frowned in thought. "Some apartment house not far from Fish Haul Pier. His name's Roger. He teaches at the high school."

Annie knew the big apartment complex on the other side of a wooded area from the park that faced the harbor and Fish Haul Pier. She wrote down: *Sherry Gillette, Roger Gillette.* Certainly if Sherry was staying at the house, her husband would likely be familiar with the house and grounds.

"Were Sherry and Jane fond of each other?"

"I only saw them together a few times when Toby and I were there for dinner. Jane loved to have us as an audience to talk about Tom's work. I thought Sherry was a big soppy self-centered drip. She usually looked like she was pouting. Jane kept telling her to act like a grown-up. That always sent Sherry off in a huff." Frankie briefly pressed her lips together. "Jane decided Sherry had to boot her husband. It didn't matter that Sherry obviously wanted to wiggle out of everything she'd said about him. I think she showed Jane a bruise on her arm or something and said he'd been mean. Maybe it was all made up. But Jane insisted Sherry had to act. And if she didn't, Jane was going to talk to some people on the school board 'because that kind of man shouldn't be around kids.' Like Tom said, Jane was always right. You know what I mean? I got the idea Sherry showed up thinking she'd get a lot of sympathy and stay for a while in luxurious surroundings, maybe tease her husband a bit. But Jane told Sherry the guy was a jerk, drop him. Tom said Jane was always sure she knew what was best for everybody."

Annie wondered if Frankie knew how hostile she sounded. Perhaps she didn't care. Certainly Jane was demonstrating care for the woman if she was trying to protect her from an abusive husband. Or was Frankie right and Jane was interfering and causing trouble?

Frankie brushed back a strand of reddish-brown hair. "Kate Murray probably knows everything about Jane. She's in her sixties and she's worked for the Corley family forever. I think she's some kind of cousin. Or maybe not. Some connection to the family, anyway." Her face crinkled. "I don't know exactly how to describe her. She oversees the running of the estate, though there's a maid and cook who come and do everything. She was Jane's personal assistant. She went most places with her, like art shows, and she was included in family gatherings."

Annie underlined Kate's name. She would know exactly who was at work in the house when Jane died. If there was a gardener or yard service, she could supply that information.

"Was Kate at the open house at the gallery?"

"Yes." There was no warmth in Frankie's voice.

Annie darted a quick glance at Frankie's stiff face. Clearly, Frankie didn't like Kate Murray.

"Did Kate seem to be on good terms with Jane?"

For an instant, humor glinted in Frankie's blue eyes. "Kate never bothers to be on good terms with anybody. She's a gruff old broad. She ran that house like a boot camp. Even Jane saluted when Kate came around."

"Who else might have been likely to drop by the house on a regular basis?"

"David and Madeleine, I suppose. They live in the original Corley house. Jane built that big mansion when she married the golfer."

"Where is the original house?"

Frankie concentrated. "David's house is on Crescent Street. The house faces Wherry Creek. Jane's house is a half mile away. Toby used to talk about how much money and land Jane owned."

Annie realized the gallery owner apparently made it his business to know all about the young painter he sponsored and the money behind him.

"Toby said it's all private land, the forest between the houses, pine woods with cypress and magnolias and bayberry. He said Jane built a private road called Corley Lane that connects Crescent and Berryhill. Her house is on Corley Lane about a quarter mile from Berryhill. Toby said the Corleys own all the land between Crescent and Berryhill."

Annie turned to her desk, pulled out a drawer for an island map. She didn't have any trouble finding Crescent and Berryhill. The streets ran parallel from Sand Dollar Road and ended at the salt marsh. A curling loop indicated the creek that wound to the marsh. Corley Lane was a thin squiggle connecting the public streets. She remembered from garden tours that the grounds around Jane's Mediterranean mansion were extensive. Annie drew a quick map, marked *A* for Jane's house, *B* for Tom's studio, and *C* for David and Madeleine's home. A private road . . . Unless there were deliveries or visitors, there would have been no one to notice anyone turning into Jane's drive. "Is there anyone other than family who might have been likely to drop in?"

"Tom might know." Frankie didn't sound certain.

Annie wondered if Tom was too self-absorbed to know or care about his wife's family or friends. "Did you talk to Tom the day Jane was killed?"

Frankie spoke carefully. "I talked to him on the phone."

"When?" Why wasn't she more forthcoming?

"Around two o'clock."

Annie marked two o'clock on her notepad. "What did you talk about?"

Frankie's lips parted, closed. She jammed the fingers of her small hands tightly together. "I was . . . I asked about crating some paintings."

"Nothing else?"

"Not anything special."

Annie gazed at her steadily. "I've heard that you and Tom were . . . more than friends."

If possible, Frankie looked even more forlorn. "Oh God, I knew it was wrong. He's—he was married. I was going to leave the island. It wasn't any good. And it was wrong." She lifted her eyes. Her lips trembled. "I told him I wasn't going to stay."

Annie looked at her and saw despair and shame and desperate unhappiness. "When did you tell him?"

Frankie brushed away tears. "Last week."

Annie was silent.

Frankie's eyes widened. "No." Her voice was sharp. "He wouldn't hurt Jane. You can't think that."

Annie knew she would not be alone in that thought. If the police knew Frankie was threatening to leave the island, that would only reinforce their sense that Tom had a huge motive for murder.

She said quietly, "When did you know Jane had been killed?"

"Tom called me that night, said it was awful, that he'd found her . . ." Her voice trailed away.

"Where were you that day?"

"At the gallery."

Annie persisted. "Were you there all day?"

"Most of the day."

"Where were you between one and five?"

Frankie's gaze slid away. "I was out and about for a while." A pause and she swallowed tightly. "That afternoon I went to the bank and stopped at the grocery. It was such a pretty day, I played hooky for a little while. I went to the park across from the harbor and took a walk."

Annie said quietly, "Did you go to Jane's house?"

A pulse fluttered in Frankie's throat. "I didn't go to the Corley house."

Annie looked into brilliantly blue eyes holding her own in a steady gaze intended to convey honesty. Instead, that straight look reinforced her suspicion that Frankie Ford was lying. "If everyone tells the truth, we may find out what happened."

Frankie jumped up. "I don't know what happened." Her

voice wobbled. "But Tom wouldn't hurt Jane." She turned and rushed toward the door.

M arian Kenyon poured ink-black coffee into a mug, handed it to Max. She flopped in an opposite chair, ripped open a sack of peanuts, poured some into her Coke, lifted the can, drank, munched. Her short black hair poked in several directions, likely from frenzied hand swipes as she typed. "What's up?" Her tone was easy, but her dark intelligent eyes watched him intently.

Max pulled up a wobbly wooden chair, turned it to face the stained table, straddled the seat. "Who was at the arraignment?"

"Defense lawyer, Dinah Whittle from a criminal defense firm in Beaufort. The prosecutor." Her lips twisted. "Our own beloved circuit solicitor Willard Posey—"

Max kept his face blank, but Marian, too, remembered the hot August when Willard Posey, self-important and pleased, had trumpeted Max's guilt in a murder case. Posey was always quick to think he had a foolproof case.

"—thundered that Tom Edmonds was a danger to society, a man who crept up behind his defenseless wife, left her dying in their family room, and now had the audacity to deny guilt despite the fact that only his fingerprints were on the murder weapon and the weapon had come from Edmonds's remote studio deep in the grounds of his wife's estate. Moreover . . . But you get the picture, yada yada yada. Tom's held over for trial, no bond permitted. It was short, if not sweet. I took the early ferry over to the mainland, just got back. It didn't take long to write." Marian screwed up her narrow face in disgust.

"I think it's hogwash. I was there yesterday when a couple of deputies picked him up at the jail en route to the mainland. He looked about as much like a murderer as my dog resembles a ballerina." A wrinkle of her nose. "Stanley's a Chihuahua." She put down the can, pushed up from her slump in the chair, planted her elbows on the scarred tabletop, looked at him like a mama hawk ready to attack. "So what's up?"

Max tried to look the essence of cherubic innocence. "I thought you wouldn't mind filling me in on everything you noticed Monday afternoon at the crime scene." He never doubted that Marian picked up the scanner call for police to be dispatched to Corley Lane, possible homicide, and that Marian arrived by the time the police had piled out of a cruiser.

The *Gazette*'s star reporter looked like Dorothy L contemplating a dish of sardines. "Who wants to know and why?" Her aura of fatigue was gone. Her dark eyes were bright, interested.

"Confidential. Let's just put it that an interested party has doubts about Tom's guilt."

"Better and better. So do I. Killers don't slink. They posture, bluff, bully, preen, charm, dismiss. They sure as hell don't slink. Be glad to share what I know—if you'll explain why an upstanding island citizen can't wait to read all about it in the *Gazette*."

Max looked thoughtful. Lucy Ransome wanted to do something. Maybe he could give her that opportunity. "Okay. You first, then I'll give you a lead to a hell of a story."

"Sweet it is, honeybunch." Her grin was impish. "Been watching old Jackie Gleason reruns. I know"—her expression was suddenly poignant—"life's always been a crock, but back then you could go see a movie and never hear the F-word and darned if the movies didn't encourage people to be good guys. Now, hello, serial killer, everybody screws everybody, and that good horse Decent pulls up lame. Anyway, what do you want to know?"

Max's answer was quick. "Everything. What you picked up at the scene. What you got from Billy later."

4

Annie drove with the windows down to enjoy the mild October morning. She turned off Berryhill onto Corley Lane. The blacktop wound under a canopy of interlocking live oak branches. Live oaks and pines loomed dense and impenetrable on either side of the road. It was like being in a nature preserve with nothing to block out the island sounds, insects whirring, birds twittering, the crackle of a passing deer, perhaps a wild boar.

A sudden break in foliage marked the entrance to the grounds. Annie slowed the car to look up at a huge bronze horse. The image shifted in her mind, the horse's lips drawn back in a snarl, an animal facing danger. Did Paul make that change as a talisman to protect Jane, the horse ready for battle?

Annie's hands tightened on the steering wheel. She hadn't called ahead. Perhaps she should have. But it was easy to rebuff a caller over the telephone, harder in a face-to-face encounter. At the least, she might have perhaps a few seconds longer to make her case in person than if she had called.

Annie turned the car between stone pillars, drove up a broad paved driveway. Sunlight gilded the golden stucco, emphasized the dark red of the tiled roof. The house rose three stories, could have graced an avenue in Miami during its heyday. Utter silence enveloped the house. No cars. No one about. No lights in the tall windows. Annie found the quiet sinister, knew she was reacting to what had happened within the opulent mansion.

She pulled into the wide paved area near a porte cochere. Silence pressed against her as she stepped out of the car. No voices, no motors, no footsteps, only birds chirping, squirrels chittering, magnolia leaves rustling. Annie had a wild sense that the enormous home was deserted, that entering would be like boarding the *Mary Celeste*, no one there, no one ever to be there.

She steeled herself and started up broad, shallow front steps. Surely that sense of emptiness came from her knowledge of violent death here. Within the house, there must be movement, the clatter of steps, the whine of a vacuum. She pushed a doorbell next to a huge carved wooden front door.

As she waited, a lean gray cat jumped up on a brick planter filled with pansies, watched her with cool golden eyes. Annie turned and reached out a friendly hand, snatched it back in time to avoid a bite.

A voice behind her said acidly, "Doesn't like strangers."

Annie faced the woman standing in the entryway, observing Annie with about as much warmth as the feline. Short-cropped, white hair framed a narrow unsmiling face with a high forehead, cold brown eyes, long thin nose, sharp chin. She was trim in a charcoal-gray-and-white-striped blouse with sleeves rolled up between elbows and wrists, light gray slacks that hung loosely on bony hips, black loafers.

"We've met before, Miss Murray. I'm Annie Darling."

"If Jane had ordered some books"—her tone was impatient—"we'll honor that. Now if you'll excuse me—"

"I need to talk to you."

"I'm very busy. Send a letter." She started to turn away.

Annie's quick temper flared. There was no need for her to be rude. "Don't you want to know who killed Jane?"

Kate Murray swung about. Her face hardened. "That's an outrageous question. You run that mystery bookstore. If you think you can capitalize on Jane's death, you've come to the wrong place."

Annie felt jolted. "I'm trying to save an innocent man from a murder charge."

"What's the idea? A guided tour of the murder scene, then a True Crime evening at your store?" Kate's tone was scathing. She started to turn away.

Annie spoke fast. "Two murders and counting, Miss Murray. Paul Martin. Jane Corley. Tom will be victim number three if he's convicted and sentenced to death."

Kate slowly turned back to face Annie, her dour face taut, still, disbelieving. "Paul?"

"Paul knew someone intended harm to Jane. He warned that person at David's birthday party. Someone followed Paul home, shot him, set up his death to look like suicide. Lucy Ransome believes this happened. I believe Lucy. Lucy sent me."

Kate yanked a cell from her pocket, tapped. "Lucy, did

you send that bookstore woman here? . . . Paul, too? . . . All right." She ended the call, jerked her head toward the hallway. "You'd better come in."

M ax propped a legal pad to one side of the keyboard, glanced at his notes as he typed.

BACKGROUND ON CORLEY HOMICIDE FROM MARIAN KENYON

911 call from Tom Edmonds received by dispatcher 4:49 P.M. Monday, October 14. Homicide One Corley Lane. Victim identified as Jane Corley by husband Tom Edmonds who claims to have discovered body. First cruiser arrives 5:04 P.M., Officers Lou Pirelli and Hyla Harrison. Chief Cameron arrives 5:08 P.M., crime van 5:10 P.M., two additional cruisers 5:11 P.M. Officers Treadwell, Collins, Ingram, and Baker secure scene. ME Dr. T. W. Burford 5:14 P.M. confirms victim dead, prelim cause of death blunt trauma to head. Investigation begins, photos, sketches, measurements. 7 P.M. Chief Cameron speaks to press. Chief says Tom Edmonds, husband of victim, last saw her after lunch, approx. 1:15 P.M., claims he was in his studio until coming into the house and finding her body in the family room at approx. 4:47 P.M. Edmonds told police Jane intended to spend the afternoon in her office, which adjoined the family room. Present in the house that afternoon

were Kate Murray, personal assistant to Jane Corley; Sherry Gillette, family friend; Gertrude Anniston, cook. Kate Murray claims she was in her upstairs office following lunch, did not come downstairs until she heard Tom's shouts. Sherry Gillette spent the afternoon reading in her room. She, too, heard Tom call out and hurried downstairs. Cook cleaned kitchen after lunch, went out side door to drive to the grocery, returned about four, carried in groceries, made coconut cake. According to police, no one heard any unusual noise during the afternoon. Police said the walls of the house are unusually thick. Body facedown midway between pool table and French doors to terrace, head toward terrace. Struck from behind.

Max pictured Jane's body. Was she leading the way for a guest to depart? Or simply leaving someone behind as she walked toward the terrace? Maybe Tom asked her to come to his studio to look at a painting in progress. Maybe Kate Murray suggested a stroll in the gardens. Maybe none of the above. As for the cook, if Jane had spoken with her—but why in the family room?—Jane could have ended the conversation and turned away to go out on the terrace, assuming the cook was returning to the kitchen. He didn't think a cook harbored murderous impulses toward her employer, but she would be vetted as well as anyone known to be present that afternoon.

In actuality, the murderer could be anyone. However, departure by way of the terrace possibly meant the murderer arrived that way. Arrival and departure through the terrace door was another indication someone close to Jane or part of the family was the killer, just as only a member of that close circle attended David's birthday party and possibly spoke with Paul.

Max glanced at the legal pad, continued to type.

> French doors unlocked when police arrived. Gardener Ross Peters saw Jane Corley strolling near a pond in the lower garden beneath the terrace at approx. half past one. She waved at him, then turned and walked back toward the house. He did not see her again. However, he spent some time at the garden at David Corley's house. Police invited the public to contact Crime Stoppers if anyone had information about persons in or around the Corley estate that afternoon. Got no response.

Max tapped the space bar, typed a new title.

GUEST LIST DAVID CORLEY PARTY

Marian's gamine face had registered disdain at his request for the guest list. "Do you think I do society, too, and maybe sweep out after hours? Hop on a bike and deliver papers?" Her eyes narrowed. "Why do you want to know?" Her tone was sharp. "Harsh words, maybe? Somebody challenged to a duel?"

Max had been quick to explain all he needed was the guest list and if she'd hold on, she'd know why. In her usual efficient fashion, Marian pulled up the story that had run in the society editor's column on the Saturday after the birth-day party. All Max needed were the names.

> David Corley, Madeleine Corley, Jane Corley, Kate
> Murray, Sherry Gillette, Kevin and Irene Hubbard,
> Toby Wyler, Frankie Ford, four off-islanders from
> Atlanta, Steve James, Harris Carson, Ken Daniels,
> Wendell Evans, and, of course, Paul Martin and
> Lucy Ransome.

Max liked to have a sense of people. He knew the islanders casually, but he wanted background. First, though, he'd record what Marian described happily as scuttlebutt. He grinned. Marian's dark eyes had gleamed as she unloaded. "BTW. The cop shop zeroed in on Tom from the get-go, but I nosed around a bit, asked here and there who might have it in for the lady. I came up with a little list. As you might expect, check out the nearest and dearest. If anyone wants to know where you picked this up, you can say you walk in the garden every night and little green men murmur in your shell pink ear. Or you looked into Madame SpookaLook's crystal ball in the fortuneteller's tent at the last church rummage sale. Whatever, but nada from *moi*. Right?"

He'd held up his right hand. "Swear to die." If anyone ever should ask, Marian could rest easy. He kind of liked the little green men in the garden. Who could prove otherwise?

Their footsteps echoed hollowly on the tiled floor of the shadowy entrance hall. Arched mullioned windows with stained glass did little to shed light. Tapestries of hunting scenes hung from gray stone walls. Annie was reminded of Errol Flynn movies on TBS except these massive stones were real.

Kate led the way past an enormous reception area framed by Moorish columns on one side and a formal dining hall on the other, again with mullioned windows set high in the walls. Her pace was brisk. At the end of the hallway, a broad stairway led to upper floors. She passed the steps, came to a huge oak door, partially ajar. She paused, took a quick breath, pushed it open.

They stepped into a different world, still Italianate, but with warm glowing Florentine colors, walls hung with Tom's paintings, comfortable furniture. They stood in what was obviously the family room, a fireplace on the north wall, a pool table with a nearby wet bar, chintz-covered sofas and easy chairs, windows overlooking the flagstone terrace and the gardens that sloped beyond.

Annie's gaze stopped at the pool table.

"Just past there. That's where she died. Blood all around her." Kate's voice was uneven.

Annie looked into dark eyes filled with pain and grief. "I'm sorry."

"Hell of a place to die. Her favorite room." Kate hunched thin shoulders. Her stare at Annie was a glower. "Jane was more alive than a hundred people. Smart, quick, clever, never afraid." She swallowed and her voice was thin. "Now she's gone." She stalked across the parquet flooring, pointed down at a too-shiny floor. "They scrubbed and scrubbed to get up her blood." She whirled on Annie. "If you've talked your way in here like a slimy vulture to feast on it, then get the hell out."

Annie met her penetrating gaze steadily. "I'm here because Lucy found a drawing in Paul's desk . . ." The wariness in Kate's gaze changed to intense concentration as Annie spoke of the open house, followed by Paul's worried demeanor, the apparent lifting of his spirits following David's birthday party, the discovery of the sketch, and the underlined words, *Protect Jane.* "Lucy doesn't believe Paul ever owned a gun."

Kate's fingers clamped on Annie's arm. "For God's sake, woman, Lucy has to go to the police."

"Lucy went. I did, too." Annie wanted to be fair to Billy Cameron, one of the finest police officers she'd ever known. "Chief Cameron listened. He admitted someone could have set everything up to make it look like Paul killed himself. Billy didn't believe there was someone who'd planned that well."

Kate loosened her grip. "Let's go out on the terrace. I don't think I can stand being in this room much longer." Again she moved fast, striding the few feet to the French door, yanking it open.

Annie followed her outside, welcoming the sunshine, trying not to remember the too-shiny floor near the pool table.

Kate gestured toward redwood furniture beneath gaily striped umbrellas. When they were settled, Kate was brusque. "Cops look at evidence. Billy's got plenty. But I know Lucy."

Kate spoke of Billy with familiarity. Annie wasn't surprised. Billy was a native of the island. He knew everybody as only a small-town native can know them, who had been married to whom and when, why two women managed to attend the same church for a lifetime but never speak to each other, which secretary was meeting her boss at a motel on the mainland, where a missing uncle was last seen and why no one instituted a search.

Kate gave her a sharp look. "I know about cops. My husband was a beat cop in Atlanta. Gunned down when he stopped a guy who'd killed his girlfriend. Kent was twenty-four, just getting started. He had dreams. He would have been a good cop, like Billy Cameron. That's when I came home to the island. I didn't do much of anything for a couple of years after Kent was killed, then I did books for some local businesses. I'm good at detail. That was before Jane's mother died. Bolton, Jane's father, hired me to run the place after Sherrybeth died in childbirth and he needed someone to oversee taking care of David. I was a cousin of Bolton's." She talked, but her expression was distant, a woman thinking, digesting what Annie had told her.

She turned a troubled gaze on Annie. "Jane wasn't herself the last few weeks. The Friday before she died, she came out on the terrace—I was weeding the pansies"—her mouth quirked—"even though Ross, the gardener, doesn't like for me to fool with 'his' beds. Anyway I was out there, and Jane came out. She didn't look . . . right. She asked me to come to her office. Once inside, she shut the door and said, 'Something's wrong, Kate. I can feel it.' I asked what had disturbed her. She turned her hands up. 'I don't know. I've been uneasy the last few days. Very unlike me. But I wondered if you felt uncomfortable, too.' I said maybe the changes in the barometer were bothering her. She looked a little grim. 'Probably I'm out of sorts because I have to decide what to do about a husband who's acting like a teenager with his first crush. Maybe it's time to yank the lead, remind him who has entrée to the success he'd like to have.' She laughed that robust laugh of hers and seemed to shake off the gloom. She was pretty emphatic. 'I'll deal with that little romance. And him. And her.' That was all she said about Tom and Frankie. So"—her dark eyes challenged Annie—"if you're right, if someone killed Paul and Tom was on the mainland, you need to look at that girl."

Annie remembered Max's story about David Corley's remarks at the men's grill. What did Jane say to Frankie at the birthday party? "Did you see Jane talk to Frankie at David's party?"

"Little difficult to see anything. Madeleine is nuts for Japanese lanterns. I say if you've got lights, use them. I could hardly tell what I had on my plate." She lifted bony shoulders in a shrug, dropped them. "I saw the girl at one point, and she looked like she had a demon sitting on her shoulder, but for all I know she had a migraine. I don't know whether Jane talked to her or not. The whole evening seemed off-kilter to me. I don't know why. I didn't feel comfortable. Madeleine was nervy and she kept darting inside to check on that yappy Yorkie." A pause. "Millie's kind of a cute little dog and she's nuts about Madeleine and both of them have been basket cases lately. Cats are better. They always smell good." Again the words filled space, then, abruptly: "I saw Paul once when I don't think he knew anyone was watching him."

Annie looked at her inquiringly.

Kate brushed back silvered hair, a gesture of impatience. "Maybe what you told me is affecting the way I remember. I was on my way inside to the bathroom. Paul was standing by the wet bar near the pool. As I consider it now, he had an odd expression on his face. He looked like a man confronting something unpleasant, definitely not a party look. I wondered what was wrong, decided he'd seen someone he didn't like. He started walking toward the end of the pool."

"Do you know who was standing near the end of the pool?"

"I don't remember who was there. People wandered around. There was a group clustered past the pool, throwing horseshoes. He was going in that direction."

"Is there anyone you can vouch for that could not have been beyond the pool?"

For an instant, Kate looked puzzled, then she gave an abrupt nod. "I get it. Did I see anyone when I went in the house? Only Lucy. She was coming across the den as I walked inside."

Annie felt a flicker of excitement. When Lucy stepped outside, it would be natural for her to look about for Paul. She might have seen him walking toward the end of the pool. Lucy hadn't noticed Paul in a conversation, but she might have glimpsed who was standing beyond the pool. If Kate's perception was correct, Paul walked toward a confrontation he didn't relish.

"Who attended the party?"

Kate's dark brows drew down in a frown. "Mostly family. David and Madeleine. Jane. Sherry." She gave Annie a quick glance. "Sherry Gillette, a sort of honorary cousin. Her stepmother was Jane's mother's best friend. I'll have to say I fault Jane there. She thought Sherry's husband was a no-good. Sherry showed up a couple of weeks ago with a bruise on her arm, but it wouldn't surprise me if she just banged into something and blamed Roger. I mean he's a social studies teacher, for Pete's sake. He's big and burly, but he looks about as threatening as Pooh Bear. Whatever." Kate was disdainful.

"Anybody with gumption could do something on their own. Instead Jane mixed in and I can tell you it never pays to get into anybody's marriage. Anyway, Sherry was here, so she came to the party. As for the rest . . . Paul and Lucy, of course. Toby Wyler from the gallery, along with Frankie. I guess Madeleine invited them because of Jane." She gave a little snort of disdain. "I'm sure Madeleine thought Toby would hover around Jane in a worshipful way. And he did, of course. Irene and Kevin Hubbard were there. Jane played a lot of golf with Irene. Probably because she'd always beat her, even with Irene's big handicap. Jane liked to win. Kevin manages the Corley properties at the marina. Jane let him handle David's allowance. Kind of a buffer between them."

Annie pounced. "Buffer?"

Kate's face softened. "David's the baby of the family. He hasn't settled down yet and it worried Jane. Bolton's will gave all the money to Jane, a dollar to David with a proviso that Jane share the estate when she felt David was ready. Bolton knew Jane would do the right thing, but that's too big a burden for anybody. I don't blame David for being hurt. I tried to talk to Jane but she got her back up, snapped, 'Dad told me to be sure he was steady. He isn't there yet.' As you can imagine, a grown man—he's almost twenty-five—doesn't like having money doled out to him. That made them edgy with each other and I hate that. David's looked really stricken since she died. At least he got to have a happy birthday before this happened. I'm glad the party was fun for him. He was on a tear that night, lots of jokes." Her smile was indulgent. "Four of his old fraternity brothers came from Atlanta. All bachelors. They drank too much, of course, but they kept things lively. None of them were at the open house on Sunday, so they aren't relevant."

"Can you get their names and phone numbers?"

"Why? They didn't know Paul."

"I want to talk to everyone." One of them might be the sort who took a lively interest in new and different people and watched and noticed. "Please find out and send me a text. Names. Phones numbers."

Kate didn't look unwilling so much as totally unimpressed with Annie's logic. "You need to talk to that girl. The more I think of it, she was upset that night. She looked like somebody falling out of a plane and the rip cord didn't work."

M ax kept his promise of anonymity for Marian as he named the file:

MURMURS FROM LITTLE
GREEN MEN

H e could hear her raspy, slightly breathy voice as he typed from his notes.

> Tom Edmonds—Not your most robust villain. Got it from the cook that Kate Murray's cat brought in a rabbit dripping blood and Tom damn near fainted. It was Jane who scooped up the wounded critter, raced off to the vet. Turned out to be a bite in one shoulder and Bugs returned to frolic in the lower garden and all should be well in bunny land, assuming his small rabbit brain has the wit to

avoid encounters with felines. How does that square with Tom battering Jane all bloody until she was dead? Sure, he was apparently dallying with Frankie Ford, he hasn't got a sou to his name, signed a prenup that a divorce with cause kept the Corley money in the family, and a local artist says nothing matters to him but his work. Might tally up to *mucho* motive for murder, but wouldn't he avoid hammers, especially one from his studio?

Kate Murray—On the scene. One tough broad. Hikes. Racquetball. Deep-sea fishes. Fought a 200-pound tarpon for five hours, got him. Cook said she slammed out of Jane's office a couple of days before David's birthday, looked "like she was ready to spit nails." What was that all about?

David Corley—Big on charm, short on steady. Everybody in town knows his dad left stacks of gold to Big Sis and she doled out money. Apparently, she was generous. David and Madeleine don't appear to be short on cash. I understand now he gets access to his trust fund. Everybody likes him. Got a smile that makes the ladies . . . Well, 'nuff said. Funny things reporters learn when they're following up a lead. I was keeping an eye on the treasurer of a local church—that story's still building—who suddenly started driving a real fancy car and hanging out in some interesting spots. Like the new gambling dive where the island's high rollers shed greenbacks faster than a porcupine flings quills. Not your usual seedy tin building behind a bar. This place is snazzy, an antebellum house tarted up fresh. They call it Palmetto Players, though it isn't written down anywhere. They're not talking horseshoes. The upstairs bedrooms have poker tables, slots, and, in one of them, a shirt-sleeved croupier who rakes in chips like Tarzan dives after Jane. Anyway, I swanked over there with a dude the boss imported from Savannah, who was playing the role of rich guy just waiting to be bilked. Had a hell of a good time, though Vince said we could only blow five hundred and to stay off the sauce.

Max wondered how Vince Ellis, the *Gazette* publisher, entered that night's expenses. $500 misc? $500 incidental? $500 research?

Anyway, we kept an eye on our grim-faced treasurer, hunkered at the table, betting on the black, watching the red come up. Got some neat pics on my cell. Which I did verrrry carefully. My dress was filmy with flowing sleeves and you can bet your iPad nobody saw me take the shots. I value my neck. Suffice to say, I was tuned up tighter than a banjo and keeping an eye on everybody. That's how I happened to notice David Corley. I'd guess the roulette wheel was in what had been a main bedroom adjoined by a study. There was no apparent door. The remodel must have covered it up. The wall was slats of green bamboo. Got my attention because David walked right past the bar and there was nothing ahead of him but a wall. He didn't have his Brad Pitt look. I figured the squat guy marching along at his left elbow might have sucked some oxygen out of pretty boy's lungs. Not buddies on a prowl. David was on his way to a little confab and there was no joy in his heart. Squat guy came up to the wall, poked a stubby pinkie about waist high, and a panel swung in. They stepped inside, but I got a peek at a guy sitting behind a black desk. The desktop had some papers on it. Not much else except a skull. Looked real. The guy behind the desk is probably a little over six feet, good physique, curly graying hair, florid face, one of those easy smiles, but his eyes were cold as a snake's. FYI, his name's Jason Brown, arrived on the island a couple of years ago. Maybe from Tampa, maybe from Dallas, no pedigree I could find. He gestured for David to sit down with one hand, picked up the skull with the other. The door closed.

Madeleine Corley—So far as anyone knows, Madeleine and her sis-in-law were on good terms. But I picked up a tidbit at the beauty shop last week. My gal has dachshund ears when it comes to gossip. She likes to see herself as a tipster to the news ace. In case you're wondering, that's me. Anyway, I was in for a trim and she said I'd never guess what she'd heard, that Bridget Olson, whose mouth runs like a trout stream, was talking to her hairdresser and she said she'd heard that Madeleine said she was home all afternoon the day Jane was killed, BUT SHE WASN'T!, and Bridget knew that for sure because she'd dropped by to ask Madeleine to help with the animal rescue adopt-a-day the next week and she'd knocked, then gone on in because the door was unlocked and she called out and looked everywhere for Madeleine and she absolutely wasn't there. The hairdresser said maybe she was out in the garden. Bridget shook her head, said she'd asked the yard man if Madeleine was around and he said, "No, ma'am, she went off that way a while ago," and pointed to a path. Bridget said probably Madeleine had just taken a walk but it was kind of exciting to think she really hadn't been where she said she was even though it turned out that Jane's awful husband killed her, so it didn't really matter. Sometime, and Bridget has a laugh that sounds like a horse's whinny, she'd have to ask Madeleine about the Mystery of That Monday Afternoon.

Sherry Gillette—The cook has it in for her. Sherry complained about the food. So take this with a grain of salt. Maybe a whole shaker. Cook said Sherry shouted at Jane—she thinks it was the Friday before Jane died—that she'd better not cause any trouble for Roger, then came running out of Jane's office. Roger's a high school teacher, social studies. The cook then went all over trembly and said she had second sight from her Irish grandmother and she'd known something bad was going to happen, that Jane Corley was not herself and went around looking spooked. Cook believes Jane had a presentiment of her death.

Frankie Ford—Nice kid. Got a heap of trouble now. People whispering about her and Tom. Kind of hate to say it, but I'd press her about her errands that afternoon. When I talked to her, she tried to act casual but body language'll get you every time. One hand kept clenching and unclenching. What're the odds she got a little closer to the Corley place than she wants to admit?

Max was thoughtful. Marian Kenyon's crackling black eyes missed little, but Frankie Ford was under enormous pressure. Maybe her hand clenched and unclenched because of the sickening realization deep inside that Tom Edmonds was not only in jail, he was likely bound for a trial and his life was on the line.

Which brought him back to the task at hand. He still wasn't convinced of Tom's innocence, but Lucy Ransome was a smart woman. Okay, smart and grieving. But she could be right and, if Lucy was right, someone who attended David's birthday party was guilty of two murders.

Max concentrated. He pulled information from the Web, scouted out stories in past issues of the *Gazette*, made a series of phone calls. He was purposefully vague, but explained he was a lawyer trying to determine how a witness might cope in a trial. Was the potential witness intelligent, defensive, quick to anger? Character traits? Would a jury pick up on a streak of meanness, selfishness? Finally, he was ready to flesh out the dossiers for the birthday party guests plus the man who wasn't there. He liked his heading: Killer Guests Plus the Man Who Wasn't There.

The phone rang.

As he scanned the last entry, Max reached for the receiver with his left hand, clicked Save and Print with his right. As sheets furled out of the printer, he noted caller ID and felt a flicker of surprise. "Confidential Commissions. Hey, Ben."

"Yo, Max." Ben Parotti, owner of Parotti's Bar and Grill, the ferry, and great swaths of island real estate, spoke sotto voce. "Boot scoot this way for lunch. Got something for you." A pause. "Oh hell, maybe I shouldn't. Hell, maybe I should. I used to play poker with Bolton." On that husky, whispered, obscure pronouncement the connection ended.

5

Annie turned into a now familiar street. A yellow VW, driven too fast, braked abruptly. Marian Kenyon poked her head out the open driver's window, the breeze ruffling her dark hair. Marian radiated excitement, practically bouncing in the seat. "Tell Max he's tops on my list right now. I got a story, I got pics"—her thumb jerked toward the Martin house—"and tonight's *Gazette* will knock 'em dead." For an instant, her monkey face was stern. "Trust me, when I get done, somebody on this island's going to be scared as hell because everybody in town's going to know Paul Martin was murdered." A fist clench, a short chop, and the VW jolted past.

Annie pulled into the Martin drive. She reached for her purse, grabbed her cell, called, burst into speech as Max answered. "I just got to Lucy's and saw Marian leaving. She's going to do a story about Paul and the drawing. Max, it was brilliant to send her here."

"Thank you, ma'am. A fair trade. What brings you to Lucy's?"

"A heads-up from Kate Murray." Annie described Kate's view of Paul Martin at the birthday party. "If Lucy noticed who was standing on the far side of the pool, we can narrow down the possibilities. Luckiest of all would be if there was only one person there. Then we'll know." It didn't take long for her to realize that Max's silence wasn't pulsating with excitement. "Don't you agree?"

"You're such a nice person." His tone was kind.

Annie bristled. "Excuse me?"

"Straight from the horse's mouth?" He was gently wry.

"Oh." Annie got it. Intelligence was only as good as its source. Had Kate played Annie like fish beguiled by a fancy lure? Maybe Kate saw Paul and interpreted his look correctly and his walk indeed signaled an approach to Jane's murderer-in-waiting. Maybe the entire story was a fabrication. Maybe Kate was laying down a false trail for Annie to follow. Maybe it didn't matter a damn who stood beyond the pool as Paul walked away from the bar. "You think she conned me?"

"Maybe she didn't. Caveat emptor. Anyway, it's smart to talk to Lucy. She's had time to think about the party. She may remember something else that will help. Meet me at Parotti's for lunch. Maybe another lead there." He clicked off.

The front door opened. Lucy Ransome hurried across the porch and started down the steps. Lucy moved with energy. The breeze stirring her white curls, Lucy looked almost youthful in a white tee and pale violet jeans. "Did Marian tell you what she's going to do?"

"She's going to bang out a story that will jump off the page." Annie never doubted that Marian would succeed.

Lucy smacked one small fist into the opposite palm. "Finally we're doing something for Paul. It isn't right that people think he killed himself." She gestured toward the side yard. "Come this way. I want to show you something." She wheeled and marched toward a wall of eight-foot stalks of pampas grass.

Annie hurried to follow. Oyster shells crackled underfoot. Annie imagined the yard in darkness, the darkness of the Wednesday night when Paul Martin died. There was a streetlamp but it was a half block distant.

Lucy walked to the end of the border of pampas grass, turned right. The thick mass of plumed stalks extended the length of the side yard as well. Beyond the house an asphalt trail led into a grove of pines. Lucy pushed through a gate flanked by the tall sentinels of pampas grass and led Annie into a secluded garden ablaze with rosy camellias and lavender-and-white rhododendron blooms. A fountain trickled softly near a gazebo. Burnt orange daylilies encircled the redbrick pool. An oyster-shell path led to the gazebo and on to the house.

Lucy gestured. "That's the door to Paul's study."

A quiet figure could easily have slipped unseen through darkness, come to the door, perhaps knocked softly, or perhaps simply turned the knob and walked inside. "Would the door have been locked?"

Lucy shook her head. "The front door is locked during the day but not the study door or the kitchen door. Paul always closed up the house at night, locking everything up before he went to bed."

Annie wasn't surprised. Unlocked doors weren't unusual on the island. Many people when home didn't lock any doors.

"That next morning—"

Lucy forestalled the question. "I don't know. I ran to the kitchen and called 911. It doesn't matter whether the door was locked that morning or not. The point is that Paul was in the study. He hadn't yet made his rounds of the doors in the house before going upstairs for the night, so the door would have been unlocked. In fact"—and she nodded energetically—"I think he asked someone at the party to come and talk to him. He went into the study that night in such a purposeful way. I think he expected someone to come." Some of the vigor left her face. "If only I'd paid more attention at the party."

That gave Annie her opening. "There might be a moment that could be helpful." She kept her tone easy. After Max's warning, Annie wasn't counting on anything definitive. "At one point, Kate Murray came inside and she said you were just going out onto the patio. I believe Paul was walking toward a group at the end of the pool, near where they were throwing horseshoes. Think about that moment and tell me who you saw."

Lucy was shaking her head. "I saw Paul going that way. I didn't pay much attention to the group. Besides, some of them were in shadow. Kevin Hubbard was standing a little sideways and the light from a lantern fell across his face in such an odd way." Her eyes narrowed in consideration. "It was like seeing half a face and that half was as empty and sad as a rusted bucket." She looked uncomfortable. "It may have just been a trick of the light."

An empty and sad expression. Annie thought about a

killer who might be watching the approach of a familiar face, now stern and set. Kevin Hubbard . . . "What do you know about Kevin?"

Lucy's gaze was troubled. "I think he has a good reputation on the island. He's had different jobs but the last few years he's been the property manager for the Corley family. They own a good portion of the buildings at the marina. He always seemed like a nice man. But he looked different that night. I didn't think about it at the time. Now, I don't know what to think."

It was silent in the garden except for the rustle of the feathery blooms of pampas grass and the soft splash of water from a stone dolphin in the redbrick fountain.

Lucy clasped her hands tightly. "I hate the way my mind works now. I'm suspicious of everyone."

Annie's answer was swift. "You should be." Kevin Hubbard might be the person Paul Martin intended to warn. If not, Kevin should be able to recall those who were standing near him at that moment.

Lucy looked toward the study door. "If we'd been in the garden the night Paul died, we would know. Or if my room were on the garden side." She saw Annie's puzzled look. "Upstairs there are two big bedrooms that face the street. Mine is on the far side of the house. I see the street from the front windows. Through the side windows, I can see the fence between our house and next door. The bedroom across the hall from me—that was Paul's—overlooks the street and the garden. That night I stood at the front window for a while. A car passed. I watched its taillights and I wondered who had been out so late. A few minutes later I went to bed. I have a clock with luminous figures. It was about fifteen minutes past midnight. But I didn't pay much attention. It was just a car. Now I wonder . . ." Her eyes held darkness. She pressed her lips together briefly, then spoke in a rush. "I want to show you Paul's study."

They walked in silence to the door. Lucy turned the handle and they stepped inside. Cypress paneling gave the small room an aura of warmth. Filled bookcases lined two walls. The surface of the oak desk was bare. A wingback chair sat near the desk. The study furniture was old, shabby, comfortable. It should have been an enclave of peace, a man's retreat. Annie tried hard not to imagine Paul slumped over the desktop, right hand trailing above the floor. Instead she pictured Paul turning his head at a knock, perhaps calling, "Come in."

Whoever came might reasonably, on a chilly fall evening, have worn a light jacket, whether a man or woman. The jacket would be half-zipped, the gun very probably tucked within, held against one side by the pressure of an arm, hands thrust into side pockets. Had there been a few moments of talk? Had the visitor perhaps sat in a wingback chair to one side of the desk? Had there been reassurances? Promises?

Annie remembered the bloodied but blank sheet of paper and pen found beneath Paul. Had there been an agreement to write a statement assuring Jane's safety? Paul might have insisted, seeing the paper as evidence should anything happen to Jane. That would have given the visitor a reason to come around the desk and stand behind Paul. Had a hand slid into a pocket, wriggled into a loose glove, seized the gun, pulled it out, pressed the barrel to Paul's temple, fired?

If so, the visitor was swift, cool, audacious, and deadly. Such action required the kind of planning Billy discounted.

After the shot, the killer waited, heart thudding, pulse racing. Would anyone come? Would an alarm be raised?

The night remained silent.

Breathing shallowly, hands perhaps a little unsteady or perhaps rock firm, the next few minutes would have sped by, the weapon rested for the moment on a corner of the desk, Paul's hands placed on the box of cartridges, the box slipped into the bottom drawer, gunshot residue from the right-hand glove smeared on Paul's palm and fingers, his flaccid hand conformed to the gun grip, creating fingerprints, then the gun placed on the floor where it might have dropped from nerveless fingers. A final look around the study. A silent departure.

Lucy walked past the desk to the wingback chair. A tasseled decorative pillow rested against the back. She pointed at a Tiffany lamp on an oak side table. "I was too upset to think about it, but the lamp was on when I stepped into the study that morning." She swung to face Annie. "Someone came that night. Someone sat in that chair. Paul never turned on the lamp just for himself. He was found sitting at his desk. And," she concluded triumphantly, "the cushion was on the floor. I stumbled over it and almost fell when I turned away from the desk."

Her small, thin face had the look of a teacher sure of her pronouncement. An equilateral triangle has three matching sides. The speed of light is 186,282 miles per second. Akhenaten's queen, elegant and imperious, was Nefertiti.

Annie looked at soft light gleaming through the vivid red, green, and amber art glass of the Tiffany lampshade. Billy Cameron could murmur about unicorns, but Annie knew

Lucy was right. Death had sat in the black leather wing chair near Paul's desk and waited for its moment.

Max looked up as Ben Parotti approached and was mesmerized by Ben's appearance. Since his marriage to Miss Jolene of a mainland tea shop and her arrival on the island, wizened Ben had blossomed into sartorial splendor, discarding dingy white singlets beneath bib overalls for Tommy Bahama cool-beach-daddy attire. But today's ensemble was over the top, the dress shirt a pale lavender, trousers in a purple that matched lowering clouds in a hurricane sky.

Ben's face furrowed when he saw Max's expression. "Miss Jolene loves her Loropetalums and she thought my pants looked just like her Purple Diamond Loropetalum." At Max's silence, he hurried on. "A shrub." A forlorn addendum. "She made the pants for me."

Max hurried to make amends. "I should have known. Purple Diamond. Neat idea, Ben. Give Miss Jolene my congratulations."

Relieved, Ben glanced toward the empty chair. "Two?"

Max smiled. "She's coming. Now, Ben, about your call—"

Ben slapped down the menus. "Back in a jiffy."

Max watched him cross the planked flooring, skirting tables as he strode toward the swinging door to the kitchen. A change of mind? Or did he want Annie here, too? Max heard quick steps, saw Annie hurrying toward him, a pale gray scoop neck tee molding softly to her, a short floral skirt revealing very, very nice legs. Her dusty blond hair was wind riffled, her gray eyes intent. A quick smile softened her serious expression as she reached the table.

He stood and thought how nice it would be to go home—now—with her and knew she saw desire in his eyes. Everything was better and brighter and sharper and happier when Annie was near.

She came around the table to touch his cheek, telling him she knew, she loved him, later, then took the opposite chair, plopped her elbows on the table, talked fast as he settled back in his chair. ". . . so I'm sure Frankie knows something she hasn't told us and Kate Murray's trying to help—I think—and if cushions could talk we'd know who came to Paul's study—"

Ben sidled up, stood at an angle to them, his eyes whipping around the partially filled dining room. "Got some specials today." He rattled them off, Manhattan clam chowder, grilled flounder, spinach quiche. He raised his pen to his order pad.

"Fried oyster—" Annie started.

"Onion bun, double order Thousand Island, fries, iced tea. Got it." Ben looked at Max.

"Grilled flounder sandwich. Iced tea."

Ben reached for the menus, held them up high enough to mask his face, spoke out of the side of his mouth. "Tuesday before Jane Corley died. Saw her stalking into Kevin Hubbard's office at the marina. Got to say up front, he's a sorry"—he looked at Annie, pressed his lips together, then continued—"jerk. A few years ago, I made a bid for some town land near the lighthouse. Several bidders. Kevin's bid came in five bucks more than mine. Maybe he was lucky. Maybe he had a buddy in the know. He wasn't buying for the Corley properties, a flyer on his own. I'd bet the house he cut corners, paid somebody on the sly for the bid numbers. If he cut corners there, he'd cut 'em anywhere. FYI. BTW." He turned away.

Annie waited until he pushed through the swinging door. "What's with the Sam Spade imitation?"

Max laughed. "Ben's the entrepreneur behind the open-air old movies at the pavilion. Bunch of Bogart movies lately." Max glanced across the room at a round table not far away where their old nemesis Mayor Cosgrove was at lunch with several city employees. "I'd guess Ben doesn't want it to get around that he thinks there might be a little bit of palm greasing going on at city hall. He wheels and deals all over the island. Some fights you don't pick unless you can prove your claim. I picked up some stuff that raises a few questions about Kevin Hubbard. You can take all of this with you." He tapped a folder. "But for now, Mrs. Darling, let's talk about us." His voice was hopeful. "We can give Tom's fate a rest until Marian turns the screws with her page-one story that blows the lid off Paul's death. We can take the afternoon off." His eyes promised delight.

Annie looked regretful and he knew his vision of afternoon delight wasn't to be. But she did look regretful. There was always tonight.

Ben arrived with their plates and a big bowl of cheese grits. "Something extra from Miss Jolene. Hot out of the oven."

Max looked from the steaming grits to Annie's fries, raised an eyebrow.

She ignored him and spooned a generous heap of steaming grits next to her fries.

Ben nodded approvingly, hunched a shoulder, tucked his chin down, and muttered like an undercover agent passing a contact, "KH looks soft, but he can kickbox like Charlie Chan," and strolled away a man absorbed in his order pad.

Annie said decisively, "I want to talk to Kevin. Ben's side-of-his-mouth lowdown has to be fate pointing the way. Plus Lucy Ransome thought Kevin looked odd that night at David's house. She said his face looked like a rusted bucket."

Max squeezed lemon over the flounder. "Wait until tomorrow. Let's put everything on hold until Marian's story comes out."

Annie looked thoughtful. "That's probably a good idea."

Ah. Maybe they would go home . . .

"Once the story runs, nobody will be surprised that we are trying to help Tom. Everyone close to Jane will look like they don't care what happened to her if they refuse to talk to us."

Max wished he shared Annie's conviction. He doubted guests at David's party would be eager to reveal much about themselves and Jane, but Marian's story would get a killer's attention. That was the prism they needed to apply in looking at those around Jane. Somebody was going to be scared, and fear can make people do stupid things. As well, the blockbuster story would give hope to Tom and Frankie and maybe prod the authorities to take another look at their case.

But this afternoon . . .

Annie licked from one finger a splash of Thousand Island dressing that had dripped from her sandwich. "We need to talk to Tom. We can tell him about Paul."

Max took a bite of the perfectly grilled flounder, the

white flaky flesh delectable. He could think of other delectable . . . But Annie had a point. Tom Edmonds must feel like a guy twisting in the wind with no rider on horseback coming his way. "Sometimes, Mrs. Darling, your ace trumps. It's a good idea to talk to Tom. I'd better stay on the island. There's a cop who deserves a heads-up."

6

Annie stood on the top deck of the *Miss Jolene* as the ferry thumped over whitecaps. She pulled Max's folder from her Sak tote. The more she knew before she saw Tom, the better equipped she would be to ask the right questions. There was no assurance Tom would see her during the afternoon visiting hours, but she'd ask that he be told she was there on behalf of Frankie. That should entice him. Once he understood that she was on his side, he might be able to give information no one else possessed.

Annie skimmed Max's Run-up to Murder, the summary of what he had learned from Marian, and David Corley's birthday party guest list. She had no difficulty identifying the presumably anonymous source of the tart comments in Murmurs from Little Green Men. She reached the final sheet: Killer Guests Plus the Man Who Wasn't There. Max had obviously made a lot of calls. It was clever of him to use the ploy that he was assessing personalities of potential witnesses. The dossiers included photos, some likely from the *Gazette*, some likely from Facebook pages. The names were in all caps.

DAVID CORLEY—25. Son of the late Bolton and Sherrybeth Jessop Corley, brother of Jane Corley. Attended University of South Carolina, washed out—probably literally—his sophomore year. Likes to bartend at parties, claims he makes the saltiest margaritas east of Juárez. Athletic. Sails, rock climbs. Loves to take chances whether it's a mountain, outsailing a storm, cards, or horses. David lived high, which meant his sister, Jane, provided him with a generous allowance.

High school tennis coach Gil Bradley—"Had a knack for figuring out opponent's weakness. Once he found it—lob, backhand, net game—he never let up. Pretty savvy about people. Lots of charm."

High school ex-girlfriend Judy Walter—"David puts a good face on everything. Everybody thinks he's great. I liked him until I went to a football game. My brother told me to get over it, guys get mean on the field. David grabbed this guy's face mask. He was a lot littler than David. He didn't get up after the play. It could have been worse, I guess. The boy's neck got hurt and he couldn't play anymore. I asked David and he said I'd seen it wrong in the lights." A pause. "I don't think I did. That's when I stopped dating him."

Fraternity brother Harris Carson—"Everybody thinks David's cool. Guys on a jury would like him a lot. Any guy can figure he's a hell-raiser, and man, they'd be right. You didn't know fun till you hit the street on a Saturday night with David. Never met a woman he couldn't charm or a dare he wouldn't take."

Fraternity housemother Heather Hastings— "What a dear boy. Everyone liked David. It's too bad he didn't settle down and study. He always made everyone laugh."

Bolton Corley longtime friend R. T. Magruder— "David makes a good first impression but he was a disappointment to Bolton. Irresponsible. He's still easy come, easy go, but maybe that's because he was still treated like a kid by Jane. I thought leaving all the money to Jane wasn't fair to her. Not that she seemed bothered. Jane was like the old man. She never minded playing the ball where it landed. I imagine all this trouble will grow him up quick."

Annie glanced at the photographs. David Corley was a very handsome man, tousled blond hair, broad forehead, wide-spaced blue eyes, straight nose, firm chin, full lips usually smiling. The photos without exception showed him having fun, a flushed and sweaty David pumped a losing opponent's hand after a tennis match, David on his sailboat with the wind ruffling his thick hair and tugging at his sweater and white slacks, David at his wedding, face aglow with pride, David edging up a steep rock face but pausing to look down with a daredevil smile.

According to Kate Murray, David had been grieved at his sister's death. Had he resented his dependence upon her enough to kill?

> MADELEINE CORLEY—24. Native of Charleston. Mother Ellen a widow. Madeleine an excellent student. Scholarships. Worked her way through college. She met David at the university. They married a year after her graduation. She trained as a fashion designer and isn't currently employed, though she has been working on a portfolio she hopes to offer to some fashion houses in Atlanta.
>
> High school counselor John Casey—"Gifted. As with many gifted people, volatile. Up or down. Responsible. Cheerful." A pause. "Perhaps"—and the words seemed chosen carefully—"because of her life circumstances—her father died from cancer when she was in middle school and her mother didn't cope well—she has a streak of anger. If things strike her wrong, she can lash out."
>
> Sorority sister Betty Taylor—"Sweetest girl in the world. A little fearful, afraid things will go wrong but that's 'cause she lost her dad so young. Sometimes she blows things out of proportion."
>
> Church acquaintance Bridget Olson—"Madeleine's always been so dependable. But she missed her turn to drive for Mobile Meals a couple of weeks ago, claimed her Yorkie was sick. I don't

like to tell tales out of school but I know the vet really well, my Mitzi has one bladder infection after another and we've tried all kinds of diets, and so I had Mitzi in a few days later and I just said something about too bad Madeleine's dog had been so sick and she said I must have heard wrong because Millie hadn't been in since her yearly checkup, fine little dog. I would have thought Madeleine told the truth about things. She's not been herself since, oh, maybe it was late September. This haunted look. But she could just have told me she forgot or she wasn't feeling up to it. There's no reason to lie."

Addendum: Marian's hairdresser told her Bridget claimed Madeleine wasn't home the afternoon of the murder. No luck yet but trying to find out name of yard man who told Bridget he saw Madeleine take a path. What path?

Lies, a haunted look, and an undercurrent of anger . . . Annie remembered the too-shiny floor in the family room where Jane was struck down. Anger . . . She pulled out her cell, dialed a familiar number. Thankfully, the ring was clear and distinct. The electronic imps that summarily prevented connections on and between the island and mainland were on their good behavior.

"Is Doc Burford there?"

"Please hold."

Annie looked out at the green water. There was the faintest hint of a dark purple line on the horizon, the first glimpse of the mainland. The cool air sweeping against her smelled fresh and clean and faintly salty. Not far away sleek gray dolphins, shiny in the sunlight, arched up from the water, slid down again into the Sound.

A deep voice barked, "Burford."

"Doc, Annie Darling. Did Jane Corley's wounds seem excessive?"

A snort. "Hard to bash someone to death without inflicting major damage. But I get your point. Coldly methodical or sheer rage." A pause. "Maybe ten, twelve blows. More than enough. Could indicate lack of medical knowledge. Cerebellum crushed. That would have been sufficient. Either making damn sure or mad as hell. Maybe both. Massive blood loss. Told Billy to look for spots of blood on perp's clothing. Thought they tossed Edmonds in jail."

"He's innocent, Doc." A crackle, a hiss, the connection was lost. Annie clicked off the cell, dropped it into her purse.

Blood on clothing . . . She turned to the next sheet. The contrast between bloodied clothing and Madeleine Corley's elegant attire in a collage of photos was mind-bending. Madeleine was a beautiful woman, soft silky hair dark as midnight, eyes of a particularly striking violet hue, and fine features, a high forehead, straight nose, full lips touched with a faint hue of coral, rounded chin, magnolia creamy complexion. She was striking in an ivory gown at a charity event, beguiling in a pale pink Oxford shirt and cream slacks and boat shoes on the deck of a sloop, regal in a summery white dress at a garden party.

Annie shook her head. To picture Madeleine wielding a hammer—bringing it down with force several times—and watching blood spatter was beyond Annie's imagination. She shook her head again, turned to the next sheet.

SHERRY GILLETTE—27. Island native. Father Arnold Booker. Mother Annette Frasier Booker. Mom left the island when Sherry and her brother Louis were little kids, never heard from again. Apparently a divorce. Arnold m. Genevieve Hastings, a local Realtor and close friend of Sherrybeth Corley, Jane's mother. Sherry and Louis were always included in Corley family gatherings, even after her mother's death. Jane was a little older and dominated the younger kids. But she continued to give them a helping hand after her father's death. Louis a top student at Washington and Lee, now working as a stockbroker in Chicago. Sherry never held jobs long. Fast food. Manicurist. Recently let go from Scentology Shop at 413 N. Main. Sells perfumes, candles, potpourri. That's about the time she showed up at the Corley house.

Next-door neighbor to Booker family Sueann McKay—"As a witness, I don't know. Sherry has kind of a silly way of acting. Quick enthusiasms, never steady about things. Of course it's hard on a teenager when she's a little too heavy and frankly not very pretty to boot. Or smart. She chased after Roger Gillette from the time they were in junior high. He's one of those diffident, won't-look-you-in-the-eye guys. Big as the side of a house, but no bluster. Still, he can get riled up.

Nuts about his Labs. I heard from a coworker that he went on a school trip and when he got home one of the dogs had a thorn in his paw and almost died from an infection. He got so mad he trashed Sherry's iPad, said she was so busy in chat rooms that she didn't take care of the dogs."

Hardee's manager in Bluffton Bill Tway—"I had to let her go. I wouldn't recommend her to anyone for anything. She didn't show up a couple of days in a row then threw a big sobbing fit when I told her not to come back, claimed her husband had kept her locked up because he didn't want her spending so much money on gas. Sounded like baloney to me."

High school history teacher LaRue Willis—"I've only met her a couple of times. Poor Roger. Bless his heart. I heard she'd moved in with the Corleys. I know Roger's looked like hell for a while."

Best friend in high school Candy Hewlitt—"I don't know how Sherry would come across to a jury. She doesn't have a lot of self-confidence. She always felt overshadowed by Louis. He was handsome. He was popular. He made straight As. She tried to compensate by making things more exciting than they were. A rough trip on the ferry and she acted like it was the *Titanic*. And sometimes the hungrier you are for people to like you, the more they try to avoid you. Deep down all she wanted was for somebody to love her."

Scentology owner Jessamine Jackson—"If Sherry took the deposit to the bank, she'd come back with a tall tale about these rough-looking men and she thought one of them followed her into the bank and she just couldn't get to the teller quick enough. Or a delivery came to the back door and she touched the knob and got such a shock and by the time she found something to wrap around the knob the truck was pulling out of the alley. Lordy, she should be writing soap operas but even daytime TV figured out nobody believes that stuff anymore. I fired her after three weeks."

Annie studied the photos. A wedding picture and Roger with curly black hair and a big wide face, a younger Sherry looking almost demure. Later photos at a school picnic revealed Roger with an unhappy look and a paunch, Sherry thirty pounds heavier. If Sherry got a better haircut and improved her makeup and lost that extra weight and straightened up her shoulders, she might be attractive. Dark-haired, she was fairly tall with large green eyes and a nice enough nose and chin. But her expression was self-pitying, dissatisfied. Annie stared into wide green eyes that looked vulnerable and lonely . . . *all she really wanted* . . .

KEVIN HUBBARD—44. Island native. BBA in finance Savannah State. Married for two years to Irene Dooley Roberts. No children. Held several jobs on the island, banking, realty, marketing. Employed for five years by Corley Enterprises as leasing manager of marina shops and offices in the marina complex. Active in civic clubs, Chamber of Commerce, Friends of the Library.

Bank president Fred Marley—"Banking takes an instinct, you know. When to make a loan, when not. Kevin's good at accounting, knows how to do a spreadsheet, but not right for banking. I suggested he find something that suited him better. He puts up a good front. You'd think he was on top of things. Lord knows he means well. He tries to please. On the witness stand? He'd probably do fine. He'll come across as a good old boy."

Kiwanis president and Estes Jewelry owner Ralph Estes—"Kevin's a great guy. He flips pancakes like nobody's business. He hasn't been as active since he got married but hey, he's got himself a babe. He used to be married to a teacher. They got a divorce and she moved to Birmingham. He'd been single for a couple of years when Irene blew into town. I hired her as a clerk. She knew her jewelry. She was decorative behind the counter, too. A Dolly Parton blonde. My wife took a dim view. But like I told her, a woman can't be blamed for looking her best. Edith didn't crack a smile. Irene only worked for me for about a year. She was looking for Mr. Right. As soon as she married Kevin, she took to a life of leisure. I'd say the upkeep there is pretty expensive. Kevin would do fine with a jury, especially if it's got a lot of ladies on it."

Johnstone Realty Jim Johnstone—"Nicest guy in the world. But a bust at selling real estate. Course the downturn hit us hard. Takes some whiz to sell oceanfront lots now. Funny thing, he's got a lot of bullshit, but he just wasn't cut out for real estate."

Friends of the Library president Rachel Morris—"Kevin was a big help a couple of years ago when we were trying to apply for some grants. He has a real eye for detail. He hasn't been active for a while. I think Irene likes a little glitzier social life. I saw them at the hospital ball in April and her dress was a knockout, crimson lace with a scalloped hem. Someone told me it was a Michael Kors evening gown. They were sitting with Jane Corley and her husband. Kevin's lucky he landed that job managing the Corley properties. He always looks pretty prosperous, too. I don't know how that would play with a jury."

Max had printed a montage of photos for Kevin and Irene. Annie understood the Kiwanis club president's appreciation of Irene. Perhaps someone had once told her she resembled Hollywood's icon of sex and beauty. There was a definite resemblance to Marilyn Monroe, shining blond hair, an inviting gaze, and full lips parted in a seductive smile. Annie glanced with interest at Kevin Hubbard, who had persuaded this flamboyant beauty—as exotic on the island as a scarlet macaw—to marry him. Slickly handsome, his dark hair was a little thin but he had deep-set brown eyes, a narrow nose, and a chiseled chin.

IRENE DOOLEY ROBERTS HUBBARD—36. Native Saint Louis. Dropped out of University of

Missouri. First marriage to a drummer in a rock band ended in divorce. Worked as a clerk in several upscale women's boutiques, on weekends sold jewelry at flea markets. Came to the island with a friend on holiday, saw job listing in the *Gazette* for Estes Jewelry. Married Kevin Hubbard a year after arriving. Turned out to be a good golfer and soon was playing with Jane Corley, whom she met through Kevin.

Women's Golf Association president Charlotte White—"Irene's very good. Her only weakness is a tendency to think she can play even better than she can. She'll try a shot to make it over the water on eight with a three wood instead of laying up. That costs her. Definitely she's fun to play with. She always thinks she's going to win. If you want someone on the stand who projects confidence, she's your gal. And, of course, men on the jury will lust for her."

Manicurist island salon Tasha Pritchard—"Big tipper. She always has a roll of green and she likes to spread the wealth. She always came in right after Jane Corley. Marked contrast. Jane tipped 15 percent. No more, no less. That's often true of people who have a lot of money. It's obvious Irene didn't grow up rich. But maybe people who come into money late enjoy it more."

It was hard to look at Irene's photos, a woman supremely sure of her beauty and her sex appeal and imagine her planning a clever murder. But larger-than-life swagger might translate into the willingness to take chances. She wasn't a safe golfer. She'd found a comfortable niche on the island after her marriage to Kevin. Ben Parotti saw Jane Corley stride into the Corley Enterprises office apparently in a grim mood. Ben also thought Kevin was willing to cut corners. Annie thought about money and women with expensive tastes and Kevin at the birthday party, his face reminding Lucy Ransome of a rusted bucket.

Her cell rang, the opening bars to the original Joan Hickson *Miss Marple* TV series. Annie retrieved the phone. "Ingrid?"

The connection was spotty. ". . . fine . . . couple phone calls . . . must be stirring something up . . . kind of a hurried, breathy voice, woman, didn't give a name, conspiratorial like somebody might be listening . . . said you weren't here . . . looked at caller ID . . . listed for Sherry and Roger Gillette . . . does . . . plot thicke . . ." The connection ended.

A hurried call, apparently from Sherry Gillette. Annie pictured a woman with masses of curly dark hair and beseeching green eyes. Interesting. Or maybe not. Was Sherry Gillette calling because she knew something about Jane's murder? Or did she want to plump herself in the middle of an exciting moment? Annie felt a flicker of distaste, dropped the cell into her purse, and looked at the printout.

> TOBY WYLER—52. Owner Wyler Art Gallery. Longtime island resident. Single. Known up and down the coast for finding and launching artists with an emphasis on American representational and Lowcountry impressionism. Had been the sole

purveyor of Tom Edmonds's paintings until Jane Corley arranged for a show in Atlanta.

Local artist Cissy Moreland—"Toby knows his stuff. But a cross-examination might unleash his inner Katharine Kuh. Kuh was a great curator but she'd blow you away if you didn't measure up. Toby's not a man to mince his words either. He drives a hard bargain. He's launched a lot of artists around here. Tom Edmonds was his poster child until now. Or maybe that romance was already over. I understand Jane Corley ticked him off when she insisted on taking over managing Tom's career and would only let Toby have paintings on consignment, not an exclusive. But he gave Tom a big show just recently."

Local contractor Carl Colson—"Will he have to testify about his current financials? I'd say there might be a problem there. I'm sure I'll get my money pretty soon, but I've got subcontractors to pay. I'll continue with the addition to the gallery as soon as I get paid."

Toby Wyler was broad faced with bushy black hair, piercing dark eyes, a bold nose, thick black mustache, and jutting chin. He affected Tom Wolfe–style white suits à la Mark Twain and a wide-brimmed panama hat. He was pictured at the show for Tom Edmonds, bending low over Jane Corley's hand. Jane's expression was curious, a slight smile, an almost imperceptible quirk to her full lips. In another *Gazette* photo he stood behind a lectern, obviously at ease and enjoying himself. The caption read: *Art curator extols local painters.*

Toby Wyler was a man accustomed to the ways of artists. Using a sculptor's mallet as a weapon would be very natural and he was surely familiar with Tom Edmonds's studio.

The darkish line of the horizon had expanded. Only a few more minutes and the ferry would land. She moved on to the last guest at David Corley's party.

> FRANKIE FORD—23. Native Little Rock, Ark. Father Charles a Methodist minister, small rural church in Bluffton. Mother Corrine Harrison Ford, dec. Only child. BFA in art history University of South Carolina. Worked on the island summers in college as a waitress, summer after junior year at Wyler's Art Gallery. Full-time after graduation. Particular interest 20th-century American painters.
>
> Church secretary Martha Crawford—"Miss Frankie is as nice a girl as I've ever known. After her mama died, she pitched right in and did her best to help her father and she was always at the church when they needed an extra hand. She's right handy with tools, always helps make the booths for the fall festival and she can paint a backdrop that makes you feel like you're in Gay Paree at the Moulin Rouge or at the inn in Bethlehem."
>
> Sorority housemother Lucinda Merriweather— "Lovely girl. Went to church every Sunday. Of course, she's a clergyman's daughter, but even so . . . I understand she owes quite a bit on her student loans. She always worked hard. Any jury

would think she's a peach. Her friends . . . let
me see . . ."

Annie did sense that Frankie was uncomfortable about
her connection to Tom. Yet she'd stayed on the island and
continued to care more for a married man than she should.
A girl from her background surely had strayed a long way
from what she had been taught.

> Former boyfriend Buddy Howard—"I don't know
> about a courtroom. She's kind of fragile. Really
> fun and smart, but she can lose it when things go
> wrong. I mean, I was just kidding around with this
> other girl, didn't mean a thing, but when Frankie
> found out, I think she would have shot me if she'd
> had a gun."

Marsh grass wavered in the breeze. The tug headed for the
deep water of a bay. Slash pines rose dark and somber on either
side of a small clearing. The ferry eased her way to the dock,
bumped against the rubber tires lashed to the concrete pilings.
Annie took the steps down two at a time and hurried to her
car in the center lane. She slid behind the wheel, smelled diesel
fuel, car fumes, salt water. As she waited for the ramp to lower,
she ignored the photos of Frankie. She knew what Frankie
looked like. As her eyes slid past the photos to the entry on
Tom Edmonds, she was struck by the stark contrast between
Frankie in happier days and Annie's memory of Frankie this
morning. She turned on the motor, read fast.

THE MAN WHO WASN'T THERE

TOM EDMONDS—29. Native of Greenville. Only child. Parents divorced. Father Charles a bush pilot in Alaska. Mother Doreen high school history teacher. Graduate BFA University of South Carolina, MFA ditto. Winner art awards in high school and at the university. Oil paintings recognized in recent juried shows. Establishing a reputation as a modern Edward Hopper.

Gazette feature by Marian Kenyon about Tom as a local artist. "Edmonds's talents range from watercolors to oil painting to sculpture to wood carving to silversmithing. On his desk sits a quote from Edward Hopper carved in mahogany: 'Maybe I am not very human—what I wanted to do was to paint sunlight on the side of a house.'"

Art critic Mario Costello—"I haven't decided whether to classify Edmonds as a figurative realist or a postmodernist. Then he'll do a painting that reminds me of a young Gauguin. Fascinating possibilities. He's a very young man. I can testify as to his stature as an artist, but beyond that . . . I'm sorry to hear he's facing trial. On the several occasions that I spent time with him, I had the impression of a man consumed by art. I rather thought he and his wife had a good relationship. Of course, it's always wise for an impecunious artist to have a sponsor, and she was a very attractive and very wealthy woman."

Art professor Mark Quilley—"Never knew him to think about anything but his art. Like most artists, bound up in an interior world, the only reality the brush in his hand, the canvas on the easel. Funny to me that a man like Tom can see colors most of us can never imagine but the people around him might as well be stick figures."

The pickup in front of her belched an oily plume of black smoke from its exhaust. Annie punched the window buttons and tried not to breathe. As the car rolled up the slight incline and onto the concrete pier, she dropped the last sheet onto the passenger seat. Loblolly pines made the road shadowy but perhaps not as shadowy as her thoughts. The Hopper quote ran through her mind: "Maybe I am not very human—what I wanted to do was to paint sunlight on the side of a house."

7

Billy Cameron's face was set in his stolid cop look, impervious, tough, seen-it-all, spare-me-hokum. "We got facts, Max. Marian spins a sob-sister yarn with the best of them, but nothing changes facts. I will admit that when she was working on the story"—his tone was grudging—"she called, filled me in, shot the question: 'Does new information concerning the death of Paul Martin reopen the investigation into the murder of Jane Corley?' I told her what I'm telling you, nothing alters the case against the accused."

Max opened his briefcase, pulled out a folder with another copy of his findings. He placed the folder on Billy's varnished yellow oak desk. "Jane Corley was a wealthy and powerful woman." His tone was mild. "She controlled the Corley money. Her brother, David, depended on her largesse. David may have been in hock to the Palmetto Players."

Nothing moved in Billy's steady gaze.

Max knew Billy was familiar with gambling spots on the island, whether in rusted-tin-roof shacks or a stately mansion. "David was seen at PP with a bulky escort walking toward Jason Brown's office." Max tapped the folder. "Madeleine Corley claimed she was home all afternoon that Monday. She wasn't. Kate Murray professes shock at Jane's death, but the cook says Kate was furious with Jane a week before her murder. Jane and Sherry Gillette quarreled. Jane was interfering in Sherry Gillette's marriage. The week before she died, Jane entered the offices of Corley Enterprises where Kevin Hubbard keeps the books and Jane looked like a woman who wasn't happy."

Billy folded his arms across his burly chest. "Give it up, Max. I'll share a piece of evidence if you give me your word you won't leak it to Marian."

Max studied Billy's confident, untroubled face. Billy was smart and careful. If he found evidence, the evidence had been there. Max had an empty feeling in his gut. Maybe Lucy Ransome was wrong, maybe the drawing was irrelevant, maybe Paul referred to some other Jane entirely, maybe Paul had always had a gun in his lower desk drawer, maybe they needed to rethink what they were doing. "I won't leak anything."

Billy looked sympathetic, then he was brisk. "Officer Harrison executed a search of the outside premises of the Corley mansion."

Max pictured Hyla Harrison, red hair often drawn back into a severe bun, her somewhat pale face sprinkled by freckles, unsmiling, serious, intent, trim in a crisp uniform.

"She followed protocol, started on the far side of the terrace, worked her way back and forth, checked patio furniture, drains, shrubbery. She hit the jackpot in a big urn outside the door into the family room. There was wadded-up cloth stuffed into a clump of great blue lobelias. She saw a stalk listing to one side, used her gloves, carefully pulled the stalks apart." He loomed up from his chair, a big man who could move lightly. He stepped to a bank of metal filing cabinets, pulled out a drawer, riffled through files, retrieved one. He came around the desk, opened the folder, and handed it to Max.

Max wasn't surprised by the clarity of the photographs. He doubted there was any technical phase of investigation that Hyla Harrison wouldn't perform with excellence. Color, of course. Five photos. 1. 10/21—Dingy wad of cloth stuffed down near the base of the plant. 2. 10/21—Gloved hands holding the flower stalks apart, cloth visible. 3. 10/21—Cloth contained in oversized clear plastic bag, identifying tag visible: Hidden cloth found in urn next to door on terrace of Corley home. 4. 10/22—Unfolded to full size: Front view XL artist smock, polyester-cotton, chamois color, streaked with oil paints, darker splotches ID'd as human blood. (10/23 test confirmed blood spatters from homicide victim Jane Corley.) 5. 10/22—Back view XL artist smock, polyester-cotton, chamois color, some paint smudges, no blood stains.

Billy took the folder from Max, replaced it in the file cabinet. When he settled back in his chair, he built a steeple with his fingers. "We found matching fibers from both the studio and family room. The smock was one of a half dozen Edmonds kept in an armoire next to the north wall in his studio. Sorry, Max. This time you're backing the wrong horse."

Sunlight slanted through a series of small windows, accessible only by a ladder. The remote windows emphasized the reality that the only means of entering or exiting the long narrow room was through steel doors. A mesh screen rose five feet from a counter that divided the room. Chairs sat on either side. A uniformed officer with an impassive brown face led Annie to the third chair, then withdrew to stand with her back against a dun-colored wall, arms folded.

The only other visitor was four chairs down from Annie. A rotund guard with a sleepy gaze stood next to the wall behind a forlorn woman hunched forward to stare through the mesh. She murmured in a voice too soft to be overheard. A young man with a soft downy fuzz on his cheeks turned his face away. Annie saw him swallow convulsively.

A big metal door swung open on the prisoner side of the mesh. Tom Edmonds moved slowly. A balding, stocky guard with a thin black mustache jerked an impatient thumb. Tom paused and looked toward Annie. She saw that he had no idea who she was. Perhaps that was not surprising. The only time they'd met was at the open house the Sunday before Paul Martin died. He hesitated, the guard said something.

Tom watched her as he came toward the counter. He dropped into the chair. "They said Frankie sent you." His brown eyes were wary. "That's nice of her. I guess she feels sorry for me because I don't have any family here." He spoke formally as if speaking of a distant acquaintance.

Annie dropped her voice, although she didn't think the guard behind her was interested in what prisoners and their visitors said. The guards were there to wait and escort visitors out.

"I'm Annie Darling. Frankie asked my husband and me to help and we have new evidence that proves you are innocent." Quickly she described Max and Confidential Commissions, the drawing in Paul Martin's desk, Paul's death, and the fact that Tom was absent from the island the night Paul died.

Tom's eyes widened. "You mean they're going to let me out?" He looked around at the guard standing by the door, arms behind his back.

"Right now the police don't believe us. That's why I'm here. I hope you know something that can help us find out what happened."

He let out a breath, his face abruptly defeated. "They still think it's me." His voice was dull.

"Yes, but if we can find different evidence, the police will have to listen." She wished she could grip his thin shoulders, give them a shake. "We've already discovered a lot. We know the murderer was at David's party."

Tom put his long-fingered hands on the opposite counter. Even through the mesh she could see the flexibility and suppleness in those hands, still stained by paint. He clenched and unclenched his fingers. "Somebody at David's party?"

She could imagine those lean fingers holding a brush, firm on the handle of a mallet. She jerked her eyes away and rattled off the names. "David and Madeleine Corley, Sherry Gillette, Kate Murray, Kevin and Irene Hubbard, Toby Wyler, Frankie Ford. You weren't at the party, but you were at the art gallery open house on Sunday and all of those people were there. Did you see Paul Martin talking to any of them?" Even as she finished, she saw his blankness.

"That night . . . we sold three paintings. Jane was pleased." For an instant, an expression of incredulity touched his face. "Jane . . . I couldn't believe it when I found her lying on the floor. The sun was coming through the French windows and the parquet flooring had this rich golden color. Except for the blood. The blood was bright, bright, bright red." His voice quivered. "I don't know if I can finish the sculpture. I needed for Jane to be here. I needed to have her in the studio and look at her face—the planes of the cheek, the strength of her jaw."

Annie felt a curl of dismay. A woman—his wife—died and he was afraid her death might prevent him from creating a sculpture.

Oblivious, he continued in the same querulous tone. "That sculpture can be the best thing I've ever done." Now his look was earnest. "Jane was"—his face crinkled in thought—"like the most alive person you ever saw. She walked into a room and everything changed. It was like she had electricity. I can get that. Marble's cold but think about the *Pietà*, *The Kiss*. If you have the right subject, there's magic." He slumped back in the hard wood chair. "Now, she's gone."

Annie gazed at him and knew Tom was innocent. If she had ever had any doubts of his innocence, she didn't now. Jane alive meant everything to him as an artist. Yes, he was self-absorbed enough to do whatever he had to do for his work. Yes, he had very likely married Jane to advance his career. Had he ever loved her? Perhaps not, but he had been attracted by her over-whelming vitality. He loved Frankie, but Frankie, too, would take second place to the work in progress or the painting he had to do or the sculpture he envisioned. If Jane had lived, Tom might very well have turned away from Frankie because the sculpture of Jane was—to him—as essential as breath itself.

He felt her gaze, looked up. "I don't think the painting will be enough. Maybe it will. It's one of my best, the way the sunlight touches her face, streaks the water. Maybe it will."

"Who wanted Jane dead?" The question sounded harsh. Perhaps she wanted it to be. "Who killed her?"

He blinked those large brown eyes, seemed to bring her into focus. "Who?" It was as if this were the first time he had considered the question.

"She was struck from behind with your mallet. Only someone familiar with you and your studio would know about the mallet."

"My mallet." Again he looked aggrieved. "It was just the right weight and balance when I worked."

Coldness enveloped Annie. His work. His tool. Was that all that mattered to him? "How far is your studio from the terrace?"

He brushed back a lock of curling brown hair. "Maybe three hundred yards. The location's perfect. A path at the bottom of the rose garden leads into the pines. It's a nice walk. Peaceful. The building's in a clearing, so light comes through the skylight and the windows. Wonderful light."

Annie persisted. "Was everyone at David's party familiar with your studio?"

He looked vaguely puzzled. "Yeah, Jane liked to show it off. They'd all been there."

"Do you lock the studio when you aren't there?"

"Never did." He suddenly looked worried. "Maybe with everything that's happened, the studio should be locked up. You know how people kind of hang around places where bad things have happened even though the house and grounds are really private. Especially the studio. Will you ask Kate to be sure it's locked? It would be awful if someone got in there and messed things up."

The totality of his self-absorption was stunning. Did he ever see anything around him except in relationship to himself? She had doubts. Still, if anyone should have had a sense of Jane's ups and downs, surely it was the man who lived with her. She spoke without thinking, trying to understand. "Did you and Jane share a bedroom?"

Those long strong fingers combed through soft brown hair. "Well, yeah. She was my wife." His eyes slid away from her.

Annie felt a quick certainty that yes, indeed, they shared a room and a bed and that he had been drawn to her vitality as a man and a lover, despite Frankie's growing hold on his affection.

He was awkward suddenly. "You had to know Jane. She was"—he spread those lean hands—"a remarkable woman."

"Someone who knew her well—and knew your studio—killed her. Who was angry with Jane? Or feared her?"

His broad forehead furrowed in thought. "It was kind of like the sun and planets. Everybody was dim when Jane was around." He seemed to search for words. "I think she was worried about something, those last few days. She was kind of like . . . different. Kind of like she was looking over her shoulder."

He was inarticulate, but Annie understood his meaning. Tom had picked up on an aura, Jane sensing danger. "Did she mention anyone in particular?"

Tom gave a *whuff* of suppressed laughter. "Jane mentioned everything and everybody all the time. David was driving her nuts. He always wanted money. She was irritated with Madeleine, I saw them in the garden one afternoon the week before Jane died. I'd never seen Madeleine look like that." His artist's eye had noticed. "Almost sloppy, the way she was dressed and she had that little terrier in her arms and it kept yipping and Madeleine was talking like she couldn't get words out fast enough and Jane was shaking her head. I ducked out the other way. You don't want to get too near when women are tossing words at each other. Same thing with Sherry. Every time I saw Sherry and Jane, Jane was issuing orders and Sherry was tossing her head—she needs to cut that hair—and clutching her throat. I think she saw too many reruns of the old silent movies." He threw back his head, clapped his hands on his throat and his expressive face mirrored in turn: Shock. Dismay. Despair. Fury. Tom did them perfectly, a pitch-perfect mimicry.

Annie wondered what had been the subject of Madeleine's encounters with Jane.

Tom shook his head. "Too damn many women in that house. Kate Murray wanted to be the big cheese. She and Jane had it out over a redesign of the rose garden." He looked doubtful. "Nobody kills somebody because of a bunch of damn plants."

Annie agreed. Unless the quarrel had been deeper, a struggle for dominance and the disagreement over the garden a final precipitating quarrel. "Who inherits?"

He looked blank.

"Jane's estate."

"I get some of it, the house and the studio and all my paintings. Kate can have the house. The studio has sleeping quarters, so I'm fine with that." He flicked a glance at the mesh and counter. "If I ever get out of here."

First things first.

"How about David?"

"He gets half the estate. Kate and I split the rest."

"How much money is that?"

He brushed back a tangle of hair. "A lot, I think. Maybe eight or nine million to David and maybe four million for Kate and me."

Annie thought it very likely that his knowledge of sums was truly imprecise. He didn't think about money. But he always thought about his work. Money made all the difference there.

He shoved a hand through his hair. "Who else did you say was at the party?" He finally seemed to be taking an interest.

"Kevin and Irene Hubbard."

Tom squinted. "Jane liked Irene. They had a lot in common. Big women with big egos. You know, I just remembered . . . at the open house Irene was watching Jane with this kind of speculative look. It seemed odd, but I know Jane was pissed about Kevin. She thought he was all blow and no show and maybe she needed to get somebody else to handle the properties. Properties." His voice was thoughtful. "I guess that's what Jane considered me. And my paintings. Toby did a lot for me, but we didn't have anything in writing. Jane said it was stupid to limit myself to one gallery. Toby thought I owed it to him to stick with him like we'd agreed, but what was I supposed to do? Tell Jane to bug off? The gallery in Atlanta was a big step up." His expression was forlorn. "I don't know if they'll cancel the show. Maybe not but I was supposed to be there. Could you find out for me? It's the Fernandez Gallery."

Annie thought it made a good deal more sense to be worried about trial and conviction, but clearly that wasn't Tom's priority. "We'll check it out. We'll explain that we're sure there's been a mistake and you'll be released soon."

"Yeah. Great. Thanks." Then he drooped. "But it seems kind of nuts to me, somebody from David's party killing the doc because he knew Jane was in danger, then getting my mallet and going after Jane. Somebody we knew."

"When did you last see the mallet?"

He turned his big hands over. "I hadn't worked on the sculpture for a couple of days, so I don't know whether it was there Monday. I was thinking about stuff. I took a walk. I didn't go back to my studio until after lunch and then I was making some sketches."

"Were you there all afternoon?"

His eyes slid away. His reply came just a beat late. "Yeah. I didn't leave the studio in the afternoon until I went up to the house and found Jane."

Annie studied him. Downcast eyes. Long fingers twisting together. If all they'd found out was true, he was innocent. Why was he lying about his presence in the studio in the afternoon? She had a quick memory of Frankie Ford and her overwhelming relief when told of Paul Martin's sketch and the fateful birthday party. Frankie had obviously been afraid Tom might be guilty. And Frankie had conveniently been out and about the island that afternoon.

"Were you in your studio when Frankie came?"

He seemed turned to stone. "Frankie didn't come to the studio." The words were stiff. He swallowed twice. "I was in the studio all afternoon. I didn't go up to the house until almost five." He pushed back his chair, came to his feet. "Tell Frankie . . . tell her I wish I knew something to help. But I don't." He turned, shuffled toward the door.

As soon as her Thunderbird purred off the ferry, Annie found a parking place and popped out long enough to drop two quarters in the coin slot of a newspaper rack and snatch out the afternoon's fresh edition of the *Gazette*. She would be home in less than five minutes but she didn't want to wait. She slid into the car and opened the paper. Her eyes widened. Two big headlines. One ran above the lead story, the other below the fold. This front page would catch every reader's eye.

ARTIST ARRAIGNED IN WIFE'S MURDER; JAILED IN BEAUFORT

by Marian Kenyon

WAS TOM EDMONDS FRAMED? EARLIER DEATH QUESTIONED EXCLUSIVE TO THE *GAZETTE*

by Marian Kenyon

Annie ignored the lead story. Instead her eyes dropped to a three-column photo of Paul Martin's office with a view of the desk and a chair to one side and the caption—*Sister insists Death sat in a chair by doctor's desk*—and then to Marian's story.

> The late Paul Martin, a native of the island, is a homicide victim, according to his sister, Mrs. Lucy Ransome, who spoke with *Gazette* reporter Marian Kenyon today.
> Dr. Paul Martin was found dead of a gunshot wound to the head in his study at his home on

October 10. Police evaluated forensic evidence and concluded the death was self-inflicted.

This morning Mrs. Ransome discovered a sketch in the desk of Dr. Martin's study that convinced her that Dr. Martin was murdered and did not commit suicide. (Photo of sketch on page 4.) Mrs. Ransome said that Dr. Martin often made a sketch when he was preoccupied about some concern and that he had appeared worried ever since they attended an open house at Wyler Art Gallery the Sunday before his death.

The open house was in honor of local artist Tom Edmonds, who is now in jail on a charge of murdering his wife, Jane Corley, on October 14. The sketch made by Dr. Martin contained inscriptions in handwriting identified by Mrs. Ransome as her brother's. The sketch was dated October 8.

Dr. Martin drew a rearing horse that appears to be the statue of the horse outside Jane Corley's home. The drawing differs from the statue in that the drawing depicts a horse snarling, possibly in response to danger. Dr. Martin also sketched three witches dancing around a cauldron. The inscription reads: *Evil in a look. I saw it. I'll deal with it at the party.* A final sentence written by Dr. Martin was underlined twice: *Protect Jane.*

Mrs. Ransome related this sequence of events: Her brother attended the open house at the art gallery Sunday, October 6. Afterward, he was worried and preoccupied. He drew the sketch the following Tuesday evening. He attended a birthday party for David Corley, Jane Corley's brother, Wednesday night. Thursday morning Dr. Martin was found dead in his study of a gunshot wound to the temple. The following Monday afternoon Jane Corley was bludgeoned to death in the family room at her home by a sculptor's mallet belonging to her husband, Tom Edmonds.

Police yesterday charged Mr. Edmonds with first-degree murder. Mr. Edmonds denies the charge.

Mrs. Ransome said today, "Paul drew the sketch. I believe some event occurred at the open house October 6 that suggested to Paul that Jane Corley was in danger and he decided to speak to someone at David Corley's birthday party to warn them that nothing must happen to Jane. I believe the person who intended to kill Jane Corley came to our house and shot Paul. Police found a box of cartridges in Paul's desk that matched the weapon that killed him. I believe Paul was murdered, that the murderer brought a gun and cartridges and staged Paul's death to appear as a suicide. I had never heard my brother mention owning a gun. I believe the person who shot Paul also attacked and killed Jane Corley the following Monday. Tom Edmonds was not on the island the night Paul was shot, so I am certain that Mr. Edmonds did not kill his wife."

The *Gazette* confirmed that Edmonds was not on the island the night of Dr. Martin's death. Edmonds was in Atlanta as a guest of the Fernandez Gallery and was at the home of Lorenzo Fernandez.

Police Chief Billy Cameron said Mrs. Ransome had contacted him. Chief Cameron said he had no evidence to suggest that Dr. Martin's death was anything other than self-inflicted. He declined to comment further.

Circuit Solicitor Brice Willard Posey said the state will seek the death penalty for Edmonds. "The crime was brutal. Ms. Corley was savagely attacked and battered to death in her own home. The murder weapon was a mallet from her husband's studio. The only fingerprints found on the mallet belong to Edmonds. Although it is not necessary to establish a motive, the circuit solicitor's office has information indicating that Edmonds was involved in an extramarital affair. Edmonds's whereabouts on the night an island physician took his own life has no bearing on the case against Edmonds."

Posey commended Chief Cameron for "excellent police work and the compilation of a strong case."

Mrs. Ransome vowed to continue her efforts to establish the truth of Dr. Martin's death and has asked anyone in the vicinity of the Martin house at shortly past midnight October 10 to contact her. She is seeking a description of a car that passed the Martin house at approximately that time. Mrs. Ransome concluded that if police refuse to investigate Dr. Martin's death, she will consider hiring a crime expert to evaluate her brother's study as the possible site of a homicide.

Maxwell Darling, owner of Confidential Commissions, told the *Gazette* he has been retained to determine the truth of what occurred on October 14 when Ms. Corley was murdered. Confidential Commissions is an island agency that assists individuals seeking information. Darling declined to identify his employer. He has invited anyone with information about Jane Corley's murder to contact him.

Annie folded the *Gazette*, her thoughts veering from Marian's riveting story to her uneasy feeling at the jail that Tom Edmonds hadn't told everything he knew, to Max's dossiers of those at David Corley's birthday party, to Doc Burford's blunt conclusion that Jane's murderer must have been spotted with blood, to Sherry Gillette's call to Death on Demand.

She fastened on the oddness of Sherry's call. Why had she called Annie? They had never met, though Annie likely had seen her in passing at the open house.

Annie reached to start the car, stopped. She pulled out her cell, noted waiting messages from Laurel, Henny, and Emma, swiped to call Ingrid.

Ingrid's tone was grim. "I saw the *Gazette* story. It made me feel sick, just like everybody who knew him." A strained breath, then she continued. "Lots of calls for you. All of them came after the *Gazette* was out. Another whispery one. Pulsating with drama. She wouldn't leave her name or number. I didn't have the heart to tell her we have caller ID. I resisted saying, 'Thanks for your call, Sherry.'"

"Do you have the number?"

"Sure."

Annie tapped in the name and number. "The other calls?"

"The Wiley Coyotes are on your trail." *Wiley Coyotes* was Ingrid's dry nomenclature for Laurel, Emma, and Henny. "They saw the story in the *Gazette*, too. They're on the warpath." That accounted for the messages on her iPhone. "I told them you and Max are trying to find out what happened. They want to help. They're in a bridge tournament tonight but they'll see you here at nine sharp tomorrow."

Annie ended the call. So the Intrepid Trio was reporting for duty. She felt buoyed with optimism. Between them, crusty Emma, resourceful Henny, and perceptive Laurel had a web of intelligence that enveloped the island as thoroughly as the steel-strong thirty-foot strands spun by banana spiders.

Now . . . She swiped the number Ingrid had given her. If Sherry Gillette never considered the possibility her call might be announced by caller ID, she likely didn't have the service on her phone.

"Gillette." The voice was undeniably male and not at all cordial.

"Is Sherry there?"

"Who's calling?"

Annie made a swift decision and tapped End. Hopefully she was correct in her assumption that the Gillettes didn't have caller ID. Or—her smile was wry—if they did, Sherry Gillette might wonder why Annie Darling was calling her. In any event, Sherry had to wait until tomorrow. Annie wanted to talk to her privately. From the unpleasant tone in the male voice, which Annie assumed belonged to Roger Gillette, perhaps Jane Corley's opinion of him was well-founded.

In any event, they were doing everything possible for Tom Edmonds. She frowned. It seemed obvious when she spoke to him at the jail that he was holding something back about the afternoon his wife was murdered. Still, he wasn't on the island the night Paul Martin died. If Lucy Ransome was right, Marian's story in the *Gazette* would come as a devastating shock to a murderer basking in success.

A nnie drew her cardigan tighter around her shoulders. The chill of the late-evening air presaged cooler days to come, but part of the coldness that enveloped her was the image she had trouble pushing out of her mind. "Someone else could have taken one of Tom's smocks."

The porch swing creaked as Max gave a push with his foot. In the dusk their garden looked shadowy and secretive. "Tom's mallet. Tom's smock."

"Why would he be dumb enough to wad the thing up and stuff it in an urn?"

"Maybe he heard someone coming. Or thought he did. Maybe he heard some noise in the house and was afraid Kate or Sherry was going to find him. Maybe he had to move fast."

She twisted to look at him. "Maybe the person who killed Paul Martin took the mallet and the smock from the studio and planned all along to frame Tom."

Max was silent. His face was thoughtful. And skeptical.

M ax's breathing was deep and even. All was right in her world. Except she couldn't sleep. Annie watched the shifting pattern of wind-tossed branches against the ceiling. Images flitted. Tom's big hands with the spatulate thumbs . . . Lucy Ransome's blue eyes blazing with determination . . . the leather wingback chair at an angle to Paul's desk . . .

Doubt tugged at Annie. Perhaps she and Lucy imagined a horrific scene that never happened. The bloodied artist's smock stuffed behind a shrub was one more piece of evidence against Tom. Max agreed that they would keep looking, keep talking to people, but she knew he didn't expect to find evidence to clear Tom. The bloodied smock was one piece of evidence too much for Max to believe another hand held the mallet.

Annie closed her eyes, pictured gentle surf rolling to the shore. The song of the surf, soothing, encompassing, forever . . .

8

The peal of the phone shocked Annie into muzzy wake-fulness. She swept out a hand to grab the receiver, saw fluorescent numbers on the nightstand clock. Two eighteen. No good news comes in the dark watch of the night, unheralded, destroying peace, making breath hard to find. "H'lo." Her voice was thin, high, shaky.

"Fire. Martin house. Two-alarm. Scanner." Marian's words pelted her. "On my way."

Max's Maserati squealed to a stop. A police cruiser, lights whirling, blocked the street. Firemen aimed hoses from two trucks at flames bursting from one side of the Martin house. The men were dark shadows silhouetted by distant streetlamps, lights spilling from neighboring houses, and searchlights mounted on the fire trucks.

Max pulled up to the curb. Annie slammed out of the passenger seat. Max was right behind her when they reached the squad car. Hyla Harrison stood with her back to the house, barking into a megaphone: "Stay back. Remain clear of emergency vehicles." Billy Cameron, unshaven, hair scarcely combed, T-shirt hanging out over his jeans, stood next to a cruiser, talking into a cell phone. His face was grim.

Smoke flecked by burning embers swirled above the house, spiraling up into darkness. A clump of neighbors watched from the front lawn across the street. Annie grabbed Max's arm. "There's Marian."

They crossed the street, picking their way carefully past the fire trucks, and joined the reporter and somber onlookers, many in pajamas and robes. Marian lifted her husky voice to be heard above the roar of the fire and rumble of water and brusque commands. "Nobody's seen Lucy." She craned to see better. "That guy"—she pointed at a stocky man in Lucy's front yard with the firefighters—"apparently he called in the alert. He lives next door."

Near the first fire truck, a shirtless man in boxers gestured to his right toward dark windows in the front of the house and shouted, "Lucy's room is there. The corner one."

Annie felt a clutch of horror. There was no fire yet on Lucy's side of the house. Flames poked from lower-floor windows of Paul's study and danced on the roof above. Soon the other side of the house would also be enveloped in fire.

Two firemen moved swiftly across the lawn, placed a ladder against the wall. Bulky in protective clothing and boots, a helmeted fireman wearing a mask clambered up the rungs. A long steel tool dangled from a strap around his left wrist.

Annie reached out, held tight to Max's arm. Quickly, he

pulled her close. She pressed against his side, comforted by his nearness as her mind grappled with horror. Lucy had not been seen. Lucy in that house amid suffocating smoke.

One of the searchlights moved, settled on the window, illuminating the panes and the frame. Braced near the top of the ladder, a fireman gripped the long tool and battered the window. The thuds and the crackle of shattering glass sounded over the fire's roar and the whoosh of water. In another moment, perhaps two, the window was knocked from its frame. Carefully, heavily, the fireman clambered into the room.

Despite the deluge of water on the columns of flame, small tongues of fire flickered across the roof, coming nearer and nearer the gaping window. A hiss marked contact between water and fire. Smoke thickened, the acrid odor souring the night air, making Annie's eyes water.

In the glare of the searchlight, the masked fireman looked otherworldly, inhuman when his upper torso appeared in the broken-out window frame with flames shooting skyward from the roof above him. He leaned out, yelled, "Hold the ladder steady. Unconscious woman in sling."

Two firemen braced the bottom of the ladder as the rescuer eased a limp body dangling from a webbed harness over the sill.

Max's arm was taut beneath Annie's clutching hand. "If the roof gives way . . ." He broke off.

The webbed harness descended in jerks and spurts and seemed to move with frightening slowness, although it was only a minute or two before the men on the ground unsnapped the harness and lifted the limp figure away from the ladder and onto a waiting gurney. An EMT tech blocked their view, but when the gurney was rolled across the lawn toward the ambulance, bumping over hoses, there was an oxygen mask clamped to the face.

Marian was already moving. She reached the back of the ambulance as the techs slid the gurney inside. "Is she alive?"

A nnie wrinkled her nose, but the smell of smoke clung to her even in the antiseptic waiting room. "Why don't they tell us anything?" Annie paced back and forth in front of the now untenanted desk. She wondered if there was anything more dismal than a hospital emergency room at three o'clock in the morning.

Max spoke quietly, though they were alone in the cheerless room. "Maybe they don't know anything yet."

Minutes passed and Annie's hope waned. It was another half hour before a door opened on the other side of the counter. A tired-faced nurse walked toward them. "Are you here for Lucy Ransome?"

Annie clasped her hands together. "Yes."

"Next of kin?"

Annie spoke before Max could utter a sound. "Yes."

The nurse was matter-of-fact. "She's stable. Smoke inhalation but the doctor expects a full recovery. She'll be in intensive care probably until midmorning. You can check back then."

Annie gave a whoosh of relief.

T he front door of the *Gazette* was locked, as might be expected, but light spilled through the windows of the newsroom. The street lay silent and deserted in the darkness.

Max pulled out his cell, swiped. "Hey, Marian. We're at the front door . . . She's conscious and in intensive care . . . Yeah. Thanks." He dropped the cell in his pocket.

When the door opened, Marian stood back for them to enter. She, too, smelled of smoke. Her gray sweatshirt and pants sagged. She was pale without makeup. Her hair stuck out at odd angles. She jerked a thumb. "Just finished the story. I'll add in the update on her condition. Want some coffee and stale doughnuts?"

They settled in the dingy break room. Marian rustled through a drawer. "Got some instant from Starbucks." She punched the microwave and in a moment slid a mug of hot water to each of them, flipped narrow thin packages across the table.

Annie reached for the sugar bowl. Normally she drank coffee unsweetened. Right now she wanted any extra jolt of energy she could find. She hesitated when her fingers encountered a sticky film on the outside of the bowl, but this was no time to be squeamish. Marian pushed an oblong box without a lid toward them. There were three glazed doughnuts and one tired-looking chocolate long john. Max shook his head, Marian snagged a glazed, and Annie picked up the long john.

Marian dipped the doughnut in coffee, ignored drips onto her sweatshirt, took a bite, spoke in a mumble. "Arson. Like that's a surprise. Fire Chief pretty sure it was gasoline. I hung around as they started the investigation. Nasty smell. When stuff burns, all kinds of noxious stuff gets crisped. Like vinyl flooring. Fire started in three spots. They found melted remnants of one-liter pop bottles and even a few scraps of rags that had been stuffed in the necks. A garden window was pushed up, screen pulled off. The arsonist got inside, splashed gas around, then tossed in a lighted rag from outside. That's why the damage was spotty. The whole thing could have gone up if the bottles had been made into what we used to cheerily call Molotov cocktails. Anyway, flames spread from the desk to a chair that had sat beside the desk—"

Annie remembered the black leather wing chair that sat to the left of the person behind the desk.

"—and the Oriental rug in front of the desk. Amazing what they can figure from what looked like a blackened mess to me. That whole side of the house is unstable. Smoke goes up, of course. That's why Lucy was unconscious when they got to her." Marian rubbed one temple. "Jesus, I'm glad she's going to be all right." In her dark eyes was the horror of unintended consequences.

Annie reached across the table, touched a tense arm. "It might have happened anyway. Lucy was telling people what she thought. She wasn't going to quit."

"Yeah." Marian wasn't convinced. "Maybe. But my story spelled it out."

"It was the study that was destroyed." Max's tone was thoughtful. "If somebody wanted to shut Lucy up, the fire would have been set on the other side of the house."

"Maybe the objective was to destroy the study." Marian's dark eyes still held horror. "But everybody knew Lucy lived there, that she was asleep upstairs. The arsonist didn't give a damn if she burned, too?"

Annie reached for the copy of yesterday afternoon's *Gazette* lying open on the table. She turned a page, tapped the photo of the black leather wing chair. "If we're right, whoever came that night and made it look like Paul Martin shot himself sat in that chair. The light on the table next to the chair was on the next morning. Lucy said Paul was sitting at the desk. He wouldn't turn on that light unless he was expecting a guest. Lucy and I figure the murderer had a glove in one pocket and wriggled a hand into the glove just before pulling the gun out to shoot Paul. That means there could have been some prints in the study, maybe on the chair."

Max pulled out his phone.

Annie's eyebrows rose.

He gave a brief grin. "I'm not calling anybody at this hour. I'm going to text Billy." He tapped swiftly, handed the phone to Annie.

She looked at the blue letters and the confirmation Message Sent and read aloud: "Lucy Ransome threatened to hire crime expert. Prints available on leather chair by desk?"

Marian studied the photo of the chair. "That chair only matters if someone killed Paul, made his death look like suicide. We think Paul intended to warn someone at David Corley's party. It figures that Paul did exactly what he intended to do and that means his visitor was someone at the party. We need to know"—she scrunched her face in thought—"whether any of these people had ever under any circumstance been in Paul Martin's study: Kate Murray, Sherry Gillette, David Corley, Madeleine Corley, Tom Edmonds, Frankie Ford, Toby Wyler, Irene Hubbard, Kevin Hubbard. If not, a single print anywhere in that study has to be explained." Despite fatigue, her dark eyes gleamed. "The press conference's set for ten A.M. I'll have some questions."

The Maserati idled behind Annie's Thunderbird. Usually both cars turned south on the island's main north-south road, their destination the resort shops on the marina, which included Death on Demand and Confidential Commissions. Instead Annie signaled left to head north for the small-business district near the ferry landing and Parotti's Bar and Grill, her objective the turnoff to the hospital. She'd spoken with Pamela Potts, who was directing shifts of Altar Guild ladies at Lucy Ransome's bedside. "I want to tell Lucy she can stay with us when she gets out of the hospital. I'll ask if she wants us to get someone started on repairs. At least now she can be confident that the police will pay attention to what she told them."

Max was ready to turn right when he heard a ping. He checked the rearview mirror. No one behind him. He pulled out the cell, glanced, saw Billy's reply to his early-morning query: *Surfaces degraded by soot, smoke. Premise in question.*

Premise in question?

Max's eyes narrowed. Yes, his text assumed a murderer returned to destroy evidence. Why else would anyone set fire to the Martin house?

Max swiftly made a call.

"Broward's Rock Police." Mavis Cameron's tone was formal, though, of course, she knew the identity of the caller.

"Hi, Mavis. Max Darling. Can I speak to Billy?"

"Chief Cameron is in conference."

"Will you ask him to call me?"

There was an instant of hesitation. "He's had a number of calls this morning. I am keeping a log for him." Her tone remained formal.

In other words, don't hold your breath.

"Thanks, Mavis." He ended the connection. He and Annie were meeting at the ten o'clock news conference. Maybe they weren't going to hear what they'd expected.

He drove carefully, alert for a deer bounding out from the

pines. One of the charms of the island was exuberant sub-
tropical growth, pines and live oaks crowding either side of
the road with a thick undergrowth of ferns and tangled vines.
Deer, possum, wild boars, cougars, cotton rats, and raccoon
thrived. The curving road was still in shadow, the sun not
yet high enough to spill over the top of the loblollies. Usually
the drive to the island's southern tip wrapped him in a cocoon
of peace, but this morning the final sentence of Billy's text
was a refrain in his thoughts: *Premise in question.* Annie's
reassurance to Lucy—that her brother's death was surely
now going to be investigated—might also be in question.

He parked in an oyster-shell lot and strode through a
slight mist. He rounded a row of palmettos. This early the
boardwalk in front of the shops was empty. Most shops
didn't open until ten. Water slapped against the piers of the
marina. Many slips were empty, the charter boats departing
early for a day of deep-sea fishing.

As he stepped out of the shadows, a trim, athletic figure
hurried down the steps from the boardwalk. David Corley
jogged toward him, jolted to a stop a foot away. The breeze
from the marina tugged at his thick blond hair. He was
unshaven, eyes staring. He looked as if he'd pulled on the first
clothes at hand, a ragged crew sweater, navy sweatpants, and
scuffed running shoes.

David jammed a hand through his tangled hair. "I got to
talk to you."

Annie served mugs of coffee to the waiting trio at the
table nearest the coffee bar, dark Italian roast strong
enough to hike the Cinque Terre trail for Emma, cappuccino

with a dash of brown sugar syrup for Henny, and seasonal pumpkin spice latte for Laurel. Annie indulged her passion for chocolate, topping Tanzanian peaberry with whipped cream and swirls of chocolate syrup. She gestured toward folders at three places. "Max's summaries of Marian's background and bios on the birthday party guests. And everything I picked up."

She glanced in the mirror and was surprised that she didn't look an utter hag with only four hours of sleep. Makeup hid the dark shadows below her eyes and she'd chosen a vivid carmine lip gloss. While Emma, Henny, and Laurel read the dossiers and summaries and her bits and pieces of information, she drank coffee, waiting for the life-lifting caffeine-and-chocolate jolt.

Emma flipped her folder shut, tapped the cover. "Good work."

Laurel was thoughtful. "Interesting that Jane had a presentiment."

Henny said quietly, "Last night when I read the *Gazette*, I almost called. I had a sense Marian's story about Lucy and Paul might trigger trouble. Now I wish I had."

Annie understood. She felt, too, as if she'd not looked ahead to imagine a killer's response. "I'm afraid the paragraph about Lucy hiring a crime expert might have caused the arson. Lucy's lucky to be alive. I dropped by the hospital a little while ago. Lucy's doing well, though she still coughs a lot and says her throat hurts. Pamela brewed green tea, added honey and fresh lemon, and Lucy felt better after she drank it. I told Lucy we'd find out who caused the fire."

Henny's dark eyes were grave. "Do you think the intent was to kill Lucy?"

Annie drank her delectable brew, wished she didn't remember the hungry flames crawling across the roof of the Martin house and the choking pall of smoke. "Maybe. But the fire was set on the other side of the house from her bedroom. Maybe the plan was to destroy Paul's study and any evidence there. But whoever set the fire knew she was asleep upstairs." Her voice shook a little. "Knew and didn't care."

Emma's gaze was intent. "Does Billy Cameron agree?"

Annie looked at her in surprise. "What else could he think?" The connection between the *Gazette* story with Lucy's claim that Paul had been murdered and the torching of the house was obvious cause and effect. "There's a press conference at ten. We went by the *Gazette* after we left the hospital."

Henny looked relieved. "The press conference will set everything straight. In fact, Billy may be arranging for Tom Edmonds's release right this minute. Billy will scour the island now that it's clear he's dealing with two murders. Still, we may be able to offer some help. Sometimes people won't talk to the police."

Emma's strong square face folded in a ferocious frown. "The guest list for David Corley's birthday is key." She brushed back a straggly spike of magenta-hued hair that matched her caftan.

Laurel was emphatic. "Absolutely."

Annie tried not to look surprised at Laurel's immediate grasp of the salient point. That wasn't fair to her mother-in-law. Laurel might be ditzy. She wasn't dim. This morning she looked—no surprise to Annie—her customary gorgeous self. Smooth hair golden as sunlit honey framed a patrician face with Mediterranean blue eyes. Stylish as always, her striped sweater was a mélange of fall colors above boot-cut gray twill slacks.

"Given the circumstances"—Laurel nodded toward Henny—"the guests will be careful in what they say. But I always know where to find out what really happened at a party. I asked Virginia—" She looked around inquiringly.

Annie nodded as did Emma and Henny. Virginia Taylor was Laurel's housekeeper and she had a large extended family.

"—and her cousin Tina works for the Corleys. I talked to Tina last night." Laurel opened a multipatterned tote bag and pulled out a sheet of paper and a brocade glasses case. She perched Ben Franklin glasses on her nose, which made her look, to Annie's exasperation, on the sunny side of twenty. "Tina said she was too busy serving and clearing up to pay much attention to the guests. She said Mr. Corley had way too much to drink and was loud and boisterous. Tina's very active in her church. Missionary Baptist. She said the party had an odd edge to it. She couldn't put her finger on it, but she said, 'Folks supposed to be having a good time sure had frowny faces when they didn't think anybody was looking.' Tina thought the problem might be with the hostess. 'Miz Corley hasn't been herself for a week or so, wandering around holding Millie. I think she was making the dog nuts, too.'"

Annie spoke slowly. "I wonder about Madeleine. According to Tom Edmonds, Madeleine and Jane were having some kind of heavy talk in the garden the week before she died. When he saw them, he turned around and went back to his studio. Kate Murray said Madeleine looked awful at the birthday party. A woman at the beauty shop claimed

Madeleine wasn't home the afternoon Jane was killed. Madeleine told everyone she hadn't left the house, but the gardener told Bridget Olson that Madeleine left the garden on a path."

Emma reached down for her capacious knit bag, which had been known to contain everything from a tin of smoked oysters to a pirate treasure map to a compilation of Yogi Berra quotes. Emma's favorite and often-repeated Yogi quote: "If you don't know where you are going, you might wind up someplace else."

Emma drew out a small pad, flipped it open, marked a numeral one. Her stubby fingers gripped a Montblanc pen with a Year of the Dragon design. "Billy will obviously interview everyone at David's birthday party. However, that's official and not guaranteed to get straight answers. We can make unofficial inquiries." She drew four columns, one for each of them. Her gimlet-sharp gaze flicked to Annie. "I'll put Madeleine on your list."

Annie spoke quickly. "Sherry Gillette tried to call me a couple of times. I'll find out why. Put David Corley down for Max."

Henny was decisive. "I'll talk to Irene Hubbard and Kate Murray. Irene tried out for a role recently in *The Pajama Game*." Henny was an accomplished actress and among her island successes were appearances in *Little Women*, *Blithe Spirit* (Elvira, of course), and *The Mousetrap*. "Irene's flamboyant. But nobody's fool. As for Kate, she's brusque, intimidating, but we've worked on rummage sales together. I think she'll talk to me."

"Excellent." Emma was pleased at the responses. "That

leaves Toby Wyler and Kevin Hubbard. I'll deal with them."
Her expression was wolfish. "That takes care of the guests."
She glanced toward Laurel, who had an expectant expression,
then at Annie. "I wonder who else should be contacted."

Annie pressed fingers against her temples. She had a dull
headache from lack of sleep, but she knew Emma was depend-
ing upon her. Definitely Laurel must be included. "The gardener at the Corley house."

Laurel waved pink-tipped fingers. "I enjoy men who are
earthy. I'll speak to the gardener."

There was an instant's pause. Henny lifted a hand and
placed her fingers across her lips. Emma's gaze was speculative.
Annie gazed determinedly at the second of the watercolors
above the mantel.

Laurel's smile was dreamy. Then, with a little head shake,
she continued briskly. "And that sweet child Frankie Ford."

Annie hesitated. She, too, thought Frankie was appealing,
but . . . "Frankie was evasive about where she was Monday
afternoon."

Laurel's blue eyes were knowing. "One lover is drawn to
another as surely as the sea seeks the shore."

Emma cleared her throat. "Right. Laurel takes the gardener and the girl." Her brusque tone returned the moment
to the matter-of-fact. "Anybody else?"

Annie nodded. "A week or so before Jane died, Marian
was out at the Palmetto Players. She saw David Corley being
escorted in to see the owner. Nobody looked happy."

Emma raised an eyebrow. "If David owes Jason Brown
money, he'd better pay up."

Henny raised both eyebrows. "Emma, what are you keeping

from us? How do you know the name of the guy behind the Palmetto Players?"

Emma's square face was thoughtful. "Had a second officer on *Marigold's Pleasure*. He played a little too loose with Caribbean stud, ended up owing the house about forty K. He welched. Pretty soon he had a broken leg. Last I heard he was working on a yacht out of Miami."

Laurel pushed the half-glasses higher. "That explains Madeleine's distress."

Annie pictured an office where a burly man kept a skull on his desk. "Max can try, but the guy probably won't say anything."

Emma was brisk. "Still, he may learn something."

Annie could be brisk, too. "There are other questions that need to be answered." As Emma glanced at her watch, Annie quickly set out what seemed pertinent to her. "Frankie was hugely relieved when she heard Lucy's story. What did Frankie see that made her suspect Tom? Kate Murray gave no hint that she and Jane had quarreled. Why? Was David Corley in a panic to get money because of gambling? Sherry Gillette shouted at Jane a few days before she died. Why? Madeleine seemed nervous and apprehensive at the birthday party and a friend didn't find her home the afternoon Jane died. Where was Madeleine? Kate Murray remembered Paul looking somber as he walked toward the end of the pool. True or false? Would Jane's death give Toby Wyler control of Tom's paintings again? Ben Parotti dumped on Kevin Hubbard, thought he was dishonest, and Ben saw Jane heading into Kevin's office and she didn't look pleasant. Why?"

There might have been a gleam of approval in Emma's

gaze, in addition to a flicker of surprise. "Well put." Then she glanced again at her diamond-encrusted watch. "It's a quarter to ten."

There was a quick flurry, purses retrieved, chairs pushed back. Annie had no doubt that the four of them would be in the front row at the news conference.

M ax gestured toward a chrome-and-web chair in front of his desk. "Coffee?" Barb set the coffeemaker to turn on automatically and there was a heady scent of Colombian.

David Corley swiped a hand across his bristly cheek. "Yeah. Sure. Whatever."

Max poured two mugs, brought one to David, then settled behind his desk. He kept his expression unaffected but he was startled by the change in David's demeanor from unflappable cool guy to a harried, distraught man. "What can I do for you?"

David hunched forward, holding the mug in both hands, ignoring the coffee. "I got the *Gazette* yesterday." He stared at Max, his gaze troubled. "The story about Doc Martin blew my mind. Then I heard on TV this morning about his house. I didn't even take time to eat breakfast. I went right to the police station and tried to talk to the guy in charge. I guess I didn't handle it right. They asked if I had information and I should have said, yeah I did. Instead, I said I wanted to know what the hell was going on. My brother-in-law's in jail and if all this stuff in the paper was right, Tom didn't have anything to do with hurting Jane. I said I wanted the lowdown. If somebody else killed Jane, they had to get busy, find out what happened. They took me off to a little room and this woman wrote everything down and said they'd get back to me. And there I was out on the street in front of the police station and I didn't know anything more than when I got there. Then I remembered in the *Gazette* it said somebody hired you to find out who killed Jane." He reached out, put the mug on the desk and some coffee slopped over. "Who are you working for and what do you know?"

Max leaned back in his chair, kept his tone casual. "My clients are confidential, but I can share some information. Tom Edmonds is innocent because he was not on the island the night—"

"Yeah, yeah, yeah. I get that. I want to know if the *Gazette* had it right that Doc Martin talked to somebody at my birthday party and that's why he got killed. My God, is that true?" He cracked the knuckles of his right hand.

"According to Lucy, that's exactly what happened. It started at the open house—"

David made a chopping motion with his hand. "I read all about it. I didn't notice a damn thing." David spoke the words like they hurt. "A couple of days after that, I talked to Jane." His jaw quivered. He took a breath. "She asked me if I picked up on something peculiar at the open house, that she'd felt worried ever since, kept looking over her shoulder. Hell, I joked around. See, I think art's a bunch of baloney. I said, yeah the whole thing gave me the willies, too. I stepped into the wrong gallery and it was all this disjointed stuff and a couple of canvasses with grinning skulls. At least Tom doesn't paint that kind of crap. Anyway"—now his eyes looked at Max but they were filled with misery—"I blew her off. She tried to tell me that something was wrong, that she didn't feel right, and I made a joke out of it. God, she tried to tell me."

Max saw a man struggling to contain emotion. He kept his voice gentle. "Did she mention anybody?"

David jammed his fingers together, stared down at them. "I don't know. I needed to talk to her about something and I guess she saw I was uptight. That was like Jane, you know." He lifted his face. "She could be a bitch and then she'd turn around and do anything she could for you. I guess she knew I was in a tight—"

"The money you owe Jason Brown?"

David looked shocked. "How'd you know?"

Max shrugged. "Lots of people go to Palmetto Players. Somebody noticed you. What was Brown threatening to do?"

For an instant, there was a hot flicker in David's eyes before his gaze once again dropped to his tightly clasped fingers. "He said he'd ruin my credit." It was a mumble.

Max studied him. In a slant of light from a high window, there was a hint of weakness in his bristly jaw. Ruined credit? Rich kids like David didn't worry about ruined credit. Max expected the threat was much more direct and forceful.

David's head jerked up. Now his face reformed. He almost managed a tremulous smile. "Anyway, that's the point. Jane came through. She was going to take care of everything." He blew out a whoosh of air. "I'll have to admit she surprised me. I had to promise no more blackjack, no more roulette. Hell, that wasn't a problem. I sure didn't want to go back there."

Max figured David now had a pretty clear idea that the gentility of the old plantation house didn't include the man with the skull on his desk.

"Sure, I agreed, no more gambling." His face drooped. "If I hadn't been thinking about my own sorry ass, maybe she would have told me more. If she had, maybe we'd have some idea who . . . hurt her. I want to help anybody who'll find out what happened. You. The cops. Anybody. Damn, if only I'd paid attention to what she said."

Max understood his anguish, but maybe he knew more than he realized. "What did she tell you?"

David looked uncomfortable. "I can't promise any of this really means anything. She was talking and I wasn't paying a lot of attention. But this morning when I thought back"—he hesitated—"well, I don't want to toss anybody overboard but I remember she said something about Kevin." He rubbed knuckles against his cheeks. "Something about Kevin and sticky fingers."

S un splashed the front steps of the police station. TV cameras from Savannah stations were set up and smooth-faced, blond reporters in stylish suits waited with mics in hand. A crowd of perhaps twenty-five or thirty clustered beyond the cameras, jostling for a good view. The breeze off the harbor stirred Marian Kenyon's short dark curls. The blond TV reporters apparently used enough spray to prevent even a ripple in their coiffures. The blondes teetered on high heels, gripped their mics. Marian kept one hand on the strap of her Leica. She waved her other hand at Annie and the trio.

Annie felt a touch at her elbow. She half turned, smiled up at Max. She felt a quick flicker of happiness as she always did when he was present, followed by an immediate recognition of a dark shadow in his eyes. He knew something that would upset her.

He saw her understanding, started to speak, then the front

door of the station opened. He nodded toward the steps. "I'm afraid we won't hear what we'd hoped for." Mayor Cosgrove stepped outside, followed by Billy Cameron. Annie marveled at the penguin-shaped mayor's ability to win reelection, but he was a good retail politician, never missing a beauty pageant, chili supper, or civic club luncheon. This morning he was attired in a natty silver gray Palm Beach suit, pink oxford-cloth shirt, and gray tie with pink stripes. Annie wished she could toss him a cane and top hat and suggest a riff from "Puttin' on the Ritz."

In contrast, Billy looked stolid and weary. He was clean-shaven and dressed in crisply starched khaki shirt and trousers. Dark smudges beneath his eyes told of little sleep. He stood a pace behind the mayor, gazed out with an unreadable expression.

Mayor Cosgrove puffed up his chest, carefully keeping his head erect for the best camera view.

The nearest TV blonde shouted, "Did a newspaper story"— she was careful not to mention the competition by name—"unmask a second murder on the island in less than a week and lead to arson that put a victim's sister in the hospital?"

The portly mayor showered her with a condescending smile, white molars gleaming. "Island residents can rest assured that I"—dignified emphasis—"am making sure that proper investigative procedures are followed and sensationalism in the press is ignored."

The blonde wasn't fazed. "The hospitalized woman spoke out about her brother's murder and—"

The mayor held up a pudgy hand. "Only facts matter. Fact one: Paul Martin's death, sadly"—his face momentarily reflected sadness—"was self-inflicted. The police investigation left no stone unturned. Forensic evidence found gunshot residue on the doctor's right hand. His fingerprints—"

Annie looked past the mayor at Billy, but his face was still unreadable. Did he believe the twaddle the mayor was spouting?

"—on the barrel of the gun, a contact wound on his right temple. Fact two: The murder of Jane Corley is a separate investigation. There is no linkage between Dr. Martin's death and Jane Corley's murder." His tone was long-suffering. "Notwithstanding unfortunate reportage, there is no confirmation of the information provided to the *Gazette* by Mrs. Lucy Ransome."

Marian stalked close to the steps, confrontation in every line of her skinny frame. "Did Mrs. Ransome show police the sketch drawn by Dr. Martin the night before his death?"

The mayor drew himself up. "Dr. Martin's sketch is irrelevant—"

Marian interrupted. "Did Mrs. Ransome state for the record that Dr. Martin seemed relieved from anxiety after the birthday party at the home of David Corley?"

"We cannot know the inner workings of Dr. Martin's—"

Marian cut him off. "The sketch exists. On that sketch Dr. Martin wrote: *An open house, a hard heart. Evil in a look. I saw it. I'll deal with it at the party.* Moreover, he wrote and underlined twice: *Protect Jane.* Dr. Martin attended an open house arranged by Jane Corley at an island gallery on Sunday. Dr. Martin drew the sketch Tuesday night. Dr. Martin attended a party Wednesday night at the home of David Corley. Jane Corley was in attendance. Dr. Martin was shot later that night. Jane Corley was murdered the following Monday. Now, Mayor

Cosgrove, please explain how the sketch has no relevance to the deaths of Paul Martin and Jane Corley and"—her voice rose—"how arson at Dr. Martin's house is unrelated to this sequence of events."

The mayor's plump cheeks flamed.

Annie knew he would never admit he'd made a wrong decision. Possibly, too, he resented Annie and Max from their previous encounters and Marian because she never gave up on a story once she began.

The mayor's deep-set, small eyes glinted. "Police Chief Cameron's thorough work has resulted in the arrest of the guilty party in the death of Jane Corley. Tom Edmonds, her husband, was involved in an extramarital affair. A hammer that belonged to him and has only his fingerprints was used to kill his wife. There is further material evidence that is linked to him. The *Gazette*'s sensational article apparently gave some person interested in freeing Mr. Edmonds the idea of setting Dr. Martin's house on fire to suggest that the murderer was someone other than Mr. Edmonds. Fortunately, I and the Broward's Rock Police Department understand the arson was nothing more than a diversionary tactic."

They stood at the end of Fish Haul Pier, the nearest spot from the police station for a somewhat private conversation. Max admired the way the breeze molded Annie's soft peasant blouse against her. His mother brushed back a sliver of blond hair and smiled at him. Henny tapped the fingers of one hand on the railing. Her dark brown eyes narrowed in concentration. Emma stood with arms akimbo, her blunt face corrugated in a ferocious frown.

Max had a sudden empathy for the man in white tie and tails in a ring with Bengal tigers. He thought Jane's murderer might prefer the tigers to the unleashed efforts of Annie and the Intrepid Trio. Each talked fast, Emma's deep voice brusque, Laurel's husky pronouncement emphatic, Henny's brisk comments decisive, Annie's clear tenor outraged, all of them furious with the mayor's intransigence.

"We're all agreed." He hoped to stem the rush of words, all trumpeting fury at the mayor and a determination to find out what they could and prove him wrong.

Four sets of eyes turned on him.

"Definitely we can talk to people. I got Annie's text just before the press conference saying I should check out David Corley and Jason Brown. I've already talked to David. He came by to see me this morning. He'll help us. He said Jane kind of told him she was spooked about something but he was wrought up about his gambling debts and didn't listen. She came through and promised to cover him. He did say that Jane talked about Kevin Hubbard having sticky fingers."

Emma's smile was cool. "Thanks, Max. I'll remember that when I talk to Kevin." She looked at each in turn, a general deploying her troops. "Very well. Our mission is understood. Proceed as planned."

9

Overhead, long-necked, black-wing-tipped southward-bound ibis shared the sky with vees of geese. The morning was perfect for a stroll along the boardwalk overlooking the harbor, a pleasure Annie intended to enjoy before perfect October weather gave way to northerly winds and chilly rains. But rain might as well be slanting down for all the pleasure she could take in the day. As she drove, she glanced at the Broward's Rock Police Station at the crest of the slope leading down to the harbor. The view from Billy Cameron's office included the harbor with the *Miss Jolene* now at her berth and, on the horizon, the spread arms of a shrimp boat and a distant plume of smoke above a cruise ship on its way to Florida.

She felt confident Billy was in his office directing a careful and thorough investigation into the arson of the Martin house. Billy hadn't returned calls or texts from Max, nor one from her. Did that mean he accepted the mayor's conclusion that the fire was set in hopes of getting Tom Edmonds released? If so, suspicion was sure to settle on Frankie Ford. She was the only person who cared about Tom's fate. How could Billy believe Frankie set fire to a house occupied by a sleeping woman? The thought was sickening.

But someone splashed gasoline in Paul's study and tossed a burning rag through the garden window into the house with Lucy upstairs.

Annie drove past Fish Haul Pier, turned left into a pine-shaded road that led to the three-story apartment complex on the other side of woods that bordered the Harbor Pavilion. In midmorning there were plenty of empty parking spaces. She slid out of the car and walked fast toward the outer steps of the apartment house. She and Max and the Intrepid Trio might be the only hope for Tom Edmonds. They would do their best.

M avis Cameron pushed through the door from the corridor into the working space behind the front counter of the police station. Her angular face reflected distress. "Billy expects to be tied up all day." She didn't look toward Max. Instead her gaze slid away to the window with its view of the sparkling harbor.

Max was equable. "If he has a moment, ask him to give me a ring. He has my cell number."

She stared at the countertop. "I'll tell him."

Outside, Max went down the steps quickly. Mavis had obviously felt uncomfortable. Why? There were several possibilities. Billy agreed with the mayor and believed Tom Edmonds to be guilty and the fire a diversion. Or Billy was simply too involved in his duties to deal with Max today. Or Billy had decided to play a lone hand. If he came out in public disagreement with the mayor, the mayor was quite capable of sending Billy on short notice to a faraway conference or, in a worst-case scenario, placing Billy on unpaid leave for insubordination. Whatever, Mavis obviously felt constrained to keep her mouth shut with Max, even though she and Billy were longtime friends of theirs.

Max reached the Maserati. Once behind the wheel, he sat unmoving. As soon as possible, he wanted to talk to Jason Brown, owner of the Palmetto Players. But one sentence in Marian's story had burrowed into his mind, Lucy's hope that someone had seen the car that came up their street the night Paul died. He'd wanted to ask Billy if a hunt was under way for that car, but Billy was incommunicado. So Jason Brown would have to wait. Finding out about the car was more important.

Max reached Calhoun Street and parked behind the police cruiser in front of the Martin house. In fine weather, he usually left his car windows down, but now he pushed the button and the windows slid up. Closing the car would help seal out the rank smell of charred, still-sodden wood. In bright sunlight, the caved-in roof and scorched paint were a stark reminder of leaping flames and struggling firefighters.

A lawn mower hummed a few houses down. Squirrels chittered in the elm trees across the street. His nose wrinkled as he walked along the front hedge and around the corner of the stalks of pampas grass. The stench overpowered the scent from honeysuckle and a pittosporum shrub near the side gate. Yellow tape marked the garden and what remained of the house as off-limits.

He saw the damage clearly from the gate. The study was

a mess of charred and twisted wood. Wide planks supported by concrete blocks provided a limited walkway above the caved-in floor. Hyla Harrison knelt on a board near a blackened mound.

Max estimated the distance of the mound from the hulk of the burned desk and figured the shrunken heap she studied was all that remained of the black leather chair near the desk.

Hyla sprayed powder on a portion of the hump that looked like leather, a strip that had in the capriciousness of dancing flames escaped damage. He felt jubilant. No arsonist took time to lounge in a leather chair before setting a blaze. Billy, always thorough, might or might not accept the mayor's conclusions, but he understood that a vagrant print from one of the birthday party guests on that chair would have to be explained.

"Hey, Hyla. You're looking for fingerprints."

She looked over her shoulder. "Crime scene. Don't get any nearer." She returned to her careful application of powder.

"Anybody in the neighborhood see anyone over here last night?"

She made no reply.

"Is someone from the department going door-to-door asking about last night or the night Paul Martin was shot?"

No reply.

"How many gas-filled pop bottles were emptied?"

It took a moment, but Hyla replied gruffly, "Estimated at five."

Max turned away from the gate, walked slowly along the hedge, then paused and looked back, considering what he knew. Say there were five one-liter bottles. They wouldn't be easy to heft or transport. Probably the arsonist carried them in a cardboard box and left the box to be consumed in the blaze. The first challenge was bringing the box to Calhoun Street. That almost certainly required a car.

Lucy Ransome heard a car just past midnight after she said good night to Paul and he entered his study.

A car brought death the night Paul was shot, likely a car brought destruction last night.

Max walked to the end of the hedge of pampas grass. The feathery fronds rippled in a slight breeze. Lucy remembered that a car passed the house. But no one intent upon arson or murder would park near the Martin house. He shaded his eyes, looked up the street. Out of sight of the house . . . That would be important.

In the Maserati, he followed the street beyond the curve. Only one more house on this side of the street, two on the other and then Calhoun ended at a cross street. Turn left and the street ended at the marsh. Turn right and the street led to the main island road. From there a driver could go anywhere.

If he were setting a fire, he would avoid the dead end at the marsh. He turned right and lowered the windows. The Maserati barely idling, the car glided slowly east. Not too far. There was the cardboard box to carry. He had no way of knowing which of the houses were occupied the night of the fire, but all appeared to be inhabited with no sign of the empty look that settles upon untenanted houses. Definitely you don't park in someone's drive if you have arson in mind. Not too far . . . Perhaps thirty yards past the intersection he saw a familiar island sight, narrow ruts that disappeared into the woods beneath low-hanging overhead limbs, one of those lanes that meandered, perhaps leading to a remote house, perhaps dead-ending at a lagoon.

He parked just past the lane. He walked a few feet into the lane, waited for his eyes to adjust to the gloom. He gazed down, his eyes slowly crossing back and forth. The car would have been left out of sight from the street, but not too far. The gray, sandy soil was soft but, he felt a stab of disappointment, the ruts didn't appear to hold any tire marks. The lane was narrow. He took a few more steps, stopped, looked down. Maybe, just maybe . . .

He reached for his cell phone.

The hat was a bit summery, but what man who loved flowers would not be enchanted by a wide-brimmed pink straw with a turquoise band? Laurel adjusted the brim. She passed the rearing horse at Jane Corley's gate. She didn't approach the front steps, wending her way instead on a path bordered by bougainvillea. As arranged, Ross Peters awaited her at an arbor twined with Carolina jessamine vines that would flaunt sweet-scented yellow blooms in December. He never questioned her claim on the phone that she was gathering information to help in the investigation of Jane's murder.

He was not much taller than Laurel but powerfully built. He waited with his hands loose at his sides. His face had the ruddy color of a man who spent much time in the sun and his black hair was cut in a crew. A dark blue polo revealed muscular arms and torso.

Laurel smiled at him, her blue eyes gazing deeply into brown eyes. "Thank you so much for taking time to meet me."

Had Annie been present she would have recognized his response. Men from eight to eighty immediately stood straighter, shoulders back, libidos saluting. Laurel, with her customary modesty, simply enjoyed the wonderful maleness that greeted her. Men were such adorable creatures.

"Ma'am." His voice was deep.

"I only wish"—her throaty voice exuded regret—"that I could while away the day with you, seeing the glorious flowers and shrubbery." She looked past him, her eyes widening. "Those tea roses seem to be tipped with gold. Shall we walk in the rose garden and I can explain how you can help us?"

"Yes, ma'am." His tone was fervent. They strolled to rock steps at the top of the garden. They stopped and he spread his arms and spoke of the varieties of roses: ". . . almost four hundred bushes . . ."

"Simply splendid. I would love to learn more about the roses but"—she was clearly regretful—"I'm afraid I must take us back to that dreadful day when Jane was attacked."

His eagerness seeped away. He hunched his shoulders, stared at the ground. "Wish to God I'd been here in the afternoon." He jerked his head toward the beautiful blooms, white, pink, yellow, and every shade of red from burgundy to crimson to vermilion. "I worked here in the morning but I spent the afternoon over at the other place."

"You take care of all the Corley properties?"

He nodded. "Everything. Planting. Trimming. Thinning out the woods. That afternoon I saw Jane on the terrace about one thirty. She waved at me. I was just leaving to walk over to David's place."

Laurel's smile was bright. She looked around with interest. "Is there a path to David's house?"

"There are paths everywhere." He pointed at the base of the garden and an oyster-shell path that snaked around a pittosporum hedge. "That's the way to the studio. That's the place where Tom paints. And that path over there by the cabana—"

Laurel looked beyond the gleaming waters of a lotus-shaped pool.

"—goes down to Wherry Creek." He turned, gestured at another oyster-shell walk near the arbor that plunged into the pines. "That's the quickest way to David's house."

Laurel clasped her hands together in admiration. "That looks like such an enchanted walk. Perhaps you might show me the way."

Peters almost bowed. "I'd be pleased to show you the way."

Laurel noted that the path near the arbor was only a few feet from the terrace. She glanced back at the French windows. Anyone arriving at the entrance to the family room would be visible for perhaps a space of thirty feet between the woods and the house. She agreed that it was unfortunate Ross Peters had not been near Jane's house after he saw her on the terrace.

Peters slowed his long stride as they passed the arbor, led the way into the pines. The scent of the woods was pleasant. "Jane liked for things to be wild. You can't see more than a foot or so off the path. It's about two hundred yards to David's house." As they walked he pointed out chain ferns with deep purple stems, resurrection ferns with long slender fronds, and a glimpse of cinnamon ferns near a lagoon.

The path opened out behind the antebellum home.

Laurel gave a little cry of admiration. "How glorious to have a creek so near."

Ross shaded his eyes. "Water was the best means of transport in early days. That's why we're coming up behind the house. It faces the creek. Course, time changes everything. The road that runs past Jane's house curves around and that's how cars get to David's house. The creek's on one side, the house on the other. There used to be a dock right in front of the house, but that was torn down when the street came in and now"—he gestured—"the dock's over there. The creek curves around." He gestured. "David keeps a skiff and a kayak there." The rowboat at the end of a line moved in the wind. A kayak rested on one side of the dock. "I was working over there." He pointed at a partially trimmed oleander hedge.

Laurel glanced up at the verandah. "Did you see anyone?"

He folded his arms. "Somebody suggesting I wasn't over here? I told the police and they were fine with it. I told them I was sorry I couldn't help them. I wish I'd been at Jane's place. Maybe nobody would have got to her if I'd been there. But I was here, like I said. David can vouch for me. He came out about two thirty and took the kayak out. He headed out toward the Sound. Madeleine came out on the terrace about three, chasing after Millie. That little terrier can scoot like her tail's on fire. I don't think Madeleine saw me. She looked like she had a million things on her mind."

"Which way did she go?"

Irene Hubbard's smile was big wattage. Henny decided she was a natural to play the Perle Mesta character in *Call Me Madam*. Henny admired the silvery swirl of sequins on a faintly gray jacket above pearl gray trousers. Irene's ice-blue blouse reflected the blue of her eyes. Definitely stylish. But there might be a hint of uneasiness in her wide-open, ingenuous gaze.

Irene turned one hand and sunlight reflected the ruby red of an ornately set stone. "I'm devastated about Jane. I'm happy to help you in any way I can." But those blue eyes were cool and wary.

Henny settled back comfortably in a wicker chair in the sunroom overlooking a lagoon. Pale lemon walls, thin rectangular windows, and a profusion of cut flowers looked like a design right out of *Southern Living*. The tiled table between them held iced teas and a plate of cookies.

"I knew I could count on you, Irene. Since you and Jane spent so much time together, I'm hoping you might know if she was worried about anything."

Irene gripped her glass. "Worried?"

Henny maintained a look of hopeful inquiry, but she felt as eager as a pointer hearing a rustle in the woods. Irene was stalling for time. Irene did not want to pursue what might have been causing Jane to worry.

"I don't like to gossip." Irene pressed her lips together. "But Jane's dead. We all have to be honest, don't we? I know she was concerned about some family matters. Tom was fooling around on her. I think everyone in town knew about Tom and Frankie. Including Jane. That's why I wasn't surprised when he was arrested. I always liked Tom." It was as if she consigned him forever to the past tense.

Henny's smile was brilliant. "You'll be happy to know Tom's not a suspect now. I don't know when he will be released"—if ever—"but the arson of Paul Martin's house proves Tom is innocent."

"That's good news." Irene's tone was metallic, her eyes wary.

"Now we have to pool what we know, see if there is

anything helpful we can give to the police." Henny continued as if the question weren't loaded with danger. "Did you see Jane that day?"

"That day?"

"The day she died."

Irene's face tightened. "Of course not." Her voice was sharp.

Henny gestured. "You were here, I suppose?"

A pause. "I played a round of golf on my own that afternoon."

Alone. Henny looked into steel blue eyes. "Were there many others out on the course that day?"

Irene added a teaspoon of sugar to her tea. The clink of the spoon was sharp against the glass. She shrugged. "I never pay any attention. I concentrate on my game."

Henny looked around the expensively decorated sunroom. What she had seen of the lower floors indicated the expenditure of a great deal of money. "Your home is quite lovely and decorated in such good taste. I know Kevin must be quite proud of your choices." Now Henny looked bland. "Very different from the home he had with his first wife." That home had been a modest ranch style, which likely reflected a modest income. Upon his remarriage, there had apparently been enough money to buy a home in one of the island's expensive subdivisions. "Kevin might be the best placed to know if anything was troubling Jane."

Irene gave a dry laugh. "Kevin's a man. You know how they are. You have to whack them over the head with a two-by-four to get their attention. He just dealt with Jane over business. He'd be hopeless when it comes to what women are thinking."

"Someone saw Jane going into Kevin's office a few days before she was killed and she didn't look happy. Was Jane giving Kevin a hard time?"

Irene's face was stony. "That's nonsense. Kevin and Jane got along great."

"So if Jane was upset recently, it had nothing to do with Kevin."

"That's right." Irene took a sip from her tea, carefully placed the glass on the tiled tabletop. She opened her eyes wide. "Of course, David was a trial to her, but other than family, I don't think she was worried about a thing."

And, Henny thought, you have a gorgeous seaside lot just outside Vegas that I should buy. Irene wasn't willing to offer anything helpful. But there was one more possibility. "You were at David's birthday party. Paul Martin spoke to someone that night and the conversation must have been brief but intense."

"I wasn't paying any particular attention to Paul."

Henny gazed at her thoughtfully. "Did you talk to him?"

There was a tight silence. "Not that I remember."

Henny persisted. "Did you see him talking to anyone?"

Irene shrugged. "Paul visited with that girl who's involved with Tom. But he had his back to me. Frankie kept looking past him. She was watching Jane. It looked to me like she was trying to stay as far away from Jane as possible." A bark of laughter. "Probably a smart move. At one point Paul and David were having some kind of heavy conversation. Kevin says Paul always tried to help the family handle David, and David was sure drinking too much that night. It looked to me like David was trying to reassure him. He kept turning his hands up, like, hey, everything's cool. Later, Madeleine was hanging on to Paul Martin's arm. I felt sorry for him. I think

she's neurotic. She looked like a woman ready to fall apart."
Her tone was disdainful. "I'll bet doctors get tired of high-
strung women who act like they're about to flip out." She
smoothed one carefully mascaraed eyebrow. "I read that stuff
in the *Gazette*. Nobody looked threatening. I think the stuff
about Paul's death is a bunch of hooey. He shot himself.
People do. Jane probably tackled Tom about Frankie and Tom
lost his temper and took his little hammer to Jane. It's kind
of like golf. No point in getting too fancy. Keep it simple. Hit
the damn ball. Jane got killed because her husband had the
hots for another woman."

Henny eyed her steadily. "Last night someone set fire to
the Martin house. Firefighters rescued Lucy in time. She
could have died."

Irene's smooth face never changed. "I heard about the
fire on TV. If I were the cops, I'd wonder if somebody didn't
read that story and think a fire might be Tom Edmonds's
ticket out of jail."

Emma Clyde concentrated upon appearing genial and
nonthreatening. She was well aware that neither was a
natural default for her. She'd chosen a beige caftan with all
the pizzazz of a monk's habit and horn-rimmed glasses befit-
ting a retired accountant. She arranged her Mount Rushmore
features in an expression of bland entreaty. "It's good of you
to see me on short notice. I know you want to do everything
possible to help track down the dreadful person who killed
Jane."

The office was fairly small. Likely Jane Corley hadn't
seen a reason for her property manager to enjoy boardroom

opulence. Emma considered Kevin Hubbard as a character in a scene. Kevin might have been an aging matinee idol in an old film, thinning black hair smoothed back, sideburns slightly too long, carefully cut mustache, aristocratic features but a mouth that betrayed weakness. He was attempting to project confidence, but his brown eyes flickered nervously from Emma to his shiny manicured nails to a swirl of dust motes in sunlight spearing through a window that overlooked the marina.

"Absolutely." He sounded hollow rather than resolute. "How can I help?"

"I understand you often dealt with David Corley's financial problems."

There was a slight lessening of tension in the sharp shoulders beneath the obviously expensive houndstooth sports jacket. He leaned back, his expression avuncular. "I tried to keep peace in the family." He raised a dark eyebrow. "Easier said than done, I'm afraid. David, well, he's young and he likes to have a good time. Jane wanted him to be steady, but he didn't even have a job. I'm afraid Jane was a bit put out about him."

"Was she unhappy with him recently?" Emma looked inquiringly over the horn-rims.

Kevin was a beat slow in answering.

Emma read the competing thoughts that flitted through a not-very-subtle mind: . . . *I could dump on David . . . but he's keeping me in charge . . . better not rock the boat too much . . .*

He fingered his thin black mustache. "He's a good kid. I know, I know"—a deprecating smile—"not really a kid. But David has youthful enthusiasms and he wasn't ready to settle

176

down yet. I'm afraid Jane was pretty aggravated about his debts. But Jane's death has brought him up short. The boy looks like hell. In fact, I just got off the phone with him. He wanted to know if I knew anybody who had it in for Jane. He said he isn't going to rest until he finds out the truth, whether it was Tom or someone else."

"Yes." Emma's tone was silky. Kevin was feeling comfortable now, hinting at a motive for David but carefully refraining from any kind of accusation. He obviously hoped she'd hustle out to seek the facts of David's money problems, which, of course, ended when his sister died. "It certainly appears there's some question who should be suspected. From the story in the *Gazette* yesterday, it appears definite that Tom Edmonds was in Atlanta the night Paul Martin was shot." She shook her head. "It's dreadful how often money is the motive for murder."

"Well"—he laced his fingers together, shook his head dolefully—"it would be a matter of money for Tom as well and there's no proof the doctor was murdered."

Now was the moment. Kevin was at ease, suspicion liberally showered on others. Emma removed the horn-rims. When she chose, her primrose blue eyes could be as icy as an Arctic glacier. She stared at him until he moved uncomfortably in the chair. "When did Jane discover you were cooking the books?"

Sherry Gillette's purple sateen blouse was unbuttoned to a provocative level. Tight black leggings emphasized too-thick thighs. She flung back her head, possibly envisioning herself as a free spirit on the verge of enlightenment.

Scarcely combed dark curls swirled to her shoulders. "If only I'd been downstairs. I almost went down to talk to Jane that afternoon." A smothered sob. "Jane might be alive now if I'd been there."

Sherry pushed up from the ottoman where she had sat cross-legged listening to Annie. "But"—and she flung out a dramatic hand—"I was just so much in myself that day. I hope you understand."

Annie gazed at her coolly, concluded that Sherry was a self-absorbed drama queen enjoying her proximity to a sensational crime. Coming here to see her was a waste of time. Annie had hoped Sherry knew something. She was in Jane's house the afternoon of the murder. But it seemed evident that Sherry simply wanted to be a part of the excitement. "Why did you call me?"

Sherry pouted at Annie's brusque tone. "Kate told me you were trying to find out more about that day"—her tone capitalized the last two words—"and I was there." Again she tossed that untidy hair. She didn't want to be left out.

Annie was poised to get up and leave. "Did you talk to Jane?"

Sherry paced with both hands upturned. "That wasn't to be. I was too distraught that afternoon to spend time with dear Jane. But now I have to wonder . . . If I had only stepped out on my balcony with my mind uncluttered, who knows what I might have seen." Her green eyes slid to see if Annie was watching. "But that day"—her voice dropped—"I was struggling with my own heartbreak. My husband . . . but perhaps you, too, have known the trauma of a love gone wrong." A soulful sigh.

Annie wasn't deflected. She pounced on what she saw as

a fact, although it might be as hard to grasp as a darting minnow. "You stepped out on the balcony."

Sherry pressed red-taloned fingers to her slightly plump cheeks. "I was buffeted by emotion. I couldn't breathe. I threw open the doors and rushed out. My mind was awhirl. I was looking down at the garden."

Annie felt suddenly breathless. Sherry might possibly be playing her like a guileless fish, but there might be a kernel of truth in the rush of words. Sherry's eyes weren't bemused or confused. Her eyes gleamed with satisfaction.

"What did you see?" Four simple words.

Sherry's full lips curved in a slight smile. "If I'd seen someone crossing the terrace, that fact might be of interest to the police." Her tone was arch. "Whoever came out of the woods and across the terrace must have gone inside. Why else come? I can understand not mentioning a visit because who wants to talk to police?" She gave a little shudder. "Anyway, since Tom's guilty, I don't suppose it matters if anyone else talked to Jane that afternoon, though it seems to me that every fact should be known." She was enjoying her nearness to the room where death occurred. She wanted to tantalize, hold attention to the very last moment before revealing what she had seen on the terrace.

Annie glanced around the room. Several magazines lay atop a pine coffee table, no newspaper. "Did you read yesterday's *Gazette*?"

"Newspapers are boring, don't you think?" Sherry waved a hand in airy dismissal.

"Not yesterday. A story made it clear that Tom's innocent."

Sherry's eyes widened. "Tom's innocent?"

"Without doubt." Except to certain stubborn public officials. "Paul Martin knew Jane was in danger and—" She broke off when she realized Sherry wasn't paying attention.

Sherry stared across the room. "Tom's innocent? That means . . ."

Annie tried to decipher the fleeting expression that crossed Sherry's expressive face. Surprise? Wonderment? Excitement? Annie cleared her throat, thinking *Earth to Sherry.* "If you saw anyone, it could be very helpful."

Sherry gave her a coy look. "I will have to think. They say that even in a high emotional state, such as I was in"—a long breath—"the mind sees more than it realizes and perhaps later something will jog a memory to the surface."

The slippery fish had squished from her grasp. Sherry might have been willing to reveal what she had seen when she doubted its importance. Not now. Instead, she wanted to mull over her knowledge, decide how and when to speak out in a way of achieving a maximum response.

Annie gave one last try. "I'd go right downtown. Talk to the police. You will be a star witness."

Sherry crossed her arms, gave herself a little hug. "Oh, then I really must take my time, be sure of what I saw. You'll understand." She bounded to her feet. "I must have solitude, the better to think."

Annie didn't resist the bum's rush out into the hall, though she gave the closing door a glare. As she hurried down the apartment stairs, regretting the time she'd wasted, Annie carried with her a memory of a plump face alight with excitement. Annie stopped at the ground floor, pulled out her cell, sent a text. She was pulling out of the apartment parking lot when she heard a ping. She stopped at the exit, glanced. Not the reply she'd hoped for. Instead a summons from Emma. Imperious, of course.

As Marigold instructs the inspector—" Emma's sharp blue eyes looked from face to face, expecting rapt attention. Her forceful gaze remained an instant longer on Henny to be sure she was taking notes as Emma had requested.

Annie reminded herself that forbearance is, if not a heavenly virtue, a decided test of character. She would remain calm, attentive, and agreeable even though she loathed Emma's insufferable detective. Annie concentrated on delectable fried oysters in a bun so fresh the sesame seeds practically saluted. Parotti's never disappointed her. She noticed Ben industriously scrubbing the top of the clean table next to theirs. His back was to them, but his ears might as well be flapping.

"—succinctness is the hallmark of a good mind. Since we have others to see this afternoon, please pluck only the important information from each interview." Emma switched cool blue eyes to Max.

Max's lips quirked in a quickly suppressed smile, then he described his foray to Calhoun Street, Hyla Harrison seeking fingerprints on an unburned portion of the leather chair next to the desk in Paul's study, and his search for a place a murderer might have felt safe in parking. ". . . a few feet into a lane, I found a patch of bent and twisted and smashed ferns. A car had obviously backed and turned, leaving tread marks between the ruts. Of course, a teenage couple might have used the lane for romance. But tire prints couldn't have been there long, since we had rain last week. I texted Billy and he sent Lou Pirelli. He made a cast."

Emma looked pleased. "That shows Billy's looking at everything."

There were murmurs of approval.

Max speared a shrimp from his creole. "I have an update on David Corley. He called a little while ago, said he didn't know if it was worth checking out, but Sherry Gillette tracked him down at the marina and flounced down to his boat and every guy on the dock was watching. He thought maybe she was making a scene just for attention, but she made all kinds of hints that she saw someone on the terrace the afternoon Jane was killed. When he tried to pin her down, she was evasive, told him she didn't want to get anyone in trouble. He said he got mad and asked if maybe she remembered Jane was dead and she'd better tell the cops if she had anything to tell, and she turned and ran up the pier. He said he called the station and somebody took the information but as far as he could figure out, the police don't give a damn what he tells them."

Annie jabbed a French fry into a mound of peppered ketchup. "Sherry's the most exasperating woman on the planet. Lots of hints. Dramatic gestures. Phony emotion. But"—she frowned—"I think she actually was on her balcony that afternoon. I texted Billy, told him Sherry may know something. Or it may all be a big bid for attention. No reply from Billy."

Laurel's classic features were composed, though her dark blue eyes were regretful. "I may know who she saw."

The silence was absolute as each of them looked at Laurel.

Laurel beamed at each in turn. "Ross Peters is definitely a strong handsome man of the soil. He's coming over this weekend to give me some pointers"—a pause and a wicked smile—"on the design of a potting shed."

"Ma." Max's tone was gently chiding.

Laurel fluttered pink-tipped fingers at him. "Oh yes, the matter at hand. Ross was working in the garden of the David Corley house the afternoon Jane was murdered. David wandered down into the garden about two thirty. He stopped and chatted for a minute about football. Ross said David seemed to be in a good humor. David ambled down to the dock and took out a kayak. He headed toward the Sound. Madeleine Corley rushed out a little later, chasing her terrier. Ross said when she caught her, Madeleine scooped her up and buried her face in her fur, then snapped a leash on her collar. That was about three. She and Millie left the terrace, heading for the path to Jane's house. Ross said he turned a corner on the hedge and had his back to the house and dock, so he didn't see either Madeleine or David again. He didn't remember if the kayak was on the dock when he headed back to Jane's house, ready to call it a day. He heard the sirens when he was about halfway there and started running. He arrived about the same time as the police. He said Tom was shaking and seemed to be in shock." Laurel looked complacent. "Ross could not have been nicer."

Annie was not surprised. Of course he was nice.

Laurel maintained an expression of innocent pleasure in the gardener's friendliness. "As soon as I reached my car, I informed Billy by text."

Emma nodded in satisfaction. "Billy will never be able to complain that we did not keep him informed. Interesting that Madeleine never mentioned leaving the house. That must be explained."

Annie remembered the garrulous woman at the beauty shop and her insistence Madeleine wasn't home that afternoon. Maybe Billy would find out. But he would not make that effort unless he was convinced someone other than Tom killed Jane.

Definitely, they were keeping him informed, but Billy might possibly feel like an elephant annoyed by a swarm of sand flies.

Henny regretfully pushed away her plate of grilled bratwurst and Hoppin' John. "Wonderful. I can't manage another bite."

Annie agreed with Henny about Miss Jolene's Hoppin' John. No one, except possibly Max, could make a better version of the black-eyed peas, rice, and ham hock dish. And the bratwurst was a delicious pairing, a variation on the usual red cabbage and German potatoes.

Henny said dryly, "I should drop a pint for luck over at the Hubbard house." Hoppin' John for good luck was a Southern mainstay on New Year's Day. "Irene's as nervous as a snake with a hurricane coming. She claims everything was just fine between Kevin and Jane. While I was there, I looked things over. Kevin and Irene have spent lavishly. Their place is a lot fancier than where Kevin used to live and I never heard anything to indicate Irene came from any money."

Emma nodded toward Max. "Since David Corley wants to help, ask him what Kevin earned." She looked at Henny. "I'm not surprised Irene's jittery. I asked Kevin a simple question." Her smile would have chilled a Mafia don. "'When did Jane discover you were cooking the books?'"

There was a pause as she looked from face to face.

Annie folded her arms. Darned if she'd beg Emma to divulge what she knew.

Max glanced at Annie, managed not to smile. "I suspect the answer wasn't so simple."

Emma considered his comment. "Perceptive of you." Still, she waited.

Henny's gaze was admiring, though her dark eyes were amused. "Caught him by surprise, did you?"

Emma nodded regally, her spiky magenta hair reminding Annie of wavering cordgrass tipped by purple as the sun plunged behind pines.

Laurel smoothed back a lock of golden hair. "No doubt, of us all, your inquiry was the most pertinent, the most telling, the most"—even Laurel seemed stumped for a moment, then concluded in a rush—"the most brilliant." Her blue eyes widened in admiration.

Satisfied, Emma cleared her throat. "Kevin stumbled and mumbled, swore he hadn't cooked the books. I administered the coup de grâce." Now her smile was downright menacing. "I said I'd be glad to recommend my accountant, since I knew it was important to have an impartial audit to clear the air after Jane's murder and of course he'd be delighted to cooperate, wouldn't he? I doubt if he's picked himself up off the floor yet." Her bark of laughter was triumphant. "Now"—she scooped up a last forkful of spinach quiche—"let's see what we can find out this afternoon. I suggest a rendezvous at the police station at five P.M. By then, we will have a great deal of information for Billy." Her tone was utterly confident.

10

The elegantly appointed room with ornate molded cornices, sea green drapes framing old-fashioned windows, Chippendale furniture, and a Louis XV desk might have had an Old World charm except for the skull on the corner of the desk and the unstudied toughness of the man watching Max with an expressionless face. The presence of a steel-eyed subordinate standing a pace behind the desk and also watching added to the tension.

Max sat as comfortably as possible in a Hepplewhite armchair that seemed uncommonly hard. Perhaps his discomfort arose from that steady gaze, icy and challenging. Even seated, Jason Brown's height and burly physique were evident. He emanated power. Now an iron gray eyebrow was raised. "You aren't anybody. Not a cop. Not a lawyer."

Max could have pointed out the error. He indeed had a

law degree, but he didn't practice law, so there was no reason to quibble. He maintained a pleasant expression.

Brown folded his muscular arms. "You got in here by sending in a card." He picked up a card with the Confidential Commissions logo on one side, read Max's message on the other: "'How hard were you pushing David Corley to pay up?'" Brown's smile didn't reach his dark eyes. "Who the hell says I was pushing Corley?"

"One of your men"—Max's tone made the inoffensive noun a substitute for *thug*—"escorted David in here for a little heart-to-heart." Max glanced at the underling. "Word has it David lost big at roulette and David's like a lot of rich guys on a stipend, lots of splash, not much cash."

"I don't talk about guests."

Max's smile was sunny. "I don't need to know anything more about the Palmetto Players. I know enough to be sure David Corley was asked to pay up. All I want to know is when—or if—David convinced you he was good for the bill."

Brown absently ran a thumb alongside a small scar at the base of his jaw. Seconds passed. Finally, he grunted, opened the center drawer of the desk, picked up a small leather-bound notebook, flipped past several tabs. He glanced down, then lifted those cold brown eyes. "Wednesday, October 9."

"Did he say where he was going to get the money?"

Brown glanced at his minion.

The man came around the desk, stared down at Max. "Out."

Laurel Roethke parked her jade green convertible in the Fish Haul Pier lot. She left the top down. Few cars were ever stolen on the island. A car would be missed almost immediately and unless the thief had big-scale water wings, the only way off the island was by ferry. She strolled to the boardwalk and out onto the pier. As always, fishermen sat on camp chairs with bait coolers at their feet and rods held over the water that slapped softly against the columns of the pier.

Laurel was pleased as admiring glances followed her. Men did love pretty dresses, especially when soft material flowed in the breeze. Really this dress was a favorite, so feminine and the most graceful design, violets against pale cream. She loved hearing the water swirl around the pilings and hearing the cries of the gulls as they circled, hoping for a tossed-away fish. A catamaran skimmed past the pier, tilting up for a daredevil ride. She heard the laughter of a long-limbed girl and her muscular and attractive shirtless captain.

Laurel smiled, sent a silent wish across the water: *Enjoy being young, my dears. Each day comes but once.*

Running steps sounded behind her. She turned.

Frankie Ford slid to a stop in front of Laurel, spared one quick glance over her shoulder. "I can't stay long." Her voice was low, breathless. "Mr. Wyler thinks I'm running some checks to the bank." Frankie's pale face reflected dread. Her eyes looked haunted, her cheeks hollow. "Why don't they let Tom go?" Her voice broke. "Somebody set fire to Dr. Martin's house. Why would that happen unless somebody didn't want anyone looking again at the place where he died?"

Laurel hated to add to her burden, but she should be prepared. "There's some thought that the fire was set by someone who wants Tom to appear to be innocent."

"Nobody but me would care—" She broke off, if possible looked even more upset. "Oh my God. I didn't. I wouldn't. That's awful."

"The only thing that will help Tom is if all the truth comes out." She gazed at Frankie kindly. "You went to his studio that afternoon." She spoke with assurance and knew she was right when Frankie's gaze dropped. "I don't think Tom was at the studio. Later, when he claimed he'd never left his studio until he went to the pool and then across the terrace and found Jane, you were afraid he'd killed her." Laurel felt confident in her declarations, based on Annie's conclusion that Frankie was evasive about her whereabouts when Jane was killed and that Frankie had been terrified of his guilt until she heard about the drawing Lucy Ransome found.

Frankie came alive, face turning pink, hand upheld in dismay. "I never really thought he was guilty. But it was scary that he said he was in his studio all afternoon. I know what must have happened. He found Jane dead and panicked. I'll bet he ran back to the studio and stayed there, trying to think what to do. And then, oh I know how his mind works, he decided the easiest thing was to stay there until it was time for him to finish like he always did. When I came about a quarter after three to the studio, he was gone. He must have been up at the house. I couldn't wait. Toby gets impatient if I take too long over errands."

"Why did you go to the studio?"

Frankie brushed back a strand of reddish-brown hair. Her expression was odd, as if she looked back over a chasm that memory could scarcely bridge. "I was going to tell him I was going to look for a job in Atlanta." The words came haltingly and Frankie's eyes held anguish.

Laurel reached out, patted her arm. "What did you expect him to do?"

Frankie looked away. "I don't know." Her voice was dull.

"I couldn't stay on the island. I couldn't keep on the way it was. I can't live my life being . . ." She trailed off.

Laurel understood. Frankie was young, desperately in love, unwilling to be a mistress.

Frankie lifted that rounded chin, but her face didn't look young. There was an empty, sad expression. "I don't think he would have come. Only painting really matters to him. That's why he didn't kill Jane." Now her voice was hot. "He wouldn't do anything that could ruin his life as a painter."

Laurel suspected she was right on all counts. Now the question had to be whether Frankie would commit murder rather than lose Tom. "Where did you park?"

Frankie looked utterly bewildered.

"You drove your car. You came to the studio. Where did you park? I assume you didn't want Jane to know you were there."

Again Frankie seemed to be looking back at a long-ago moment, one that had little reality to her now. She spoke as if the information didn't matter. "Instead of turning in at the main entrance, I went about half a block and parked. There's a bike trail through the woods there. I took that. At one point, the trail crosses the path to the studio."

"Did you see anyone?"

She shook her head.

"Did you hear anything?"

She looked weary. "I didn't hear a car or see anyone on the path, only a dog yipping in the distance."

Emma was brusque. "Fine painter. If he gets the chair for murdering his wife, prices will double." She turned a thumb toward a haunting painting of a marsh scene.

Toby Wyler's dark eyes appraised her. She didn't miss the gleam of avarice in his gaze, reflecting a gallery owner's pleasure when a well-heeled buyer was uncanny enough to reveal intense interest.

Emma had already noted that the cards beneath the paintings did not contain a purchase price. Whatever she bought was going to cost several thousands more than before her revealing comment. She wasn't concerned. They were fine paintings and, thanks to Marigold Rembrandt, she could afford to indulge herself. However, Mr. Wyler was going to provide a great deal of information before she signed a check.

She turned bright primrose blue eyes toward him, considered his white suit that emphasized the coal black of his hair and mustache, found the effect theatrical. "It's fascinating to learn more about a woman's actions when she has only a few days to live. What time did you see Jane that day?"

His eyes narrowed. "What day?"

"The day she died."

He moved a little on the balls of his feet, like a boxer on guard. "I didn't see her on Monday."

Emma raised her eyebrows. "I must have misunderstood. But"—she brightened—"you were at the party."

"Party?" The pleasant tone was belied by the center of coldness in his eyes.

"David's birthday party. You were there."

"Yes."

Emma wandered to the wall, looked up at a large painting. He could likely price it at twenty thousand. "I rather like this. But part of the attraction would be the backstory. Painted by a man accused of murder. I was thinking of a dinner party and showing it to my guests. But"—a little sigh—"it would only be special if I could share something none of them knows. A little bit of history. How Jane looked that night, something she said." Emma shook her head, walked to the counter, and picked up her purse. "I'll think about it."

She was at the door when he spoke. "It's a real fine painting. I can let you have it for thirty thousand. And I don't see any harm in talking a bit about Jane."

Emma turned, careful to maintain an eager expression.

"The problem"—his voice was doleful—"was that Jane was a good friend. It's hard to look back and remember the last time I saw her. But she wanted the best for Tom's paintings. And so do I. Can I offer you a glass of sherry and I'll see what I can recall of the birthday party?" He gestured toward an art deco sofa with an excellent view of the painting chosen by Emma.

Emma smiled and graciously settled on the soft cushions. In a moment, he returned with two glasses of sherry. Emma sipped and listened.

". . . not my kind of party . . . not that I don't enjoy a few drinks, but David and his friends were drunk . . . sorry to say Jane was not in a good mood. Every time I saw her, she was crossways with somebody. She took David aside, gave him hell, but he blew that off. And"—he gave a deprecating shrug—"I came in for my share. She was unhappy about the slow sales at the open house. I told her some of my best customers were in Hawaii and I was sure I could place the three big landscapes when they got back. I was right. They came in yesterday and bought them. Too late for Jane. And she had sharp words for Madeleine. Probably told her to do something about David but short of tossing the rum in the swimming pool, I don't know what she could have done. Then"—his glance was sly—"Irene Hubbard came up to Jane. I couldn't see Jane's face, but I thought Irene looked pretty desperate." He fingered his bristly black mustache. "Just before the party ended"—for the first time his tone was unstudied, without malice—"Jane looked around the room with a strange expression, like something was wrong."

Henny Brawley admired chintz-covered furniture and bookcases with bright jackets that had the appearance of use, not simply there as decor, and felt an instinctive sadness that Jane Corley met an unexpected and painful death surrounded by familiar possessions in a warm and charming room. She must have known happiness here. The care and taste evidenced by the furnishings reflected a woman who valued beauty without ostentation. The reddish-gold of the walls recalled late afternoons in Florence. Tom's paintings were hung to best display the vibrant splashes of color, the vigor of his brushstrokes. Henny glanced in passing at the pool table and noted an occasional rug had been skewed at one end, likely to hide the blotch left on the heart-pine floor after blood was cleaned away.

Kate gestured toward a sofa with plump cushions. She sat opposite Henny in a rattan chair, brushed back a lock of white gray hair. Her gaze was stern. "You know I'd do anything necessary to avenge Jane. But the police seem to think they have the right man. Maybe Lucy's wrong about Paul and the meaning of that drawing."

Henny met that fierce stare directly. "The fire at Lucy's house was deliberately set."

Kate's face furrowed. "I know. I suppose you could be right

that Paul was murdered and the fire set to destroy some evidence. Though"—and her tone was impatient—"Lucy said the police went over his study from top to bottom, so what was there to find?" She shook her head. "I'm afraid it confirms what I've thought all along." Her lips set in a hard line.

Henny looked at her inquiringly.

"That woman. She chased after Tom. Oh, I don't think it would have come to much. He knew what Jane could do for his career." A shrug. "I'll admit I can't see him using his precious mallet on Jane. He thought too much of his tools. I'd heard him talk about that mallet, how the handle was worn just right for his hands. The man is obsessed with his hands."

Henny was a little surprised by Kate's disdain.

Kate's tone was wry. "Do you think I'm intemperate? I'll admit I don't admire cheaters. But I don't think he'd have the gumption to plan a crime. I don't put it past him to connive with Frankie, let her do the dirty work. For my take, that's what happened. She killed Jane. And maybe Paul, too. She'll do anything for Tom. Including arson." She leaned back in the chair, thin face forlorn, brown eyes grieving, body sagging. "Damn, it's hard, talking about Jane like this." She was dressed in a black turtleneck and black slacks, which emphasized the paleness of her face.

"When someone dies unexpectedly"—Henny's voice was gentle—"we're left with so many things we wish we hadn't said, moments we'd change if we could. I know it's intrusive, but everything we learn about Jane's last days may be helpful. About a week before she died, I understand you came out of her office apparently quite angry."

For an instant, Kate's face was stiff. Then, voice clipped, she said, "Everyone who lives here knows me. I'm loud. I say what's on my mind. I was really exasperated. Jane was being stubborn. As it turns out, she came around, agreed to pay off some debts of David's. But in the meantime Madeleine was having fits. David owed money to some people who weren't above making threats. I told Madeleine it was all nonsense, but she didn't believe me. She left in tears. Clutching the damn dog, of course."

"Nonsense?"

Kate waved a dismissive hand. "The threat was right out of a B-grade movie, a hoarse voice on the phone promising unspeakable tortures to woof woof unless David paid up. But Madeleine was so upset I had it out with Jane." She sighed. "Of course we got everything straightened out between us before she died. Thank God. But still, I hate to remember how we butted heads that day."

A nnie pushed the bell, then half turned to look at the sun glancing off the water of Wherry Creek. The black shutters and gray planks of the porch had been recently painted. A late-afternoon breeze stirred the fronds of Whitmani ferns in large pottery vases. A swing at one end of the porch looked inviting and would offer a glorious view of the creek.

The door opened. A grumpy-looking girl, probably eighteen or nineteen, held a feather duster in one hand, a cloth in the other. She squinted watery blue eyes at Annie. "Yes?"

Annie tabbed her as temporary help not enamored of her job.

"Is Mrs. Corley at home?"

The maid glanced behind her, then looked at Annie. She

leaned forward, spoke in a light whisper. "She just got home and ran upstairs. She said she doesn't feel very good and not to disturb her." There was a speculative look in those watery eyes.

"It's really important that I speak to her. About the afternoon of the day Jane died."

The girl stared at her avidly, but she shook her head. "She said she didn't want to see anybody. She didn't want any phone calls or anything."

Annie took a chance. She opened her purse, slipped a twenty from her billfold. "Do you know where she'd been?" For all Annie knew, Madeleine had been on an errand and been struck with a migraine. But anything unusual was worth checking out.

The girl stared at the twenty, then, with another glance over her shoulder, eased the screen open and stepped out on the porch. She reached for the twenty, folded it, and quickly stuffed the bill into low-hanging jeans. "I don't have a GPS, lady. But something funny's going on. When she ran in the house, she wasn't wearing any shoes."

No shoes. How odd. "Was she carrying them?"

The girl shook her head. "I would've seen them. I can tell you, this is a weird place. I'm here for my cousin Gloria but I told my cousin—she's been home for almost a month with a sick baby, he's having a hard time and they can't seem to figure out what's wrong, so I'll stay till he's okay—you couldn't pay me enough to work here permanent. Mrs. Corley has this wild look in her eyes. For the first couple of weeks, she wouldn't go anywhere without that mutt and I'd find her holding him out in the garden and crying. I asked her if he was sick or something and she snapped my head off. Like I told Gloria, she's some kind of saint if she sticks it out here. But, she needs the money. Single mom." She opened the screen, started to step inside.

"Jesse, come up here." The voice was hoarse.

"Oh man"—a quick whisper—"I better go up. Want me to tell her you came by?"

Annie almost left her name, then shook her head. It wouldn't do any harm for Madeleine to wonder who had come in search of her.

As Annie slowly pulled away from the curb, she glanced in the rearview mirror. She saw a flash of blue on the upper verandah. Someone stepping inside? Had Madeleine hurried out to glimpse her visitor, then quickly withdrawn? There was something odd going on in that stately old home, Madeleine arriving home and rushing inside without shoes. Where were her shoes?

Annie drove slowly. Could Madeleine possibly be aware that Laurel had talked to the gardener and that he told Laurel Madeleine took the path to Jane's house the afternoon of the murder? That wasn't likely. There was no reason for Madeleine to connect Laurel's talk with the gardener to Annie's arrival. Besides, Madeleine arrived home upset and barefoot before Annie came.

Annie slowed for a stop sign, saw an empty school bus likely on its way to take students home from school. Barefoot . . . She tucked that bit of knowledge away. For now, Madeleine's choice of footwear or its lack didn't matter. What mattered was whether she had gone all the way to Jane Corley's house on the afternoon of the murder. Annie's plan to confront Madeleine, claim that she had been seen on the terrace, was thwarted. Maybe tomorrow she would be able to talk to Madeleine. But now she had some leverage to use with Sherry Gillette, who had to reveal what—if anything—she had seen from the balcony. Annie would state with authority that Madeleine had come to Jane's house and tell Sherry it was time to stop playing games.

Although she had to take several twisty lanes, Buccaneer Arms was actually very near the pocket of old homes. She could have walked on bike paths much more quickly. She pulled into the same parking space she'd occupied earlier. As she crossed the blacktop to the exterior stairs, she considered her options. Should she encourage Sherry that she could be a star witness?

Annie hurried up the cement steps to the third floor, pulled open a creaky door. Or maybe she could finagle information by telling Sherry that Madeleine insisted she didn't see anyone on any of the balconies when she dropped in that afternoon. Unless she misjudged Sherry mightily, Sherry would rush to insist Madeleine should have seen Sherry because Sherry certainly saw Madeleine.

As she walked down the hallway, her elation subsided. Okay, she could then report to Billy that Madeleine had been spotted on Jane's terrace and Billy might agree to ask her when she was there and why, but the single fact of Sherry seeing her was not enough to make Madeleine a suspect.

Annie sighed. She had come this far. She might as well talk to Sherry. She glanced at the numbers. Two doors to go. Buccaneer apartments would have profited from fresh paint in the hallway, but the ceiling lights were generously bright. Dimmer lighting might have made the surroundings more attractive, diminishing the starkness of scuffs and scrapes. She reached Apartment 7, knocked.

Silence.

She knocked again, loudly, waited, noticing the bronze knocker was dull and tarnished. She didn't think it was in Sherry's nature not to answer a door. She would be curious. Annie reached in her purse, drew out a small notepad, wrote fast: *Sherry, urgent that we talk. There is some question whether you were on your balcony.* She hesitated. That was enough. Annie could imagine a very good reason why Sherry might not have been on the balcony. Perhaps Sherry saw Madeleine—if she did—from a hiding place in the family room. If Sherry killed Jane, it would be much better for her to claim to have been on her balcony all afternoon.

Annie folded the note, wrote *Sherry* on one side. And maybe, her thought was wry, she should try her hand at writing mysteries as well as selling them. All of her speculation was just that, imagining what could have happened and she didn't have any facts to back her up, just Sherry's hints that she *might* have seen someone from the balcony and Madeleine arriving home without shoes.

She looked for a letter slot in the door. The Buccaneer didn't run to such niceties. Likely there were letter boxes in the ground-floor foyer. Annie pawed through her purse. Lots of interesting flotsam—a key she didn't remember, a shiny blue marble, a ticket stub to a Braves game, a cellophane-wrapped, tired-looking praline—but no Scotch tape. Maybe she could slide the note beneath the door. She bent down, stiffened, stared.

Officer Hyla Harrison's auburn hair was drawn back in a tight bun. As always her French blue uniform was immaculate. She spoke to Annie while still studying the stained floor. "Could be blood. Looks like blood." She knocked firmly on the door. She waited a moment, tried again. No answer. She pulled a cell from a pocket. "The manager can help us." She tapped the phone, was answered on the second ring. "Ma'am, this is Broward's Rock Police Officer Hyla Harrison. I'm upstairs at the apartment of Mr. and Mrs. Roger Gillette. We've had a call that the occupant may need assistance. Can you bring up a key, please." She put away the cell, reached into a knapsack she'd placed on the floor. "I'll make a test while we're waiting."

Annie waited tensely.

Kneeling, Hyla gave a swift spray from a canister. She unsnapped a small flashlight from her belt, turned it on, held steady the sharp white beam.

Annie and Officer Lou Pirelli, broad face intent beneath his curly dark hair, both bent forward.

As Hyla aimed the beam, a reddish smear perhaps six inches from the doorsill turned pale green. Hyla was immobile for an instant, then she came to her feet. She flicked on her lapel-pin camera with one hand, retrieved her cell with the other. "Buccaneer apartments, third floor, Apartment 7. No response to knocking on the door. Stain on floor sprayed. Test positive. Yes, sir."

She returned the phone to its holder. Pulling on plastic gloves, she leaned toward the door, careful to keep a good distance from the green-and-red smudge on the floor. Now the knocking was thunderous. "Police. Open the door. Police."

Loud enough to wake the dead . . .

Annie leaned against the opposite wall, fought away dreadful visions.

A door down the hall popped open. A tiny woman with

frizzy gray hair and an anxious expression peered out. "What's going on?" Her voice was shrill.

Hyla ignored her. Using only the tips of the gloved fingers on her right hand, she tried to twist the knob. The knob remained rigid. The door was locked. Hyla nodded at Lou. "Get the manager. We need to check inside."

Lou moved fast and the sound of his thudding footsteps echoed up the stairwell.

"Oh my, oh, oh my. Has something awful happened?" The neighbor clung to the doorjamb, her eyes wide and anxious.

Hyla turned. "Ma'am, everything is under control. We are simply responding to a call. Please remain in your apartment. Thank you."

Annie wasn't surprised to see the woman withdraw and shut the door. Hyla had an air of authority that few would question and never twice.

Hyla once again knocked.

No response.

The exterior door at the end of the hallway opened and she heard a cheerful whistle. A country music song . . . Annie recognized the old tune, "Friends in Low Places," a rowdy, fun song, a perennial on the jukebox at Parotti's. The whistler was about half the length of the hall when he broke off, stopped, and stared, looking from Hyla to the door to the apartment. He was big, muscular with a reddish face and a mass of curly black hair. His green-checked shirt was rolled to the elbows and a little tight across the chest, his brown khakis wrinkled. A backpack dangled from over one shoulder.

Annie wished she was anywhere other than that hallway. Until he saw Hyla in her uniform, Roger Gillette had sounded like a man who had enjoyed a good day, his expression pleased and satisfied. Now he was puzzled. He walked slowly toward them.

"Hey, why are you standing in front of my door?" He moved a little faster, the backpack sliding down. He grabbed the strap with his left hand.

Hyla's face had its cop look, serious, intent, noncommittal. "Sir, may I see your identification? Officer Hyla Harrison."

"What for?" He was perhaps a foot from Hyla now.

"We responded to a call that a resident might be in need of assistance. There is a bloodstain on the floor outside the door to Apartment 7." She didn't look down but she watched his gaze drop.

Gillette stiffened, looked bewildered. "Blood?" His head jerked up. "That stuff's blood?"

"Yes, sir. Your identification, please."

Slowly he reached to a back pocket, pulled out a billfold. He flipped it open, handed it to Hyla, but he was looking at the door now. "Where's Sherry? Hey, Sherry?" He was loud, but his voice had a scared edge. He jammed a hand in the pocket of his khaki pants, pulled out a set of keys, moved forward.

"Sir." Hyla's tone stopped him short. "If you don't mind, I'll open the door. I want to be careful not to touch the knob." She held out his billfold.

"You think . . ." His voice cracked. Slowly, he took the billfold, dropped the keys into her hand. "The fourth one." Now his face looked like a man staring at something he doesn't understand, something threatening, dangerous, incomprehensible.

Footsteps sounded in the hallway. The woman's tone was querulous. "I know you're in a police uniform, but you don't have a search warrant and—" The voice broke off.

Neither Roger nor Annie turned to look. They watched Hyla insert the key, turn, never touching the knob. The door swung in.

Roger Gillette took a step forward.

Hyla moved in front of him, barring the way. "Stay here, sir. Please."

But he pushed forward to stand next to her. Then his face crumpled. "Oh my God. Oh my God . . ."

11

The Buccaneer Arms was only a couple of football fields in distance from the police station, separated by Pavilion Park and thick woods. Fast-moving police, including Billy Cameron, arrived in less than five minutes.

Annie and a stricken Roger Gillette, his body shaken by recurrent tremors, were sequestered at the end of the hall near the stairway farthest from the Gillette apartment. Officer Boots Townsend, a fairly new addition to the staff, stood stiffly by them, though his light blue eyes looked longingly toward Officers Harrison and Pirelli outside the open doorway and he strained to hear as they spoke to a grim-faced Billy Cameron. Annie tried to eavesdrop as well, but their voices were too low to be heard. Roger slumped against the wall, oblivious to them.

Footsteps thudded on the stairway. Marian Kenyon burst into the hall. The reporter's dark eyes noted Annie, had a flash of understanding and commiseration for Roger, settled on Billy Cameron and, standing a few feet away, Billy's wife, Mavis, who doubled as dispatcher and crime scene tech. A blue-canvas carryall rested on the floor by her feet.

Townsend turned toward Marian, held up a thin hand. Sandy-haired and youthful despite a valiant attempt at a goatee that looked like orange peach fuzz, he looked like a high school chemistry teacher confronting an untended Bunsen burner with a blue flame flaring too high. "Ma'am, crime scene. No admittance."

Marian flicked him a brief glance. *"Gazette."*

Townsend looked blank, started to move as Marian took several steps toward the apartment.

Annie spoke up quickly. "She's a reporter. Chief Cameron knows her."

Townsend hesitated and Marian was past him. "Hey, Chief." She had her notebook in one hand, stubby pencil in the other. Marian had an electronic notepad, but she preferred pencil and paper for initial notes.

Billy glanced her way, pointed to a spot about ten feet from the open doorway.

Marian nodded, skidded to a stop there. She understood boundaries. She was near enough to see and hear, not close enough to impede the investigation.

Marian's shoulders hunkered. From the back, she looked like a cat crouched to spring, and Annie knew Marian had spotted the smudged blood with the telltale splotch that had turned green.

"Why are they just standing there?" The raspy voice seemed to come from Annie's elbow.

Startled, Annie looked around.

A tiny woman with a topknot of white hair above a lined leathery face stood in her doorway, peering down the hall. "If something bad's happened, how come they don't do nothing?"

Annie gave her a reassuring smile. "They're waiting for the medical examiner. The police can't investigate until he officially pronounces death."

Officer Townsend cleared his throat. "Witnesses are asked not to speak to anyone."

The old lady's nose wrinkled. "Put it in a sock, sonny. The lady's just being polite." She looked down the hall again. "I worked in a hospital for forty-nine years. I could tell 'em if somebody's dead." She glanced at Annie. "Seven always made a lot of noise."

Annie realized the neighbor was referring to the Gillette apartment.

"A carrying voice. Heard her on her balcony a while ago. Then she closed the sliding door."

Officer Townsend pulled out a small notebook. "Your name, ma'am?"

"JoJo Jenkins. RN, retired." But she was craning to see past Annie. "There's Doc Burford. Good man. I'd forgot he did autopsies and things for the county. Guess they'll move things along now."

The officers clustered near the open door moved out of the way as the medical examiner thumped past. His big face beneath a mop of grayish-brown hair was somber. T. W. Burford, MD, ME, chief of staff at Broward's Rock Hospital, resented death. Even more, he resented untimely death.

Big-shouldered and burly, he carried a satchel that looked small in his huge hand. He stepped carefully over the blood smudge, disappeared from view.

He was out in the hall within a couple of minutes. He, too, had a carrying voice. "Death caused by blunt trauma to back of head. Likely within the last hour. Massive blood loss. Look for stained clothes. No weapon readily visible. I can say better after the autopsy, but it looks like there's some detritus embedded in the wound. Maybe a heavy stick from the woods." He jerked his head to the north. "Lots of broken sticks in the Pavilion woods. Lots of luck finding it. Time your exit when nobody's in the lot, spring for the woods, heave it away."

Despite the closed door, sounds from the hallway seeped into the police break room, doors slamming, rapid steps, the discordant jangle of ringing phones.

They sat quietly around a long Formica-topped table, the toll of another death reflected in each face. Max's lips were set in a grim line. He made occasional notes on a legal pad. Henny Brawley's chiseled features were somber, a strong contrast to her elegant attire chosen for cheer, a drape-front rose cashmere sweater and white slacks. She clasped a chipped coffee mug, looked down into its depths as if seeking answers. Emma Clyde's square jaw jutted. She stared into space, her cold blue eyes thoughtful. Occasionally, she gave an almost imperceptible nod, apparently approving an internal dialogue. Laurel Roethke's expression was . . . misty.

Annie thought for a moment, decided she understood, once again felt a swift rush of affection. Laurel was sad, sad for Sherry, sad that her desperate need for attention led her to a bloody end, sad that her husband was the first to see her body, sad that Annie had not arrived in time to find out the truth and keep Sherry safe.

"I should have made her tell me this morning." Annie's voice was husky.

Laurel reached across the table, took her hand. "Oh, my dear, none of us can make others do as we wish. Sherry made a decision and the result for her was forever bad."

The door opened. Weariness creased Billy Cameron's broad face, emphasized dark smudges beneath his eyes. He stepped inside, carrying a folder, and walked to the table. He stood at one end, spread the folder open on the table. "I appreciate all of you coming and making statements." For an instant the grimness of his expression was lightened by a brief smile. "Some towns have volunteer firefighters. I guess Broward's Rock has volunteer peace officers." Something else glinted in his eyes, perhaps a touch of malice. "The mayor's got his nose out of joint, says there ought to be a law against people snooping. But a man's free tonight who might not be if Annie hadn't come to the Gillette apartment when she did. Roger Gillette has every minute of his day accounted for and a friend brought him home from school because Roger's car is in the shop. The friend saw him walk into the apartment house and they both wondered at the patrol car there. Officers were already on the scene because of Annie's call. Roger walked up the stairs and found Officer Harrison and Annie outside his door. When Harrison opened the door, Sherry Gillette was dead. We know he didn't kill her because a neighbor heard her on her balcony not more than a half hour earlier. Roger was in class. Time of death is always dicey to pin down. If he'd come home, found her, called for help, we'd still be questioning him because she hadn't been dead long, maybe less than a half hour when she was found. Roger Gillette's broken up, but he isn't in a cell right now. Funny thing, all this stuff about a rocky marriage. Probably true, but I'd say the guy was nuts about her, knew she was a mess, tried to deal with it. But he's not in jail tonight for a murder he didn't commit." Billy glanced at Annie.

Laurel reached over and patted Annie's hand.

Billy was somber again. "Unlike Tom Edmonds. The mayor doesn't agree, wants to hunker down and hold Tom. I told him no way. Obviously the murders of Jane Corley and Sherry Gillette are connected. Tom was in a cell when Gillette was killed. I told the mayor, we're starting from scratch. We have to go over everything again. Here's how I see it. Paul Martin was right. Paul knew Jane Corley was in danger. He thought he could discourage anything serious by confronting someone. On his drawing, he made it clear he intended to issue a warning at David Corley's birthday party. We'll take him at his word. Paul spoke to someone at the party. Paul was shot later that night." He glanced at his notes. "Lucy Ransome heard a car at shortly after twelve the night Paul was shot. A neighbor called 911 at two fifteen A.M. the night of the fire. So far, the responses are what you'd expect. David and Madeleine were cleaning up after the party the first night. The second night they say they were in bed—together. Ditto the Hubbards. No alibis for Kate Murray, Frankie Ford, or Toby Wyler. We'll keep pressing. But you people talked to them when they weren't on alert. I want gut reactions." He nodded toward Emma.

"Toby Wyler." She leaned back, folded her arms, looked majestic in a sea blue caftan. "I may have to use him in a book one of these days, the way he kept stroking his mustache, especially when he was ingenuously fingering other attendees at the birthday party as likely suspects. As for the new status quo, he's as satisfied as Poppa Bear back in a big chair. Tom's safely in his corral again. I asked some art friends about the gallery. They'd heard sales were down, had been for a year or so, and he owed money for some remodeling. Hard to say if he'd commit murder to stay solvent." Her smile was thin. "People do. He mostly presented an aura of complete confidence, but that mustache got a workout. Big contrast to Kevin Hubbard, who was as antsy as a West Pointer facing an unexpected inspection with porn hidden under the mattress. Hubbard may not be guilty of murder, but he looked like he'd spotted debtor's prison when I asked him about the accounts."

Billy's gaze moved to Henny.

Henny gave a brief nod. "Irene Hubbard's strung tight. I don't know whether she's afraid Kevin will be accused of stealing—or murder. On the other hand, Kate Murray wasn't worried about the fact that she and Jane quarreled. Kate raised hell with Jane about not paying David's gambling debts because someone in Jason Brown's outfit threatened to kill Madeleine's dog if David didn't pay up. Kate was gruff but she said people who don't have kids—and she looked at that snarly cat of hers—get all tied up emotionally with their animals and Madeleine was absolutely distraught. Kate insists everything was all straightened out before Jane died because Jane agreed to stand good for the debt."

Billy made a note. "Did Madeleine know the dog was safe?"

Henny turned graceful hands palms up. "I have no idea."

"We'll find out." He sounded determined.

Max was casual. "David had plenty of time to tell Madeleine before Jane died. I had a tête-à-tête—short—with Jason Brown. Not a chummy man. David was a damn fool to get in hock to him. It looks like David's in the clear. According to Jason, David told him on the Wednesday before Jane died that he was going to get his money. That confirms David's claim that Jane had agreed to cover the debts."

"If the debt was going to be paid"—Billy figured out loud—"Madeleine had no reason to want Jane dead." His face wrinkled. "Killing a woman so your husband will inherit money to save your pooch seems like a stretch anyway."

"Still"—Laurel's voice was regretful—"Madeleine walked toward Jane Corley's house at two thirty that afternoon. Possibly you should ask Tom Edmonds where he was when Frankie Ford came to his studio shortly after three."

Billy frowned. "If Edmonds saw his sister-in-law, he kept quiet about it."

"Since he claimed he never left his studio until he went to the pool and stopped for a drink, that rather precluded his reporting on anything he saw." Laurel's tone was mild.

Annie mentally gave her mother-in-law a thumbs-up. Laurel had reasonably explained why Tom wouldn't have mentioned anything he couldn't have seen or heard from his studio. In fact, Tom might know something that could change the direction of the investigation. She saw Billy make a note.

Laurel beamed at Billy. "Shortsighted of Tom. But once you lie . . . Perhaps now if he is reassured that he is no longer a suspect, he might be more forthcoming."

Billy nodded agreement. "I'll be on him like a bat on a june bug. He and everyone around Jane Corley are going to answer some tough questions."

Annie felt tension draining away. They had succeeded in their efforts to free Tom Edmonds and expose Paul Martin's death as murder. Now a determined police chief was on the hunt.

Billy tapped his pad. "We'll find out where the guests at David Corley's birthday party were at critical times, including this afternoon between two and three." He looked at Annie. "You talked to Mrs. Gillette this morning."

"Yes." Only this morning . . . Annie tried to keep the wobble away from her lips.

Billy understood. "From what I've been told, she loved to grandstand. This was the time when she meant what she said, but you couldn't know that. I looked over the transcript. The day of the murder, she didn't say a word about seeing anybody. Lou talked to her. She was hysterical, wondered if she and Kate Murray were in danger. She kept crying and saying she'd been in her room and hadn't heard a thing. It's possible she confused the time of the murder with the time Tom called 911 and that's why she didn't mention seeing anyone who came earlier in the afternoon. Once she knew Tom was innocent, she'd see the importance of another visitor. Think back to this morning. Try to strip away the histrionics. Do you have any sense of what she actually saw?"

Annie recalled the small living room with its shabby decor, the slipcovers slightly soiled, the untidy pile of magazines, a wilting fern in a raffia basket near the balcony door. The door had been open and a slight breeze stirred the fronds. She remembered the sheen of Sherry's sateen blouse and a Raggedy Ann propped in a bookshelf in one corner. She wondered if the doll had been a plump little girl's best friend and confidante. She remembered Sherry's eyes gleaming with excitement and the little wriggle she gave as she hinted at what she may have seen. "I think she really did see someone on the terrace. She almost told me but decided the payoff wasn't big enough. I wasn't enough of an audience. I think she decided it would be more exhilarating, she'd get more attention, if she contacted the person she saw."

Billy folded his arms. "She went to the marina, talked to David Corley. But"—he seemed to be thinking out loud—"Corley told her to go to the cops and he called us after she left. If he isn't the person she saw, why go see him?"

Max shrugged. "Stringing out the fun, probably. Tease David a little, get him to urge her to contact you. Maybe she went to see him so she could tell the visitor that David wanted her to go to the police. Maybe she figured he'd call the police and she could tell the visitor that she was willing to keep quiet, maybe for a nice gift. David did just as she expected. He called you. He said Lou took down the information."

"Lou dropped by the apartment house around noon but she wasn't home. He left a message on her phone, asked her to call us." Billy looked tired. "She had plenty of chances to go in another direction. She didn't."

Emma's face crunched in thought. "There may be another reason she went to see David. As Marigold always advises, follow the money. Who profits big time from Jane's murder? Her brother, David, and her husband, Tom. Sherry couldn't contact Tom, so she goes to David. Maybe her plan was to tantalize him with the fact that she could expose Jane's murderer and she would do so if properly rewarded?"

Billy looked skeptical. "That's not what David Corley told Lou."

Emma's tone was kindly. "As Marigold reminds the inspector, no one ever quite tells the police everything."

"He didn't have to tell us anything. He could have kept quiet." Billy was brusque and Annie didn't blame him. He didn't need tips from Marigold.

Henny Brawley's dark eyes were thoughtful. "Sherry had a piercing voice. Unless I miss my guess, she was probably loud at the marina, put on a show. People would have noticed her talking to him. Either he is what he seems to be, a grieving brother who wants justice done for his sister, or, if he has something to hide, he figured that Sherry's visit would be noticed and he had no option but to call the police."

Laurel's face reflected sorrow. "He may well have something to hide. He isn't very steady, but you can't help but see how much he loves his wife."

Annie blinked and knew the others shared her puzzlement. Had always-spacey Laurel finally lost contact with reality, much as a hot air balloon jolts skyward if untethered? Everyone stared at her with varying degrees of apprehension.

Laurel's gaze was dreamy. "The way he looks at her whenever they are in the same room." She glanced from face to face. "I'm quite sure of that."

Annie doubted any of them were willing to contradict Laurel's dicta in matters of the heart.

Max looked puzzled. "I agree. David loves his wife. What does that have to do with Sherry's murder?"

"Oh my dear." Her voice was sad. "Madeleine started on the path to Jane's house. What if Sherry saw Madeleine and told David she would be willing to keep quiet—for a price?"

Emma's ice blue eyes moved to Annie. "You talked to Madeleine. What did she say?"

Annie shook her head. "I didn't see her."

Emma frowned. "Madeleine was on your list."

Annie didn't appreciate the implication she had shirked her duty. "I tried." She knew her tone was sharp. "The maid said Madeleine had just arrived home and was all upset and didn't want to see anyone. That's when I decided to go to the Buccaneer. I was going to tell Sherry a witness said Madeleine was on the terrace."

Billy was suddenly alert. "You went directly to the Buccaneer from Madeleine's house?"

Annie nodded.

"Probably took all of six minutes. You found the blood spot, called. If Madeleine arrived home just before you reached the house, that's maybe ten to fifteen minutes after Sherry died. The maid said Madeleine was upset?"

Annie nodded slowly. "She'd just arrived home. She told the maid she didn't want to see anyone and ran upstairs."

"Any indication why she was upset?"

"I don't know." Annie frowned. "There was one odd thing. The maid said she ran into the house barefoot."

"Barefoot?" Emma's blue eyes took on a particular recognizable gleam, an author tantalized by an idea.

Annie was sure that Emma was instantly leagues away in the world she inhabited with Marigold Rembrandt, her thoughts racing: *Why was a grown woman barefoot? Where were her shoes? What happened to her shoes?*

Billy sat up straight. "No shoes?" He sat for a moment, broad face folded in thought. Abruptly, he looked toward the windows at dusk turning to darkness. He yanked his cell from his belt. "Hyla, institute a floor-by-floor search for a pair of women's shoes." He listened, nodded. "Right." He flicked to another number. "Lou, use flashlights and check the parking lot . . ."

A nnie loved the boardwalk in early morning, a hint of mist curling up from the marina, the storefronts mostly dark. Death on Demand's plate glass window was an exception. Golden light spilled over the miniature train winding past a station, an inn, a tavern, café, water tower, a flock of sheep on a dirt road, and a straggly row of wooden houses. Seven books curved in a horseshoe in front of the tracks, their covers beckoning armchair travelers: *The Mystery of the Blue Train* by Agatha Christie, *Strangers on a Train* by Patricia Highsmith, *The Insane Train* by Sheldon Russell, *The Blackpool Highflyer* by Andrew Martin, *The Silk Train Murder* by Sharon Rowse, *Murder on the Ballarat Train* by Kerry Greenwood, and *Great Black Kanba* by Constance and Gwenyth Little. Annie sighed happily. The posters with the *Vogue* covers and the other books made the display one of her all-time favorites.

Annie was smiling as she unlocked the front door. She turned on the lights and looked into emerald green eyes.

Agatha chirped. Imperiously. Coiled on the cash desk, her tail flicked.

"I'm not late." Annie knew she sounded defensive.

Another chirp. A sleek black body flowed to the floor, started down the aisle, paused, looked back, ears flattened.

Annie didn't need an announcement. Agatha was hungry. She wanted food NOW. She didn't care that it was right on the dot eight A.M. and her usual breakfast time. Maybe Ingrid had been stingy with the rations last evening. Annie tried to ease past but a paw flicked out and a tiny red welt marked Annie's ankle.

Annie didn't have a remnant of dignity and knew anyone looking inside would think she was demented, but she raced down the center aisle, skidded to a stop behind the coffee bar, yanked up a sack of dry food, filled a blue stone bowl, and placed it atop the coffee bar.

Agatha landed there at the same instant. Annie removed her fingers just in time. She provided a fresh bowl of water, then took a moment to dab an antiseptic wipe on her ankle. She always kept them handy. She turned on the coffeemaker, settled on a stool at the coffee bar.

It wasn't just the food, of course.

"I know, sweetie. I haven't been here." Cats resent any departure from their routine. That routine included the timely appearance of Staff. Agatha's Staff started with Annie, included Ingrid as necessary. Agatha occasionally deigned to accept attention from Max. She tolerated Henny, loathed Emma, adored Laurel. "You are the world's most gorgeous cat. The most intelligent. There isn't a finer cat in the world." Agatha ate but her ears indicated she was listening.

The coffeemaker pinged. Annie poured a mug. "Everything's going to be fine, Agatha. I'm back at work." She glanced toward the storeroom. As always there was much to do, books to order, books to unpack, events to plan. It was nice to be free of worry for Tom Edmonds and to know Lucy Ransome was going to get well and that finally a real investigation had started into the death of her brother. Finding out what happened to Paul Martin, Jane Corley, and Sherry Gillette was Billy Cameron's responsibility, not hers and Max's, not Emma's, Henny's, and Laurel's. Max was already at the men's grill, eating breakfast with his golf foursome before a leisurely nine holes, quitting before it got too hot. Henny and Laurel had taken the early ferry, planning a several-day shopping trip to Atlanta. Emma had sent a terse text at daybreak: *On Marigold's Pleasure. Cruising until plot thickens. Title: Head Over Heels in Murder.*

Annie raised an eyebrow. She'd heard Emma speak about writing and knew the author often started with a title, book to come. It seemed an odd approach to Annie.

Annie looked disconsolately around Death on Demand, but the bright book jackets, intriguing watercolors, even the ferns so reminiscent of the sunroom in Mary Roberts Rinehart's Washington, D.C., Massachusetts Avenue house didn't work their usual magic. She felt restless and dissatisfied. Everyone else was content to mark finis to the sad reality of Jane's brutal murder, bookended by Paul Martin's and Sherry Gillette's deaths.

Annie looked at Agatha. "I want to know what's happening."

Limpid green eyes stared at her.

Annie had a good idea of Agatha's response. She would say, "Why do anything else when you can adore me?"

Annie cautiously slipped a hand behind Agatha's head, smoothed silky fur. "I can't walk away." Not until and unless she could shed the dreadful feeling that she could have done more, should have done more to wring the truth from Sherry. Sherry might be alive now if she had told Annie what she knew.

12

The *Gazette*'s small newsroom was very quiet. Annie hurried past a couple of untenanted desks; smiled a greeting at the matronly white-haired woman who managed the Life section and knew every birth, death, and scandal in between on the island; and headed toward a far corner and an old wooden desk mounded with papers.

The slap of her shoes on the wooden floor seemed loud, out of place.

Marian Kenyon looked around. She swiveled from her screen and waved at a rickety wooden chair.

Annie dropped into the seat, wondering how to begin, but Marian saved her the trouble.

"Billy's keeping his hole card covered." Marian swiped an ink-smudged hand through tangled short dark curls. "But you can have what I've got. I hung around the Buccaneer yesterday evening, trying to catch people coming home from work. I was about to call it a night when all of a sudden cops were swarming all over the place, going door to door, scouring—love that word—the parking lot, including the Dumpster." She slapped a hand on the scarred wooden desktop. "Finally cops were bunched around the Dumpster and you would have thought they were guarding a melting reactor. I couldn't get closer than twenty yards and I only glimpsed Mavis as she climbed a stepladder to the Dumpster." Marian's nose wrinkled.

Since Mavis doubled as a crime tech, somebody obviously had spotted something in the trash that needed tender loving care as it was taken into evidence.

"I had my camera trained but all I got was Mavis's back as she plopped something into an evidence bag." Marian's frustration was obvious. "Billy's got his lips zipped. But, this morning"—her eyes brightened—"I got a little something. There is a person of interest and there will be a news conference at ten A.M."

It was déjà vu all over again on the steps of the police station, soft October sunshine, a pleasant breeze off the harbor, Billy Cameron big and powerful, face impassive, arms folded. Mayor Cosgrove was natty in a blue blazer, pink shirt, and tan trousers. A crowd of perhaps twenty pressed as near as possible. Marian Kenyon was just to the left of the front steps.

The blond TV reporter from Savannah thrust out her mic. "Mayor, can you explain why the Broward's Rock police appear unable to find the guilty party in what appears to be a rash of murders?"

The mayor's fat cheeks puffed. "Proper investigative techniques were employed, though"—he sounded sour—"it now appears that the police"—his look at Billy was cold—"missed the possibility of murder in the death of Paul Martin, and that, of course, would have entirely altered subsequent events. I remember thinking at the time that Paul Martin was not a likely suicide victim."

Annie wondered if a shout of "liar, liar, pants on fire" would puncture the mayor's composure. Not likely. He had no doubt persuaded himself that he had entertained suspicions and been overridden by a zealous police chief.

Billy stood immobile, not a muscle moving in his face.

The mic swung toward Billy. "Chief, can you account for the botched investigation?"

Billy's tone was patient. "All the evidence in the death of Dr. Martin was consistent with suicide. However, the subsequent arson of his home, apparently in response to a reopened investigation, raised the possibility that his death was linked to the murder of Jane Corley. Police have since learned that Sherry Gillette may have observed someone at Jane Corley's home the afternoon of her death. In light of Mrs. Gillette's murder, Tom Edmonds is no longer considered a suspect in his wife's murder and has been released."

"Who did Mrs. Gillette see?"

Billy spoke in a neutral tone. "Mrs. Gillette mentioned to several people that she may have seen someone from a balcony of Jane Corley's home that afternoon, but she did not contact police."

The blonde broke in. "The police report says Mrs. Gillette's body was discovered at shortly after three P.M. yesterday. When was she killed? Where? Manner of death?"

"Time of death could have been between a quarter hour before the discovery of the body at three oh-two P.M. up to an hour prior. Death occurred at her home. Cause of death was blunt trauma to the head. No weapon has been found."

"Any idea as to what was used to kill her?"

"The forensic examination revealed traces of bark and dirt in the head wound. The medical examiner believes the murder weapon was a branch approximately two inches in diameter and perhaps eighteen to twenty inches in length. A thorough search of the apartment house and surrounding area failed to uncover a likely weapon."

The blond TV reporter looked skeptical. "Who picks up a stick to kill somebody? Where'd the stick come from?"

Billy gave her a level look. "Blunt instruments are everywhere. Why the killer used a branch is unknown at this time. All we can say with certainty is that the murder weapon was a length of wood and it was both brought to the apartment and removed from the apartment."

Marian took a step forward. "Can you describe the position of Mrs. Gillette's body?"

Billy shot her a look of respect.

Annie looked from Billy to Marian, puzzled.

Marian's intelligent dark eyes never left Billy's face.

Billy nodded. "Mrs. Gillette was found facedown. She was apparently attacked as she walked away from the door. This suggests her assailant was someone she knew. The likelihood is that the killer followed her into the apartment and immediately struck her down."

Annie understood. Sherry Gillette was self-absorbed, but even she might notice and wonder if a guest came in carrying a stout branch. Instead, she had opened the door to someone who must have kept the intended weapon out of sight and struck her before she realized there was possible danger.

The blonde edged in front of Marian. "More particulars on the victim. Age? Next of kin?"

"Twenty-seven. Husband, Roger Gillette."

"Any marital discord?" The reporter's features sharpened, reminding Annie of a vulture on attack.

"Mr. Gillette's whereabouts during the time when his wife was murdered have been verified and he is absolutely not a person of interest."

The TV reporter looked disappointed. "Is there a person of interest?"

Mayor Cosgrove intervened. "The investigation has other avenues to follow." His glance at Billy was combative.

The reporter shot a look from the mayor to Billy. "Chief Cameron, is there a person of interest?"

Billy looked even more stolid than usual. "The investigation continues. Material evidence was recovered from the parking lot at the Buccaneer."

Cosgrove pressed his lips together, glared at Billy.

Marian looked from the mayor to Billy. "Chief?" Her tone was sharp.

The other reporters and the watching crowd sensed drama. Annie felt her breath catch in her throat.

Billy hesitated only a fraction of an instant, then nodded. "The search of the property around the Buccaneer apartments yielded a pair of women's webbed red leather shoes. The right shoe sole was stained with blood matching that of Mrs. Gillette. An effort had been made to wipe away the blood but it had seeped into the sole and was also found in the crevice between the sole and the upper portion of the shoe. The shoe is a size five and one half medium. The shoe has been identified as the property of Mrs. Madeleine Corley, sister-in-law of the late Jane Corley. An island resident who visited the David Corley home yesterday was told by a housekeeper—"

Annie knew this reference came from her statement to the police late yesterday afternoon.

"—that Mrs. Corley arrived home in an agitated state and not wearing any shoes at approximately ten minutes after three. Mrs. Gillette's body was discovered at two minutes after three P.M. Mrs. Corley is at present under a physician's care and has not yet spoken to police. Police have informed Mrs. Corley's husband that she is a person of interest."

A slender mustachioed reporter for a rival station stepped in front of the blonde, held out his mic. "Is an arrest imminent?"

Mayor Cosgrove broke in. "Absolutely not. The investigation will continue. The press conference is concluded." He turned and stamped inside the police station.

Marian Kenyon glared at the phone. She'd called Madeleine Corley's house every five minutes for almost an hour. Ditto her cell. Ditto same for David Corley. Okay, no one would answer the phone. But there was another way . . . She tapped a text to David Corley: *Better to get Madeleine's story out before the aft news cycle. She had to be in death apt to get blood on her shoes. What's the deal?*

A few minutes later, she heard the soft blip of an incoming text and was surprised to see a message from David Corley: *Mrs. Corley remains under a doctor's supervision and isn't able at this time to speak with police.*

Marian raised a sardonic eyebrow. Not the world's best answer but it was an answer. Marian stared at her desktop. All right. She knew, the cops knew, even the mayor had to admit, Madeleine Corley was inside the Gillette apartment either at the time of the murder or she arrived shortly afterward. The cops would have covered the apartment house like a blanket, trying to pin down the time of her arrival and departure. But maybe they missed a witness.

Max looked across the wooden tabletop of their favorite booth. Ben Parotti encouraged tasteful carvings. An *A* with both legs serving as half of an *M* had been Max's contribution. Other designs included an anchor with a lei, several hearts containing initials, what might be the Saint Louis arch, and, Annie's favorite, a simple carving of Kilroy Was Here, bald head and nose and clinging hands draped over a wall. Henny Brawley had explained the WWII graffiti to Annie and Max one winter evening over hot chocolate. During the war years, Kilroy was everywhere, the farthest reaches of desert, on board ships, flying high above jungles, slogging through snow.

Annie always wondered about those who carved Ben's tabletops. Parotti's had been a rather seedy bar and bait shop begun in the 1930s by Ben's grandfather William. Had a serviceman on leave marked Kilroy's appearance on the island? Where had the soldier, perhaps sailor, gone? Shipped to Europe, possibly the Pacific? Had he come safely home? Was the arch carved by a vacationer from Saint Louis or maybe a Cardinals fan? Were couples united in hearts still together?

"Usual?" Ben Parotti's leprechaun face was patient. October wasn't a busy month.

Annie looked up from her reverie, smiled. "In a month with an *R*, how can you ask?"

Ben nodded. "Fried oyster san, onion bun, heavy on the Thousand Island." He looked at Max.

Max had picked up some sun from his morning on the course. "I had to beat my way out of five sand traps. May have set a course record. I'll take grilled bratwurst, all the fixings, a Bud Light, and a couple of glasses of water."

Ben gave a hoarse bark of laughter. "Five sand traps? Maybe you better start practicing on the beach." He was still laughing as he turned away.

Max's look at Annie was droll. "Actually six if you count the fact that I scudded the ball about five feet in the trap on eight, had to take another shot, and then . . ."

Annie munched her oyster sandwich, the succulent oysters hot and crisp in just the right amount of cornmeal as he continued.

". . . I whacked it and it looped up like an arch—"

She ran a finger over the carving.

"—and ran right to the hole."

Her eyes widened.

His smile was rueful. "Stopped on the lip of the cup. But I had fun and I only lost forty dollars. How was your morning?"

Annie grinned. "No sand traps. But"—she was a little shamefaced—"I went to the news conference about Sherry Gillette."

He looked at her sharply. "You told her to go to the cops. David told her. She didn't."

Still . . . Annie pushed the thought away. "I know. Billy's got everything in hand. We're relieved from duty." Nonetheless, she brought Max up to date and saw one eyebrow quirk as she described the discovery of red shoes and Billy's designation of Madeleine as a person of interest. "I guess I shouldn't be shocked that Madeleine Corley is a person of interest." It was only as she said the words out loud that Annie realized how truly surprised she was. "I don't know what you think, but I think that's crazy. Madeleine . . ." A quick memory of Madeleine at the church garden party flashed in her mind, elegantly dressed in summery white with a parasol, the flowing dress making her glossy dark hair a deeper hue than ever, her magnolia fair skin and thin spare features. Only Madeleine could carry a parasol and appear utterly fashionable. Although Madeleine was likely five foot seven or eight, she was slightly built. "Can you imagine Madeleine hitting someone?"

Max rearranged the sauerkraut on the bratwurst. "I have a little trouble with it." He looked thoughtful. "How did her shoes get bloody?"

Annie felt a little sick, remembering the smear of blood in the hallway. "The blood was Sherry's. Madeleine must have been there." Her voice trailed off.

"Why didn't she call the police?" Max's question was simple.

"I guess she was scared." Maybe Madeleine had very good reason to be frightened. "The mayor cut off the news conference. Obviously he doesn't want Billy ruffling rich feathers. But Marian bayed like a hound. She kept right on their heels when they went back into the station, shouting, 'Has Madeleine Corley explained her presence in the dead woman's apartment? Were her shoes found in the Dumpster?'"

They were silent, perhaps both of them acknowledging that Marian's questions had to be answered.

Max finished his beer. "Maybe Madeleine refuses to answer questions and they don't quite feel like they have enough to arrest her. Maybe they are trying to put pressure on her."

Marian Kenyon finished her circle of the Buccaneer Arms. Drat the architect. The balconies overlooked a swath of greenery and the woods that made up part of Pavilion Park. The end of the building adjacent to the parking lot and Dumpster was bare of balconies. Side windows, probably in kitchens and bedrooms, afforded a view of the parking lot. That cut down the likelihood anyone observed the lot Wednesday afternoon. But it was worth checking out.

Nobody home on the first floor. On the second floor a young mother shook her head. "Wednesday afternoon? Colin's been sick with an earache infection. I was at the doctor's office."

When she reached the third floor, Marian huffed to catch her breath, then moved briskly to Apartment 301, buzzed the bell. She waited, buzzed again. She needed more punch for her story. She glanced at her watch. Still a good hour before her deadline. Maybe she could come up with some color here. It was like prizing open a dungeon door at the cop shop. Mum seemed to be the word. Sure, she had the red shoes and Madeleine as a person of interest but nobody would ante up as to what Madeleine had said, if anything, and nobody answered the phone at either Corley home, ditto their cells. Sure, readers would make the link between Sherry

Gillette's blood on shoes belonging to Madeleine and Madeleine's presence at the murder scene, but Marian wanted more. A nice eyewitness to something, dammit.

The door opened.

Marian felt a flicker of disappointment. She couldn't picture the big dude looking out at her spending time gazing out windows. A mane of tousled sun-bleached hair flared around a mashed-in face. That nose had been broken at least once. Boxing? Football? Back-alley dustups? He was a big guy, well over six feet, maybe two hundred and fifty pounds. A Grateful Dead T-shirt stretched over a massive chest. One muscular arm sported a dragon tattoo from biceps to wrist. Worn Levi's hung low from his waist. He was barefooted.

"Did you see the barefoot woman running across the parking lot Wednesday afternoon?"

He glanced down at his own bare feet, gave a booming laugh. "That line'd get you a couple of free drinks at the Pink Parrot. And yeah, I saw her. But you aren't bringing me my deep-dish pepperoni, so it's been good to know you."

Marian made a couple of quick calculations as she inserted a knee to block the closing door. Big, tough, tattoos, the Pink Parrot. "Do you bartend at the Pink Parrot?"

The door remained half open. "Yeah. What's it to you and who are you?"

"Marian Kenyon. The *Gazette*. I know your boss. If I sweet-talk him into giving you a couple of days off, will you give me an exclusive on the barefoot lady?"

He lifted a meaty hand to brush back a tangle of blond hair. "With pay?"

"I'll do my best."

His big shoulders lifted in a shrug. "I'm ready for a little blackjack at the Big M. All I lack is time and money. Knock twice if you set it up."

A big hand gave her a gentle push and the door closed:

Marian made her call. ". . . and Vince will cover the cost." She listened. "Hey, thanks, Ben." Ben Parotti, owner of many island businesses and much real estate, understood her frustration with the mayor and would enjoy seeing a splash of inside info in the *Gazette*. She smiled as she clicked off the phone, turned, and knocked twice on the door.

The bell jangled at the front door of Confidential Commissions. Max swung around from his computer screen when he heard the door slam against the wall. Before he could call out, David Corley stormed into his office. His eyes had a wild look. Despite his usual polo, chinos, and loafers, he looked unkempt, blond hair tangled, cheeks bristly. He skidded to a stop in front of Max's desk. "You got to help me. You saved Tom. Now the damn fools are after Madeleine." His voice wavered. "She's terrified. Right now I've got her home in bed. The doctor's there. I got a doctor from Savannah and he's saying the police can't talk to her, she's too emotionally fragile. But that redheaded woman cop's sitting in the hall. They had a search warrant. They've been all over the house and grounds. Of course they didn't find anything. It's crazy. Madeleine never hurt anybody, never in all her life. You got to help me."

Max rose, came around the desk. He reached out, touched a rigid arm. "If she's innocent—"

"Hell yes, she's innocent. I know she is."

Max recognized certainty in David's voice. But he was

Madeleine's husband. Of course he believed her to be innocent. "I understand"—he tried to pick his words carefully—"that Madeleine wore the bloodstained shoes found in the trash at the Buccaneer Arms."

David's head hung forward. He lifted his hands, pressed them against his face. "The shoes . . ." His hands dropped. His head jerked up and wide eyes implored Max. "I know what must have happened. She went to see Sherry. Probably Sherry called her just like she came to see me, and Madeleine hurried over there. She'd want to know what Sherry saw. Madeleine loved Jane. She'd want to tell Sherry to go to the police."

Max wondered if David realized how revealing his words were. He spoke in the conditional tense, what he supposed, guessed, hoped had been Madeleine's reason for going to the apartment.

"Did Madeleine tell you this?"

That imploring gaze jerked away. David hunched his shoulders. "She's too upset to talk about anything. She cries and turns her head away. If the police take her . . . They can't. Don't you see, she's not able to tell us. Why can't they understand?" He grabbed Max's arm, his grip painfully tight. "You'll help, won't you?"

A gatha jumped on top of the cardboard box. Startled, Annie pushed down hard on the handle of the box cutter, winced as the blade penetrated cardboard. "Agatha, I'll bet we've ruined a cover." She pulled the tip free, retracted the blade, placed the tool on the table.

Agatha immediately pounced. The tool skittered across

the tabletop, fell to the floor, Agatha in pursuit. To the sound of clicks and clanks, Annie ripped up the cardboard flap, sighed at the gash across the gorgeous cat's face on the cover of a new Lydia Adamson title. Then she smiled. She enjoyed these books. Definitely an omen that this book was meant for her bedside table. As she lifted out the damaged title, the phone rang. Annie ignored it, humming. Ingrid would take care—

A tap and the storeroom door swung open. Ingrid held out the phone. "For you." She covered the mouthpiece. "Couldn't help but notice caller ID. Frankie Ford. Annie, she's in a panic."

Annie held the receiver to her ear, listened to Frankie Ford's incoherent plea. ". . . please come to my house. The police are already there. I'm on my way. I called Tom. He's coming. I'm so afraid . . ."

Annie jolted to a stop behind two police cruisers, the forensic van, and Marian Kenyon's jaunty yellow VW. Two cars were parked in the graveled drive next to a modest wooden cabin. A sleek silver Mercedes AMG that shouted money, power, and speed sat behind a black Ford Taurus that had seen better days, the beginnings of rust in some scrapes on one fender, a side window with a stripe of tape.

Annie popped from her car, hurried to join Marian, who was rapidly taking photos. "What's happening?"

Without missing a click, Marian jerked one thumb toward a cluster of uniforms in the side yard. "Far as I can tell, somebody—probably Lou, he gets all the dirty jobs—is under the house. I got a tip from a neighbor."

Annie's shoulders tightened. She didn't even want to

think about the creatures nestled in hot, humid, fetid darkness, tarantulas maybe, certainly lizards, though geckos wouldn't hurt anything except unwary crickets or spiders. Brown recluse spiders always sought peaceful darkness.

Marian tilted her head to the west. "The neighbor said the police roared up and pretty soon here came Frankie Ford in her rattly car—she rents the place—and lover boy in his state-of-the-art sports car." Frankie Ford and Tom Edmonds stood in the shade of a live oak. Frankie's heart-shaped face was pale and strained. Tom bent toward her, his face furrowed in a frown. Officer Townsend was perhaps ten feet away, watching them.

Marian made an impatient jig from one foot to another. "How long does it take to look under a Minnie Mouse–sized house? I got to get back—" She glanced at her watch, gave a yelp. "I got twenty minutes to deadline. Annie, if Lou crawls out with something in his teeth, for God's sake send me a text. But"—she was turning away, muttering to herself—"whatever, I got a lead: Bloody shoes turned up in a first search, now police are off on a new hunt, both apparently connected to a trio of island murders. At press time . . ." She broke into a jog, reached the VW, yanked open the door.

Frankie heard the rumble of the VW and turned. She saw Annie and rushed across the hummocky grass, Tom striding after her. Officer Townsend kept pace.

Frankie reached Annie. "They won't tell me anything. They came to the gallery with a search warrant. By the time I got here, they were already inside and now they're under the house. You helped Tom. Can you help me?"

Annie tried to be reassuring. "Let's see if they discover anything—"

"What are they looking for?" Frankie's voice held an edge of hysteria. "Why me? I didn't even know you could get under the house."

Tom reached out, gripped Frankie's arm. "Look."

They all turned toward the house, including Officer Townsend.

Gloved hands carrying two plastic bags emerged from the crawl space beneath the house, followed by Lou Pirelli's head and torso.

Annie craned to see, but a half-dozen figures now surrounded the side of the house, blocking any view of Lou.

Annie started across the lawn, aware that Frankie and Tom, after a moment's hesitation, followed. Officer Townsend jogged past. About ten feet from the group clustered around Lou, Townsend turned, held up a hand. "Crime scene. No access. Stop where you are."

Frankie trembled. Her mouth worked, but no words came.

Tom's long narrow face looked haunted. "Frankie, it's going to be all right." But his tone was hollow.

Annie glimpsed Lou's back, smeared with cobwebs and dirt. He stood at the rear of the forensic van, but the open door hid his arm from view. When he turned away, his hands were empty.

Mavis jumped down from the back of the van, swung the panel shut, walked briskly to the driver's door.

"Don't they have to tell me what they found?" Frankie's voice shook. "I know it's something awful." Then her eyes widened. She took a step back, pressing against Tom's arm.

Annie followed her gaze.

Billy Cameron walked toward them, his heavy face somber, his blue eyes narrowed.

Tom stepped in front of Frankie, squared his shoulders. He was an unlikely Galahad, his face too sensitive, his dark, overlong hair too smoothly brushed, his lanky frame insubstantial in contrast to the police chief's stocky, powerful build.

Billy stopped in front of Tom. "I need to speak with Miss Ford." His tone was mild.

Tom hunched his shoulders. "Whatever you found, it has nothing to do with her. Does Frankie look like somebody who'd crawl around under a house?"

"Mr. Edmonds, I am investigating three murders and an arson that endangered life. Miss Ford occupies this residence. Evidence connected to arson and murder has been discovered here."

Frankie darted from behind Tom. "I've never been under that house. Why would I? What did you find?"

Billy looked at her appraisingly. "Perhaps our inquiry can be brief. However, it will be necessary for you to come to the police station now."

Frankie's eyes were huge. "Why?"

"To answer questions. I will escort you."

"I'll drive myself."

He held out his hand. "Officer Townsend will drive your car to the station. It will be searched. You will come with me."

Frankie's hand shook, but she dropped the keys in Billy's waiting palm.

Billy half turned. "Townsend?"

Townsend's blue eyes gleamed with excitement. "Sir."

He took the keys, again broke into a jog. On the drive, he slid behind the wheel of the Taurus, expertly maneuvered the car around the Mercedes.

The Taurus hiccupped, belched smoke from its exhaust, and clacked loudly down the street.

13

The car windows were down. A breeze from the Sound stirred Annie's sandy hair. Max stood by the Thunderbird and resisted the impulse to smooth back a stray lock. Annie had no idea how appealing she was when she jutted her small chin forward in determination. Her lips, very kissable lips, were slightly parted. He wished . . . But Annie had no intention of leaving this spot with its prime view of the front of the Broward's Rock Police Station even though he could imagine a much more fun way to spend their afternoon. "Heel," he told himself firmly.

"Max, aren't you listening? It doesn't seem right that they won't let us in the station. At least Billy let Tom go with her. Do you suppose they've called a lawyer?"

"Frankie may not need a lawyer. Look, I'll go inside and ask Mavis to give Frankie or Tom a note when Billy's done. We'll ask them to call you."

Annie considered his suggestion. "I suppose we could do that." She sounded doubtful.

"Sitting out here waiting isn't getting us anywhere." He knew how to appeal to Annie's Protestant-ethic nature. "There's lots to be done." Now he needed to come up with some productive tasks. He glanced at his watch. "You can talk to Marian, see if she knows what's up."

Marian Kenyon held up a hand, dribbled peanuts into her Coke can. She tilted the can and took two mouthfuls, dropped into a wooden chair in the *Gazette* break room.

Annie moved to the small squat old refrigerator in one corner, found a bottle of Nehi orange soda. As she removed the cap using the bottle opener attached to the wall, she dropped a dollar bill into a lidless Maxwell House coffee can on the counter. She settled on the other side of the wooden table from Marian.

Marian slumped in her chair, heaved a huge sigh, then sat up straight, fished around in a baggy pocket of a worn cotton cardigan. "Yeah. Here it is. Pristine prose"—a heavy rumble shook the old building—"being printed as we speak. Newsprint. A beautiful word." Her tone was mournful. "About to go the way of the dodo. That's what happens when your wings don't work. Poor old dodo bird." Her voice fell to a mumble. "See how the world likes it when everything is a damn screen. Poor old newspapers . . ."

Annie shut out the flow of words, concentrated on the printout of the *Gazette*'s lead story:

Broward's Rock police found bloody shoes in a Dumpster near a crime scene late yesterday, while a second search today retrieved as yet unrevealed evidence from beneath an island home. Both searches appear to be connected to a trio of island murders.

According to police, the searches were conducted as part of a continuing investigation into the deaths of Dr. Paul Martin October 10, Jane Corley October 14, and Sherry Gillette October 23. Dr. Martin was found dead of a gunshot wound to the temple. The death was at first deemed suicide but is now considered homicide. Ms. Corley and Mrs. Gillette both died as the result of blunt head trauma.

Police Chief Billy Cameron announced today that women's size five and one half webbed leather shoes stained with the blood of murder victim Sherry Gillette have been identified as shoes worn on Wednesday by Madeleine Corley, sister-in-law of murder victim Jane Corley and wife of island sailor David Corley. Cameron named Madeleine Corley a person of interest in the investigation.

The *Gazette* has been unable to speak with Mrs. Corley, who is under a doctor's care and, according to her husband, unable at this time to talk with police.

After obtaining a warrant, police investigated the interior of Miss Frankie Ford's rental home at 106 Menhaden Lane and the crawl space beneath the house, then impounded her car. Miss Ford is an employee of Wyler Art Gallery and a friend of Jane Corley's widowed husband, artist Tom Edmonds.

Police apparently removed some objects from beneath Miss Ford's home. At press time, Police Chief Billy Cameron had not responded to the *Gazette*'s inquiry in regard to material removed from the site. Miss Ford was taken to the police station. Police Dispatcher Mavis Cameron declined to state whether Miss Ford was being interrogated by police.

In an exclusive to the *Gazette* today, Buccaneer resident Milton Braswell said he observed a slender dark-haired woman, whom he later identified from a photo as Mrs. Madeleine Corley, in the parking lot of the Buccaneer Arms Wednesday at approximately 3 P.M. Braswell, an employee of the Pink Parrot, glanced out of his third-floor apartment from his bedroom window as he rode an Exercycle. "She caught my attention because she ran across the parking lot. I could tell she was kind of panicked. She got to this sweet little Jag sports car and yanked open the door and then she stopped. Like an old silent movie, every move was exaggerated. Run. Stop. Stare down. Head jerked around. By this time I was pretty fascinated. I keep a little pair of binoculars on my windowsill. I like birds. I grabbed them and homed in on her. Tragic-beauty face, oval, classic features. Think Claire Trevor in *Murder, My Sweet*."

Annie heard a creak and sensed Marian at her shoulder. Marian reached over, tapped the quote from Braswell. "He's a big bruiser who sounds like a PI hero. Turns out he used to be a college prof, authority on noir crime films. Didn't want to ante why he pours drinks now."

Annie returned to the story:

> Braswell continued, "The dame's staring down at her feet. She sways, then turns. Stops. Takes off her shoes. Runs, looking over her shoulder, a shoe in each hand, to the Dumpster, tosses the shoes."
>
> Braswell said he caught a glimpse of red as the shoes rose and fell. "She ran barefoot to the car, then the Jag peeled out of the lot."
>
> Braswell said Mrs. Corley was wearing a long-sleeved red blouse and black trousers. He said Mrs. Corley wasn't carrying anything in her hands when he first sighted her running across the lot toward her car. In a press conference today, Police Chief Cameron announced the weapon used to strike Mrs. Gillette was not found at the scene, in the apartment house, or in the area surrounding the apartments.
>
> The chief further announced that the medical examiner found pieces of wood bark in Mrs. Gillette's head wound and deduced that the weapon was a branch approximately two inches in diameter and between eighteen to twenty inches in length.

When contacted by the *Gazette*, Chief Cameron said the comments by Milton Braswell had
not been confirmed.

Annie looked up at Marian. "What does that mean?"

Marian looked offended. "Hey, I got my exclusive. So they didn't catch him at home yesterday evening. That's their problem. I stand by my source." Her nose wrinkled. "Though I'm afraid the big dude's story gives the mayor another reason not to put an island aristocrat in handcuffs. She was empty-handed except for the shoes. So where was the weapon? Pretty lucky for Madeleine he was on his Exercycle."

Frankie Ford's heart-shaped face was wan. She shook her head at Annie's offer of coffee. Tom Edmonds sat beside her, an arm protectively around her shoulders.

Annie filled two mugs with fresh Colombian. Tom grabbed his, downed half in a gulp, never noticed the book title in red script, *Innocent Bystander*. Annie nodded at her mug, *Truth of the Matter*.

"They'll arrest me." Frankie's whisper was tremulous. "It was awful." Her eyes looked huge, dark with remembrance. "They brought out a big stick and said it was under the house. The end of it . . . blood . . ." She shuddered.

Tom's jaw ridged. "They like to shock you. Like when they showed me my smock and it had dried blood all over it. Jane's blood." For an instant, his face looked empty, stricken. "Somebody put on my smock and killed Jane. But it wasn't

244

me. And it wasn't Frankie who took that piece of wood and used it to kill Sherry."

Annie felt tightness in her chest. So the police had found the branch used to kill Sherry in the crawl space beneath Frankie's house. No wonder she looked terrified.

Tom's face hardened. "I asked why the hell they looked there. That cop"—Tom looked triumphant—"had to admit somebody called and claimed they saw Frankie crawling out from underneath the house. That's crap. Frankie's scared of stuff. She wouldn't go underneath a house for anything. They won't listen."

Annie understood the edge of panic in his voice. No one knew better than Tom how an innocent man could be arrested and held for a murder he didn't commit. But she understood why the police weren't impressed with his argument that Frankie was too timid to crawl under a house. A murderer getting rid of a bloodied weapon wouldn't worry about spiders or snakes.

Max looked interested. "Who called the police?"

"They don't know." Tom shoved a hand through his thick dark hair. "It was a call to that number when you think you know something about a crime. Somebody used a pay phone near the ferry building."

"Man? Woman?"

"A whisper. So why would anybody who's for real sneak around? I asked him that. But he said people don't want to get involved. They're afraid of being sued. I'll sue 'em if I ever find out who called. It's all a lie."

Annie frowned. "Did the caller specifically say that Frankie was seen? Or was it just—"

"Frankie." Tom was dour.

Frankie's face was bleak. "They found a tin of gasoline and some rags they said matched the ones used to set Lucy's house on fire. Somebody put those things there, then called the police. But"—tears spilled down her cheeks—"how can I prove I didn't do anything?"

Annie shook her head.

Tom glared at her, pushed to his feet. "Are you like all the rest of them? Do you believe this stupid—"

Annie held up a hand. "I don't believe. Or not believe. But I don't think Frankie can prove she's innocent."

Frankie lifted a hand to her throat. Tom's hands clenched into fists.

Annie said quickly, "The only way to save Frankie is to find out who's guilty. Do you know what Sherry's murder proved?"

Frankie said in a small voice, "That Tom was innocent because he was in jail?"

"More than that. Sherry's murder proved she saw the murderer on the terrace that day." She turned toward Frankie. "You went to Tom's studio. He wasn't there. Did you look for him near the house?"

"No." Frankie's voice was shrill. "I wouldn't do that."

"Why not?"

Frankie's face flushed. "You know why not. I saw how Jane looked at me at David's party. It was awful. That's why I was going to tell Tom he had to make up his mind. I wasn't going to be anybody's extra. Not then. Not ever."

Tom's gaze dropped. He stared down at interlocked hands.

Annie hoped Frankie never insisted that Tom tell her what

his decision would have been. To Annie, the answer was clear in the way he evaded Frankie's glance, in the tightening of his shoulders, in those hard-gripped hands. Tom might love Frankie. In fact, Annie thought he loved her very much. But he hadn't intended to leave Jane. Was it because of her money or the opportunities as an artist? Whatever, Annie sensed he didn't love Frankie quite enough to have made that break.

Which gave Frankie a bitter reason to kill.

Tom spoke slowly. "I had to stay on the island until I finished the sculpture. I don't know if I can now. Jane—" He shook his head, lifted his eyes. In them there was dumb misery and emptiness. "When Jane walked into a room, everything else faded. Now she's dead." He was angry, but Annie was afraid his anger was at the loss of the art he could have created.

Annie didn't know which was more painful to see, Tom's anguish and its reason or the somber acceptance on Frankie's face. Yes, Tom would turn to Frankie now, but she would always take second place to whatever he wanted to paint or sculpt.

Annie didn't doubt that Frankie would be in even deeper trouble with the police if they, too, ever understood that Frankie knew she would never have Tom while Jane lived. He might have finished that sculpture and it might have lifted him to a pinnacle of success, but then there would still be the question of who owned his works, the artist or the woman who provided him with the studio.

Add to that the discovery of the branch that killed Sherry and a gasoline tin and rags beneath Frankie's house and the police would be justified in making an arrest.

Annie wondered why Frankie was still free. The mayor

would much rather see Billy arrest Frankie than wealthy Madeleine Corley. The pressure would mount on Billy. The mayor didn't like for TV stations to be talking about a rash of murders on Broward's Rock, a botched investigation with an innocent man arrested, and a murder tabbed as suicide.

Frankie swallowed jerkily. "I went a little way up the path, in case Tom was coming back. I didn't have much time. But I stopped about twenty yards along, then turned around and went to my car."

"Did you hear anything, see anything?" Earlier she'd mentioned a dog yipping.

Frankie looked uncomfortable. "I heard the dog. I thought it was Madeleine out with Millie."

Tom leaned forward. "I heard the dog, too. Madeleine's got to speak up."

"You told the police you didn't leave the studio. But you did. Where did you go?"

"I didn't know Frankie had come. When the cops questioned me, I knew they were after me. I thought if I said I'd left the studio I'd be in big trouble. So I told them I hadn't. But it was a bad afternoon. I couldn't work. I kept thinking"—his gaze dropped again—"about stuff. I decided to blow it off, take a walk. I went to the cypress pond. It was a little after three. I don't know exactly, maybe a quarter after. I took a sketch pad. In the afternoons the trees are reflected in the water and those big knobby roots have kind of an amber color."

Annie remembered the beautiful pond. "It's near the studio."

"About forty yards from the studio. On the other side of the trees is the path to David's house. When I heard a dog,

248

I thought it was Madeleine's terrier. She'd been carrying the poor dog around for weeks. Squeezed it like a beanbag. I heard the dog yipping and somebody running. I thought maybe she'd been to see Jane and something had set Madeleine off. She's kind of a bundle of nerves. Wound tighter than a high wire."

"If you'd told the police, everything might be different now." Frankie might not be close to arrest. If he came forward now, no one would believe him—or Frankie. Annie thought they were telling the truth because Frankie had earlier mentioned hearing a dog. Still, neither Frankie nor Tom had seen Madeleine. But the gardener said Madeleine took the path to Jane's house around three o'clock, so that was some confirmation.

Tom slumped in his chair. "Yeah. I should have told them. But I was scared." He took a deep breath. "I went to the pond." He stopped, swallowed. "Then I decided to go up to the house." He didn't look at either Frankie or Annie.

Annie wondered what his intent had been. Annie had a suspicion that whatever he had planned to say to Jane, it wasn't what Frankie would have wanted. He hadn't been able to work. He wanted to finish his sculpture of Jane.

Tom talked faster, the words running together. "Anyway, I went up to the house. The door to the family room was open. I went inside. Jane was . . . she was lying there. I could tell she was dead. Nobody could be hurt like that and be alive. I thought I was going to be sick. I turned to go for the phone and then I stopped. I was afraid of what Kate would say. I heard Jane talking to her a few days before . . . I don't know. I turned around and ran out on the terrace and looked around but there wasn't anyone anywhere. I thought it would be better if I went back to the studio. I got to the studio and waited. I didn't think it would ever get to four thirty. Finally, I took the path to the terrace. I stopped at the pool and had a drink. God, I needed it. I wanted to have another one but I didn't. Everything was quiet at the house. I figured I had to go ahead and find Jane. It would look weird if I didn't come up at my usual time. Look. I can tell the police now. About the dog. See, I went up to the house maybe a quarter hour after I heard the dog and Jane was dead."

Annie looked pointedly at Dorothy L, who was draped across Annie's place mat. The thickly furred white cat looked back with bright blue eyes but made no effort to move.

Max reached out with his free hand to pat the white cat's head as he placed a plate with a rasher of hickory-smoked bacon on the opposite side of the table. "Cat seal of approval, Annie."

Annie raised a questioning eyebrow and remained standing behind her chair. "Excuse me?"

"Dorothy L's welcoming you to breakfast."

Annie laughed. "For improv, that's pretty good. You and I both know she hopes I'll take a hike and she can share the breakfast table with you."

Max put another yellow linen place mat at the end of the table. "Here you go. Eggs Benedict coming up."

Annie accepted the change. She was still smiling—and noting that Dorothy L had a peculiarly satisfied expression— as Max poured orange juice in their glasses.

Max paused at the counter to pick up his iPhone. He glanced briefly. "Doesn't look like anything happened overnight."

Annie knew what he meant. Apparently the Broward's Rock police had yet to make a move. "I'm afraid they'll arrest Frankie today. Marian's interview with that guy pretty well proves Madeleine is innocent."

Max finished crunching a bite of crisp bacon. "Maybe. Maybe not."

"Madeleine wasn't carrying anything. The guy saw her crossing the lot toward her car. That means she came out the side door. Where was the branch?"

Max speared a portion of English muffin, egg, and hollandaise sauce. "She could have thrown it from Sherry's balcony."

"Next thing we know she'll be trying out for a javelin competition."

"Adrenaline."

Annie held up both hands to indicate space. "It's at least twenty-five yards from the back of the Buccaneer Arms to the woods. Madeleine's wispy. Tall but wispy. No way. Besides, if she threw the branch into the woods, how did it end up underneath Frankie's house?"

Max frowned. "She came back and got it." He shrugged. "Okay, maybe that's a little far-fetched. And I'll agree that Madeleine killing Sherry with a branch then heaving it that far sounds ludicrous. But we know she was there. We know she stepped in blood—"

The sound of honking geese lifted Dorothy L.'s head. She wasn't yet accustomed to Max's new cell phone ring. Max

grabbed the phone, glanced. "Speaking of. It's David." The
honking continued. "I told him I'd do what I could but I
haven't figured out anything to help Madeleine." He clicked
on Speaker, rested the phone on the table. "Hey, David.
Sorry I haven't gotten back to you—"

"Yeah." David's tone was strained. "I knew you'd call if
you had any news. Thing is, the cops are coming this afternoon, said they had to talk to Madeleine. She's still all shaken
up. I've got an idea. You're a lawyer, aren't you?"

"I can't represent her. I'm not a member of the South
Carolina bar. I don't practice—"

"That doesn't matter. I'll get a lawyer if we need one. But
you know about statements and things like that. You'll know
how we can best put everything."

Max looked puzzled. "Put what?"

"A statement from Madeleine. That will hold the cops
off for a while. You said you'd help. Come on over. As soon
as you can." The connection ended.

Max took a deep breath and looked at Annie. "David
may think he's being smart, but this won't get anywhere
with Billy."

"Something is better than nothing. Besides, like Charlie
Chan said, 'If you want wild bird to sing, do not put him in
cage.'" Annie picked up her plate. "Come on. Let's get over
there before they change their minds."

Max cleared his throat. "David called me. I don't think
he had a social visit in mind."

Annie rinsed her plate, spoke above the sound of water.
"I'll tell him I'm convinced Madeleine's innocent and I want
to help." She felt a sweep of sadness. "That's true. I can't

believe Madeleine ever hurt anyone." Then she added emphatically, "I can't believe Frankie did either."

D avid was waiting on the front porch. He gripped Max's hand in a firm thank-you handshake, accepted Annie's quick murmur of sympathy with a brief smile, like a scared kid who takes courage from a big sister's hug. "Yeah. She'll be glad you came. Oh hell, it's got to get better. We've got to make that cop understand. Come on."

He led the way through the spacious entry past a Chippendale table beneath a gilt-framed mirror and up old uncarpeted wooden stairs. They hurried to keep up.

Annie had a blurred sense of beautiful objects gracing the well-cared-for plantation home, Audubon prints on the stairway wall, a white porcelain Meissen vase decorated with a cascade of roses atop a marble-topped French Empire table on the landing, a black-and-red Persian runner in the upper hallway.

In the no-expense-spared beauty of the home, Officer Hyla Harrison's presence seemed doubly odd. At the sound of their steps, the trim, athletic officer rose from the straight chair adjacent to a closed bedroom door. She waited impassively as they approached.

David ignored her. He opened the door. "Maddy, hey, we got some friends who are going to help." As they stepped inside the bedroom, he closed the door firmly behind them.

Madeleine lay in a four-poster bed in a high-ceilinged room with pale green walls. The curtains were drawn at two windows. She wore a white silk negligee with ruffles at the throat. One hand, which looked shockingly thin, clutched a coverlet, the other was curved round a mop of fur. The dog's head lifted. Bright, wary brown eyes peered at them. A warning growl sounded. "It's all right, Millie." Madeleine's voice was a soft reassuring coo.

The lighting from a rose-shaded lamp was dim, but even in semidarkness Annie was shocked at the sharp planes of Madeleine's face. The bone structure seemed attenuated and there were dark smudges beneath her eyes.

Madeleine looked at Annie. "You are kind to come."

Annie stood by the bed. "I know it's been very hard." The words seemed inadequate.

David gripped a poster at the end of the bed. "Max, I want you and Annie to listen. Madeleine's weak and it bothers her to talk about it, so don't interrupt or ask anything. She'll tell you what happened and I'll write everything down and then Madeleine can sign and date it and you and Annie can sign and date, too."

Max spoke quietly. "We'll be glad to do that but I don't think this will satisfy the police."

David's jaw jutted. "That's too damn bad. This is what they are going to get and when they read it, they'll see there's no point in bothering Madeleine anymore." He came around to the side of the bed, picked up a pad from the bedside table. "Okay, Maddy. Take your time."

Madeleine fingered the lacy throat of her gown. She looked at Annie and Max. "I have to do something or the police will come here and I can't bear to talk to them." Her shoulders looked stiff. She shot a quick glance at David, jerked her eyes away to stare down at Millie's head. She cuddled the dog close to her. "Sherry called me, told me she'd

seen someone on the terrace the afternoon Jane was killed
and she wanted my advice. I told her to go to the police. She
said she didn't think she should because maybe it didn't mean
anything." Madeleine spoke in a dull monotone. "She said
she had to tell someone and would I please come. Then she
said, 'Oh someone's at the door,' and hung up. I almost didn't
go. I wish I hadn't, but then I thought I'd better. Sherry made
up so many things, but somehow I thought she was telling
the truth. I ran out to my car and drove over there. When I
got to the parking lot, I almost didn't go up but I was already
there. I decided I'd go see and make her tell me. I walked
fast across the parking lot. I didn't see anyone. I guess people
were at work. I went in that side door and took the stairs.
When I got to Sherry's apartment, I started to ring the bell
then I saw the door was open and I thought she'd left it open
for me. I called out and said, 'Sherry, it's Madeleine.' I
pushed the door." One hand came to her face, pressed against
her lips. Her eyes were wide and staring. "Oh God, it was
awful. Sherry was stretched out facedown on the floor. Her
feet were near the door and one foot was bent sideways.
There was blood all around her. I came close and started to
reach down but I knew she was dead. I turned and ran out
and pulled the door shut. I hardly remember getting downstairs. I was terrified. All I could see was blood . . . I got to
my car and started to get in and when I looked down I saw
blood on my shoes." Her voice rose and she began to cry.
"Blood on my shoes. I took them off and ran to the Dumpster
and threw them away." She turned her face into the pillow
and sobs racked her shoulders.

14

Annie looked through the windows. Billy Cameron had a great view of the harbor. An old sloop, probably built of teak, judging by its color, moved under sail, rising and falling with the swells. Gulls swarmed after a shrimp boat. A majestic osprey hovered high in the air. The *Miss Jolene* sat at the dock, ready for the midmorning run to the mainland.

The only sound in Billy's office was the rustle of paper and a faint clank in the air vents.

Max broke the silence. "I told David this wouldn't suffice."

Annie looked away from the window.

Billy laid several handwritten sheets on his desktop, looked at Max. "I just got off the phone with the mayor." Billy's voice held an undercurrent of irritation. "David alerted him. The mayor's ecstatic. To quote His Honor, 'No reason now not to settle everything. Arrest that Ford woman without delay. Obviously she's the killer. Poor Madeleine Corley. A shocking experience for her. Good of her to report what she knew. I'll call a news conference.'" Billy's big face corrugated in a tight frown. "I've stalled him off for a few hours, said I need to button down some forensic evidence. But he won't wait long before he goes over my head, gets the circuit solicitor involved." Billy gave a *whuff* of exasperation. "I can't say he isn't right. Frankie Ford has motive, opportunity, and there's no question that the length of branch found under her house was used to kill Sherry Gillette. So, the murderer put it there. The question is whether Frankie Ford never thought she'd be suspected and tossed in the stick because that's where she'd hidden the stuff used to burn the Martin house. That would argue that she's not a very bright murderer. This is a little island surrounded by a big ocean. A little midnight walk to an inlet, a toss, and the tin and rags would be gone. Same for the stick. This doesn't seem to jibe with the mind that set up Paul Martin's murder to look like suicide. For that matter, why take the stick from the apartment?"

He answered his own question. "It could be that Sherry called Frankie—or somebody else—said, 'I saw you on the terrace' in a breathless tone, moaned about whether she had to go to the police but maybe, just maybe, if she could be convinced, she'd forget all about that afternoon.

"In that case the murderer, Frankie or our unknown, hustled to the Buccaneer. Frankie Ford could have left the art gallery, crossed the street, and walked across Pavilion Park and through the woods to the apartment house. On her way she could easily have picked up a sturdy branch to use as a club. She—or the unknown—probably didn't have gloves. Most people don't carry gloves around in October, so grab a stick, get there, whack Sherry.

"The murderer probably worried about fingerprints on the stick and that's why it was carried away, that or there was already a plan to put it somewhere handy so it could be placed to incriminate someone else. Bark doesn't hold prints, but it looked like the bark had been rubbed off about where it would have been held."

"If Frankie's a dumb cluck who tossed the stick under the house, why would she have been smart enough to rub around on the bark? That's a point for Frankie." Annie was emphatic.

Billy slowly nodded. "There's an argument to be made." His tone was judicial. "On the one hand, Frankie isn't bright and threw the stuff under her house, or we're looking for somebody damn elusive and smart." His tone was ruminative, his gaze considering. "In that case, the murderer deliberately took the stick from the apartment, thinking it might be a dandy item to plant on someone. As for the rags and gas tin, they could have been stashed somewhere they were unlikely to be found that had no connection to the killer. The other possibility is Madeleine Corley of the blood-stained shoes." Billy tapped the loose sheets. "Every word in her statement could be true. Or she's spun a total fairy tale. The problem"—he looked morose—"is trying to picture her skulking through the woods clutching a stick, murder in mind. Whoever killed Paul Martin is cool, resourceful, and capable of long-range planning. Which makes me wonder about planting the stuff on Frankie. It was already public that Madeleine was a person of interest, but word gets out. We searched their place yesterday. So it wouldn't work to put the murder weapon and arson stuff there. Right now it's a toss-up between Frankie and Madeleine. Except Madeleine wasn't carrying a stick when she crossed the Buccaneer parking lot. That weighs the scale against Frankie."

Annie felt bleak. "Three people are dead and there's scarcely any link to the murderer. We know the murderer came to Paul Martin's house shortly after midnight. Lucy heard a car. But that could have been a random passing car. We know Jane's murderer crossed the terrace. Otherwise, Sherry would be alive. We know the murderer put the stick and gas tin and rags under Frankie's house last night. You'd think we'd have some hint—" Annie broke off. Her eyes widened. "Oh wow. Chitty chitty bang bang."

Max looked at her in alarm. Billy gazed at her doubtfully.

Annie yanked her purse from the floor, reached in, pulled out her cell. She swiped a number. "Lucy Ransome's room, please."

Max began, "Annie, what—"

She held up a hand. "Lucy, Annie Darling. You sound wonderful. How are you feeling . . . Lucy, please think back to the night after David's party. You opened your window and you heard a car at just past midnight." Annie took a breath. "What did the car sound like?"

Max nodded in understanding. Billy continued to frown.

"Really? You're sure? . . . Yes, it's important, very important. Thanks, Lucy." She swiped End and looked across the desk at Billy. "Okay, you thumped the scale up for Madeleine because she wasn't carrying a stick in the parking lot. The scales are now even. Lucy heard a car but it was just a faint murmur. When Frankie's car was driven off to be searched, the engine sputtered and rumbled and clacked. It wasn't Frankie who drove by Paul's house that night."

Annie traced the gilt title on the dry and crackling cover. *The Clock Ticks On* by Valentine Williams, 1933. It was an affordable collectible. Probably Henny or Emma would like to add the book to their collections. Automatically she looked at the round-faced clock on the wall of the storeroom. Half past ten. She gently restored the book to the bottom shelf, rose, and stood at a loss. She had retired to the storeroom after lunch determined to pull and tug at the tangle of three unsolved murders until she had a trail to follow. Again she looked at the clock. She was under no illusion that her unearthing (as far as she was concerned, brilliant unearthing) of the fact that Frankie Ford's car certainly hadn't driven past the Martin house the night Paul was killed would save Frankie from arrest. The mayor and circuit solicitor would brush that inconvenient information aside. At the time Annie was convinced she'd evened the odds between Frankie and Madeleine, but in the silence of the storeroom she felt an unsettling certainty that Frankie would be arrested.

Annie looked toward her worktable. Papers were strewn from one end to the other. Agatha was stretched across a mound in the middle. She imagined Max's desk and Billy's were also covered with papers and files about the murders. All of them had the same information but nothing pointed anywhere—except at Frankie and Madeleine.

Annie simply didn't believe either Frankie or Madeleine could be the mind behind Paul Martin's death. She spoke aloud. "Frankie's a sweet girl and Madeleine is incapable of planning a campaign to commit three murders." A calculating mind coolly decided to get Paul Martin out of the way so that Jane could be murdered. Someone had planned well ahead, taking Tom's mallet and smock to the family room, intending that Tom should be the suspect, probably knowing, as much of the island knew, that Tom and Frankie were having an affair. Likely the mallet was tucked near the pool table. As Jane walked toward the terrace, the murderer grabbed the smock, picked up the mallet, and swung. In the first instant when a stunned Jane fell forward, the murderer slipped into the smock and finished the bloody attack. The murderer had reacted immediately when the story in the *Gazette* suggested Max might bring in experts to search for traces of an intruder in Paul Martin's study. The murderer had set the Martin house on fire, knowing a defenseless woman was asleep on the second floor. The murderer struck down Sherry Gillette and took the weapon away, probably with the idea of planting evidence already in mind.

Agatha lifted her head and gazed at Annie with unblinking golden eyes.

Annie crossed to her chair, flung herself down. "Agatha, we've been over everything so many times I can toss out suspects, motives, and odds like a politician with a stump speech." She pulled a legal pad close, flipped to a clean sheet, wrote *Suspects in Chief* in big dark letters.

SUSPECTS IN CHIEF

David Corley. Inherits big time. Out from under older sis's thumb. Had to pay off gambling debts. Claims Jane agreed to cover them before she died. Kate Murray confirmed.

Madeleine Corley. Gamblers threatened her dog. Did she know Jane was going to pay off the gambling debts? Jane's death makes her husband rich enough to pay off any debts.

Kate Murray. Quarreled with Jane over her refusal to pay the debts. But if Jane had agreed to pay off, Kate had no motive to wish her dead. However, Kate also inherits substantially from Jane's estate.

Kevin Hubbard. Probably had his fingers in the till at the property management company. Indications Jane was getting ready to investigate.

Irene Hubbard. Big, strong, a tough personality. She'd landed in a nice patch of clover when she married Kevin. She might be willing to commit murder to protect her new comforts.

Toby Wyler. If Jane had lived, Toby was going to lose his exclusive over Tom's paintings and thereby a main source of income. Rumor had it that the gallery was in a financial hole.

Annie leaned back in her chair and sighed. Billy always covered all the bases. She had no doubt he'd checked out the whereabouts of everyone involved both Wednesday afternoon and Wednesday night. Obviously, Madeleine and Frankie still held center stage.

Billy checked things out—She stopped, remembering. She'd asked Billy to find out about the older woman who had acted oddly in the receiving line at Jane's funeral. He'd promised. She reached for the phone, hesitated. Talk about a long shot. But maybe that was the only kind of shot left. Determinedly, she picked up the receiver, rushed into speech as soon as Mavis answered. "Mavis, Annie Darling. I told Billy about a woman at Jane's funeral who was very upset and—"

"It was easy to find her." Mavis's voice was suddenly sad. "I talked to Kate Murray. She remembered the woman, said she introduced herself to David as Margaret Randall, said she was a cousin. But Kate sounded doubtful, said she didn't know of any cousins. Lou went to a genealogist at the library. Turns out she was a distant cousin of Jane's and David's, lives in Columbia. You know how it is in families. There can be rich sides and poor sides and Mrs. Randall didn't come from any money and her folks are dead. She was an only child. Jane and David were her only living relatives and she didn't really know them, had just heard about them from her mother who was a cousin of Jane's father. It's a really pitiful story. Billy sent Lou to talk to her. It doesn't have anything to do with Jane's death. Mrs. Randall's husband, Clem, has one of those weird diseases and they think the only thing that will help is bone marrow transplants and one of their children is a match but insurance won't cover it. Mrs. Randall said she talked to Jane and she was really nice and said she'd help, but she never heard anything and then Jane died. Mrs. Randall came to the funeral. Lou said Mrs. Randall started to cry, said they obviously thought she was trying on some kind of scam. Anyway, she didn't have a thing to do with Jane's murder. Lou checked, of course. Mrs. Randall lost her job as a secretary but she works at a school cafeteria and she was there the day Jane died."

Annie put down the phone. So her hunch had come to nothing. Another dead end. Annie pushed up from the chair, paced. They needed something fresh. Surely there was something undone, someone yet to ask. The suspect list was limited to the guests at David's birthday party. Paul Martin had walked past Kate Murray with an intent, purposeful look. If only Kate had turned to see who stood at the far end of the pool. Annie concentrated, recalling what other guests had said. So far as she knew, nothing helpful had been learned from any of them. If only there were another set of eyes—

Another set . . .

Excitement surged through her. In fact there were four sets of eyes and surely one of them could help. And these were observers with no dog in the hunt. Why hadn't she thought of David's college friends earlier?

Annie whirled, moved to the worktable, settled in her chair, and reached for the phone.

Max leaned back in his red leather chair. He cradled a receiver between his head and neck. "Remember, Marian, you didn't hear it from me."

"So Madeleine Corley's sending a handwritten billet-doux to the cop shop. I love it." Marian's voice crackled with delight. "The mayor won't want to talk about her so-called statement but I'll gig him like a sheepshead. For this tip, I'll spot you and Annie to margaritas at the Pink Parrot."

Max raised an eyebrow. "Since when have you turned into an habitué of the island's lowdown honky-tonk?"

"Since I knocked on the door of a damn interesting dude who bartends there."

Max didn't give advice, but he hoped Marian remembered a free spirit (as well as spirits) usually came with a cost. "We'll take you up on it. Now about the news scene, any word on—"

"Yep. Mayor's called a news conference for two P.M. He's setting an all-time record for running off at the mouth to the media. He loves the spotlight even if he gets tough questions. It's a downer that the conference is after my deadline for this afternoon's paper. But I got a second deadline." Her voice brightened. "We pub Saturday morning instead of afternoon and we don't put that issue to bed until nine o'clock tonight. We'll see what happens at the conference. My money's on Frankie. Poor kid. Too bad she doesn't have a rich husband. If she stays out of jail, I guess that will change soon enough."

Max slowly replaced the receiver. He'd plowed through his notes, recalled everything he could from all their sources, and he didn't see any way past Marian's conclusion. Frankie or Madeleine with the odds on Frankie.

He turned to his computer, e-mailed David Corley: *Annie and I delivered Madeleine's statement to Chief Cameron. He read it with care. I'm not sure of Madeleine's status in the investigation. An arrest may be announced at a news conference at 2 P.M.*

He looked at the time. Eleven. He reached for the phone, shook his head. He'd leave that line open in case David called, which wouldn't surprise him. Instead, he pulled out his cell, tapped Annie's name. He frowned when he didn't get her. Maybe she didn't want to interrupt a call in progress. He left a message. "Meet me at Parotti's. Eleven thirty. Mayor's called a news conference for two."

Kate Murray's tone was dismissive. "David said you and Max are trying to help Madeleine, but those young men don't live on the island."

Annie was equally impatient. "They were at David's party. No one has asked them if they saw Paul in a tense conversation with anyone." As strangers to the island, none of David's friends were likely to know who Paul talked to at any time. But perhaps one of them had an eye for people, was interested in facial expressions. Paul had seen "evil in a glance." Maybe it was asking too much to hope one of them might have seen the moment Paul spoke to his murderer. There had to have been some indication of stress or unhappiness or anger. "David must have his phone turned off. I left a message and sent a text and an e-mail but I haven't had any answer. I asked you about his friends earlier. Did you get their phone numbers?"

"Oh. Yes, I did. Hold on for a minute." The connection went silent.

Annie kept glancing at the clock.

It was almost a full five minutes before Kate spoke again. "Sorry. I'd lost track of where I put that slip of paper, but I found it." She rattled off the names, Steve James, Harris Carson, Ken Daniels, Wendell Evans, and phone numbers.

Annie saw her missed call from Max, listened to the

Carolyn Hart

message. Two P.M. She didn't doubt what the mayor would announce. She remembered Frankie's frightened face. Maybe by lunchtime she'd have learned something to help. She sent a text: *See you at Parotti's. Trying new tack. Will explain at lunch.*

Annie began with Steve James, got him on the first ring. He listened as Annie explained she was seeking information about David's birthday party and one of the guests. "You want to know if some guy was quarreling with somebody? Sorry. I don't remember which one he was and I have to tell you, I wasn't paying a lot of attention. We were having a hell of a time. The wine flowed and the whiskey poured. I don't remember much about the evening. I was feeling no pain when Harris hauled me out to the guest quarters and I flopped on a sofa."

Annie didn't hold out much hope but as long as she had him on the phone, she might as well confirm David's whereabouts. "David came back to the guest quarters with you."

"Oh yeah. Last I saw of him, it was almost one and he was all of a sudden hot to get back to the house, said he'd be in big trouble, didn't realize how late he'd stayed."

Annie frowned. For a guy who had apparently downed a lot of alcohol, Steve was awfully precise about the time. "Did you look at your watch?"

"By that time"—he was rueful—"I don't think I could have seen my arm, much less a watch. David was bleating like a little lost lamb. He held up this clock on the mantel, showed us the time. He was out of there in a flash."

So David left the guest quarters shortly before one A.M. Lucy heard a car at just past midnight.

The second call was less successful. Harris Carson had

no idea who Paul Martin was. He was grave about Jane's death, said he'd written a note to David. He'd thought Jane was a very interesting woman but they had only talked about painting and so far as he knew she was fine that evening. He agreed that David left the guest quarters around one. The third call was answered by an irate and sleepy Ken Daniels. ". . . who the hell . . . it's the middle of the night here . . . Got jet lag anyway . . . whoever you are, bug off . . ." The connection ended.

Annie shrugged, tried the last number. "Hell of a party." Wendell Evans's big voice boomed through the ether. "We were smashed, skunked, in Margaritaville. We didn't schmooze a lot with the natives. First time I'd seen the guys in a while. We had plenty to talk about."

Annie wasn't surprised when Evans was emphatic that he not only didn't know who Paul Martin talked to, he had no idea which guest was Paul Martin. She was ready to end the conversation, admit defeat, when his booming words began to register.

". . . only started at the house. Really got down to some serious drinking when we moved out to the guesthouse and then, hell if David didn't cut it off sooner than he needed to."

Annie raised an eyebrow. Maybe Evans thought the night was young at one A.M. How did the lyrics go. *Three o'clock in the morning . . .* "I understand David went back to the house at one."

"One, hell. He got in a twit about leaving his wife with all the cleanup, said he had to get back pronto. Turns out, he was wrong about the time."

"Wrong? The clock on the mantel—"

"Was wrong. My watch is luminous. I got up to go to the

can and I always check the time. Can't tell you why. Habit. My watch said a quarter to three. The clock on the mantel read a quarter to four. It was off by a whole hour. So David left around midnight, not one in the morning like he thought. David must have noticed the clock was off the next morning when he brought us Bloody Marys. I saw him go to the mantel and take the clock down and when I looked later the time was right. Pretty good joke on him. I should have ragged him about it then. Ended the party before we'd drunk all the gin."

Annie hung up the phone, yanked the receiver up again, tapped a familiar number. "Mavis, Annie Darling." She was breathless, knew her voice was shaky. "I have to talk to Billy."

"He's in conference with the mayor. I have strict orders not to disturb him. What's wrong?"

Annie held tight to the receiver. "Tell him . . ." There was too much to explain. The clock. The time. David's alibi that wasn't. The crafty way he'd made four witnesses aware of the time. Only one person needed an alibi the night Paul Martin died, the person who planned to kill him. "I'll come to the station. Send Billy an e-mail. Tell him I'm on my way and I know who killed Paul Martin." She hung up the receiver, flung herself across the room and into the coffee area. Several startled patrons looked up as she rushed past.

At the cash desk, Ingrid called out, "What's wrong?"

Annie gestured, called out, "Find Max." She didn't want to take the time to check Confidential Commissions. He'd called on his cell and cell calls can be made anywhere.

Time. She was conscious of passing time, Billy's conference with the mayor, Frankie's likely impending arrest, officers might even now be on their way to take her into custody. Running out of time . . . "Tell him to meet me at the police station. Tell him I know who killed Paul Martin . . ." She was on the boardwalk and pelting down the steps toward the parking lot. She slammed into the Thunderbird. She was halfway to the harbor when her cell rang.

M ax waggled the putter, took his stance, ready to imitate a pendulum—that was the advice the pro had given him after his putting debacle—when the front doorbell rang and hurried steps sounded.

"Max?" Ingrid skidded to a stop in the doorway. "Annie wants you to meet her at Billy's office. She ran out of the storeroom just now and asked me to tell you to meet her there. She said she knows who killed Paul Martin and then she was running up the boardwalk."

A nnie drove with one hand, held her cell with the other. Kate Murray's voice was thin, high, frenzied. "I just found something Sherry wrote. I wish I'd never gone in her room. But I can't pretend I didn't find it. Please, I need help. Someone to come with me. I can't face it on my own—" There was a strangled sound that might have been a sob. "Please come. I'll show you. Please, say you'll come."

Annie heard shock in Kate's voice. She sounded as if she struggled with enormous heartbreak. There was only one living person who meant enough to her to bring her to tears.

Annie gripped the cell tightly. Kate Murray had a gruff exterior, but she'd come to the Corley house when David was only a baby. David was the son Kate never had. Kate's world was dissolving around her, David guilty of murdering his sister, David soon to be arrested. "I'm sorry." Annie heard the tremor in her own voice. "I wish I could help you. But I'm on my way to the police station."

There was a quick-drawn breath. A sound of ragged breathing. Finally, harshly: "I'll go with you."

Annie heard the wrenching effort that sentence took.

"Please come. I know we have to go to the police, but it's better if we go together. I can't do it by myself. I'll be at the door."

The connection ended.

Annie knew Kate was distraught. Her voice was ragged with anguish and despair. Annie hesitated when she reached the turnoff to the harbor. A turn to the left and it was two blocks to the police station. Jane Corley's home was perhaps a half mile away. Annie looked at her watch. Only a dozen blocks. Kate had found something in Sherry's room. Sherry didn't seem the kind of person to keep a diary, but perhaps the night of Jane's death she'd scribbled something, mentioned seeing David in the early afternoon, been glad he'd seen his sister one last time, perhaps grieved that he hadn't come nearer five, been there to protect her.

Annie realized she'd made her decision as she drove past the turnoff to the harbor. Whatever Kate had found, the contents had to be devastating. The accusation must be specific, concrete. If Sherry wrote something down that pinpointed

David on the terrace, that evidence was much stronger than Annie's tale of time changed on a clock and a drunken man's recollections.

The car picked up speed. The sooner she got there, the sooner she and Kate could get to Billy.

Max leaned on the golden wood counter between the small foyer and the dispatcher's desk. "She's not here yet?" Max had been puzzled when he didn't see Annie's car parked in front of the station. Now he had the sudden empty feeling that comes when you miss a step, hit the ground hard. "She has to be here."

Mavis looked stressed. She frowned, her long face tense. "She's not here. Billy's in with the mayor and I can't disturb him."

Max turned and went to the front door, opened it, and looked up and down the street. No Thunderbird. No Annie. The hollow feeling expanded. He swung around and was at the counter in two long strides. "Mavis, listen to me."

Mavis looked up, eyes widening at his taut tone.

"Something's wrong. She was on her way. Running. As fast as she could go. She told Ingrid she was on her way here—to see Billy—and she knew who killed Paul Martin."

Mavis swallowed. "The mayor—"

"To hell with the mayor. We've got to find Annie."

Mavis rubbed one cheekbone. She looked at Max.

In her eyes, Max saw her thoughts: *Annie probably changed her mind . . . could be car trouble . . . but if she said she was coming here . . . mayor can't stand Max and he's leaning on Billy . . . under no circumstances interrupt . . .*

Mavis shot him a worried look, then muttered, "Go down the hall. Wait in the break room. I'll do my best."

True to her Texas Panhandle upbringing, Annie often felt claustrophobic when live oaks closed overhead, plunging a road into deep shadow. She drove into dimness beneath the thick green canopy on Corley Lane. She didn't see another car. That was no surprise, since the lane served only the two Corley homes. She welcomed the instant she reached the turn into the Corley estate and the expansive front lawn overseen by the statue of the rearing horse. Still, the emptiness of the drive and the silence when she stepped out of her car seemed oppressive. The Mediterranean mansion loomed over her.

She hurried up the steps, driven by urgency. She wanted to get past the coming moments. Kate Murray's grief would be painful to witness.

The massive door swung in. Kate was waiting, one hand gripping the frame. In the pale yellow light of a wall sconce, her thin face with its high forehead, long nose, and sharp chin was gaunt. She moved jerkily, one hand gesturing down the hall. "I've got it in the family room." She turned and moved heavily on the tiled floor of the wide hallway, her steps echoing.

Annie hesitated, then followed the shuffling figure with bowed shoulders. She would be glad to be out of this huge home with its old dark tapestries and mullioned windows set high in stone walls. No wonder the family had used these rooms for entertaining, chosen to spend time in the family room with Tom's vivid paintings hanging on softly golden walls and comfortable chintz-covered furniture and a pool table and wet bar. She pushed away the thought of the homey room with blood spreading near the pool table and Jane lying facedown.

Kate reached the massive oak door, the barrier between the public and private rooms. She turned the knob, stood aside, waiting for Annie.

Annie stepped into the family room, welcoming the change from stone walls and tiled floors to bright lights inset in a smooth white ceiling and walls that spoke of sunshine and paintings that pulsed with life.

Click. The slight sound seemed loud in the silence.

Annie turned and watched as Kate's hand fell away from the now firmly closed dead bolt on the door.

15

Billy Cameron stepped inside the break room, closed the door. "Mavis said—"

"Something's happened to Annie." Max fought to speak calmly, reasonably. He held up his cell phone. "I keep calling. No answer. Nothing. Billy, she left the store almost fifteen minutes ago on her way here to tell you who killed Paul. Now there's no answer. I came on the same road. She was only a few minutes ahead of me. She has to be somewhere on this end of the island."

Billy stared at Max for a quick, probing instant, then unsheathed his cell. "APB. 2011 red Thunderbird. Driver Annie Darling last seen near downtown. Check all roads north end of island. ASAP."

Max had always known that Billy moved on gut instinct. Billy heard the hollow tone of fear in his voice. Billy knew him. He knew Annie. He wasn't going to waste time demanding proof, being skeptical.

Max tried to keep his hands steady. He wanted to burst out of the station, run down the street, looking. But police could cover the island faster than he. Still, it took all his will not to storm out and look for her. He had to . . . *Annie . . . Dammit, Annie . . . where are you . . . where did you go . . . must be somewhere near.* His chest ached. Every minute that passed slammed against him like a pile driver crushing rock. *She was coming here . . .* He looked at the cell, gave a whoop. "Wait a minute. Maybe . . . I've got that app, Find My iPhone. Maybe . . ." He touched the small screen several times. "Jane Corley's house. At least the phone's in the car and it's at that address. Billy, I don't like it. I don't like it worth a damn. She ran from the store. She was coming here as fast as she could. Why's her car there? Where is she?" Again Max slid his finger. "The phone's ringing."

There wasn't any answer.

Billy was already in the hall. He shouted for Lou. "Jane Corley home. Stealth approach. No sound. No sirens."

The door to Billy's office swung open. Mayor Cosgrove's pudgy face was petulant. He started to step into the hall, pulled back as officers pounded past him. "What's going on?"

Billy was gruff. "Possible hostage situation. Better stay in my office, Mayor. Safer there."

Max's gut tightened. He figured Billy's warning was a worst-case scenario designed to keep the mayor out of the way. Surely Annie had run by the Corley house for some reason and everything was all right . . . But she'd said she was on her way to the station and she knew who killed Jane and Paul and Sherry.

The mayor scooted backward and the door slammed. Billy spoke into his phone again. "Officers, no mention of address. No sirens. No noise."

K ate Murray's brown eyes were empty. The gun in her hand didn't waver. "You can't go to the police. Damn you. You kept on snooping. Wendell Evans texted David, had a hell of a strange story to share. David called me." Her face twisted in despair.

Annie stared at her. What kind of woman would protect a man who had killed in cold blood so he could kill again and then again? "He killed three times."

"He didn't have any choice. That's what makes every-thing so awful. David had to do what he did."

Annie felt cold deep inside. That was always the answer, wasn't it? Whatever happened, whatever awful crime, it was the fault of the victims. She felt foolish. "You didn't find anything in Sherry's room."

Kate's face hardened. "When you said you were going to the police, we had to stop you."

Annie looked at the woman in a pale blue sweater and gray slacks. Her carefully brushed short-cropped white hair was quite perfect. She would look just the same when Annie was dead, a well-to-do woman sure of her place. There was strain in her face but not the heartbreak Annie had imagined. Instead, she was a quick-witted woman willing to do whatever she had to do to secure the safety of a killer she would protect at all cost. *We* . . . Kate said, ". . . we had to stop you." The beautiful room was now a place of deadly menace. Annie slowly turned, looked past the gaily patterned sofa.

David Corley stood to one side of the stone fireplace. His thick blond hair shone golden in the light of one of the overhead spots. His handsome face was empty, the strained look of defense for Madeleine gone, supplanted by deadly threat. No wonder he was so certain of Madeleine's innocence. Behind him and to the left was the closed door to Jane Corley's office, where Jane and Kate had quarreled about Jane's refusal to cover David's gambling debts.

Annie blurted, "Jane never agreed to pay off the Palmetto Players."

David's mouth twisted. "I told Jane—Kate told her—they were going to hurt me. She had to pay up. Damn her, part of the money was mine, should have been mine. It wasn't any business of hers what I did with my money. But she was all righteous, superior. 'This will teach you a lesson.' That's what she said. I told her what they were going to do to me and she laughed and said they wouldn't dare, that it was up to me to figure out how to pay them somehow, maybe sell my boat."

Annie heard rising anger in his voice. Jane had thought she could force David to take responsibility. She refused to come through with money. Palmetto Players upped the pressure on David, warned of what also might happen to Madeleine's Yorkie. David made his decision.

"It was Jane's fault." Kate's voice was hard.

"I told her I had to have the money." David sounded querulous.

Annie felt a curl of revulsion. Everything—all of David's problems—was someone else's fault. "Paul Martin knew you were dangerous."

"Damn him." David's eyes glittered. "He told me nothing better happen to Jane. He told me I had to come to his house, write out a letter that he'd keep." David's sudden burst of laughter was ugly, ugly and satisfied. "I fixed him. I had a gun. I used to go out and practice in the woods. I always hit my target. He was stupid."

"You set up an alibi. If you hadn't done that, no one would ever have known."

He laughed again, a pleased anticipatory laugh. "No one ever will know."

Annie's gaze dropped to his right hand. He held a poker, moved it back and forth. He was breathing too fast, his boyishly attractive face oddly flattened, his blue eyes burning with intensity.

Was that what Paul Martin saw at the open house, a stalker intent on prey, a natural killer anticipating death? Had there been incidents as David was growing up that were known to the family doctor, hints of cruelty and anger?

"I don't like the way you're looking at me." David's voice was unnaturally high. He began to move toward her, one light step after another.

Annie looked frantically around. David was between her and the French doors to the terrace. Kate was behind her with a gun. If she moved to her left, she would be defenseless with nothing between her and David. The sofas near the fireplace were closer to him than to her. If she moved to her right . . .

She saw the pool table. The players had been careless after the last game. Balls were skewed here and there, not tidily formed in the rack. Beyond the pool table was a door . . .

"David." Kate's voice was sharp.

He stopped, jerked his gaze toward her.

Annie eased a few steps to her right.

"Not here." Kate's words came fast. "There can't be another body here."

Annie felt as if ice cascaded over her. She had ceased to exist for them except as an obstacle that must be removed. Another body . . . her body . . .

David balanced from one foot to the other, the poker gently swinging in his hand. He looked athletic, strong, fast. His thick blond hair was perfectly brushed. He might have been balancing on the deck of his boat in a polo and khakis and boat shoes. Picture-perfect except for the wildness in his eyes. "All right. Not here. Tom's gone. He went to be with that little tramp. We'll take her down to his studio. I'll put on a smock—"

M ax stood next to Billy in the deep shadow of pines near the Corley terrace. As the sun slid lower, the air cooled. Max smelled earth and resin.

Billy spoke softly into his clip-on transmitter. "I'm going up to the house. Cover me." He looked at Max. "Stay here."

Max started to protest.

Billy shook his head. "You shouldn't have gotten this far. Stay here. We'll handle everything. Everyone's in place." He looked deep into Max's eyes. "We'll do our best."

For a big man, Billy moved lightly, easing silently to the edge of the terrace. Then he bent low and sprinted to the side of the house, stepped again into shadow, this time the dark splotch cast by one of the big vases near the French windows.

Max knotted his hands. *Annie, honey, God, please, be*

safe, be all right. I'm here. I'll come. Annie, are you all right?

" . . . and use one of his mallets. It will have Tom's finger-prints." David laughed. "Damn, that's good. They'll think Tom and Frankie did it together. That'll get rid of both of them. If they're arrested, Madeleine will be okay because a cop's sitting in the hall. God, that's perfect. Madeleine will have the world's best alibi and I'll end up with all the money."

Madeleine—now Annie understood why Madeleine had carried Millie with her the afternoon Jane died. Perhaps there had been another call threatening the dog. Of course no one had told Madeleine the debts were taken care of because they weren't taken care of. Jane had refused to pay. Had Madeleine come up to the terrace, found Jane's body? That must be what happened. David had left their house in his kayak a half hour before Madeleine. Likely he paddled out of sight, around a bend, stashed the kayak in underbrush, ran to the house. The mallet and smock must have already been taken from Tom's studio, hidden in the pool room for easy access. Perhaps he told Jane he'd arranged to sell his boat, everything was going to be all right, then maneuvered behind her, grabbing the mallet, covering his front with the smock, striking her down as she walked toward the terrace door.

Kate slowly nodded. "The police will think she threat-ened Frankie and he and Frankie killed her."

Annie knew the impersonal pronoun referred to her but

Kate didn't look at her. She was watching David and the slow swing of the poker. Was she afraid he'd lose control?

Annie took a few more steps to the right.

Kate stared commandingly at David. "Go down to the studio."

Annie took another step, another, reached the end of the pool table.

"I saw Tom's car leave. We'll take her down now, get it done." David was impatient.

"We can't take a chance. If no one's there, call me on your cell."

David turned. He was almost to the French door when Kate called out, "Put the poker back."

B illy Cameron crouched next to a large vase, his head at sill level of a window. He stared into the family room. David Corley crossed his field of vision, carrying a poker. Kate Murray stood not far from a large oak door, a snub-nosed black Glock 23 in her right hand. Annie was moving stealthily as a cat on the far side of the pool table.

Billy dropped lower, moved on his hands and knees until he was close enough to reach up and pull gently on the handle to the French door. He eased it a breath at a time, cracked the door.

". . . I'll keep her here until you call." Kate's head swung toward Annie. "Wait." Her tone was angry. She lifted the gun. "What are you doing over there?"

Annie said shakily, "I don't feel well. I need to lean on the table."

"Do you want me to get her?" David's voice was eager.

Kate stared at Annie. "The door behind you is locked. Do you think we're fools?" Then she nodded at David. "I'll see to her. She isn't going anywhere."

"Oh." Annie sounded despairing.

"Go on down to the studio, David. Hurry."

Moving like an eel, Billy retreated on the flagstones, came up on the other side of the vase. He spoke quickly into his clip-on radio.

Annie planted her hands on the rim of the pool table, pretended to wobble. "I have to hold on . . ." The odds were better now. She didn't have much time. David would call soon. How many minutes were there before he would call? Two? Three? Four? Would she soon have no minutes left? She had to time everything just right. She couldn't afford to wait too long. When Kate's cell rang . . .

Kate aimed the gun at Annie. She held the gun steady, watched with an unmoving gaze.

The silence was leaden, enveloping, threatening.

Kate's gaze jerked toward the clock on the mantel.

Annie leaned forward ever so slightly, one hand now at a corner of the table.

Kate drew in an impatient breath. She frowned.

Annie, too, looked at the clock and realized with an odd quiver in her chest that too much time had passed. David had been gone now for perhaps five minutes. He had left, moving fast. It wouldn't take long, a couple of minutes, to turn down the path to Tom's studio.

Why hadn't he called?

Kate's dark brows drew together. She yanked a cell from her pocket.

As she glanced down to swipe the name, Annie's hand dropped into the corner pocket. She felt cold hard roundness, gripped the ball. Not as big as a softball but it would have to do.

Kate lifted the cell to her ear, listened.

Annie yanked the ball from the pocket.

Kate whirled toward her, lifted her hand, pointed the gun.

Annie threw with all her might.

The gunshot sounded like a cannon.

Annie dropped to the floor, scrabbled on hands and knees. Now she'd likely be shot in the back . . . there would be another body in this room of death . . .

The French door crashed against the wall. Shouts. "Police. Hands up. Drop that weapon. Police."

The rattle of gunfire and the stench of gunsmoke.

Annie clung to Max. She pressed against his chest, buried her head on his shoulder. They stood that way, together, alone at the edge of the terrace despite the officers shepherding David Corley and Kate Murray toward the front of the house.

Max pressed his face against her hair. His voice was muffled. "When I heard the shot—" He broke off.

Annie pulled back a little, looked up into his stricken face. "Hey." She spoke quickly, reassuringly, "I'm okay. Thanks to Billy."

286

Billy's strong voice came from behind her. "Max found you. He used the app, spotted your cell phone."

Max reached out, gripped Billy's arm. "You listened to me. You came."

Billy looked from one to the other. "When I stop listening to my gut, I'll know it's time to quit. Annie said she was coming to tell me who killed Paul. Annie told Mavis she knew. I never doubted her."

16

Annie studied the shelf of Christie titles. The store was pleasantly full of afternoon customers, an ordinary day in October. The kind of ordinary day and days she'd come near to losing. She pushed away the image in her mind of Kate Murray, hair disheveled, pain etched in her face from the burn of a flesh wound suffered in the scuffle with police, pain and despair as she realized that David had been captured.

More than a week had passed. Annie still woke in the night, breaking out of hag-ridden dreams of a once-beautiful room filled with menace. The week had been tumultuous, the arrest of David Corley on three counts of first-degree murder, the arrest of Kate Murray for conspiracy and attempted murder.

Gazette coverage stated that a duly Miranda-warned David Corley had talked and talked and a full confession had been obtained. Kate Murray, on the other hand, declined to answer questions, though her attorney had released a statement in which she denied knowledge of the crimes and insisted she'd acted under duress in holding Annie Darling hostage. As Marian Kenyon had regaled listeners at the Pink Parrot: "Of course that doesn't explain why she had a gun and shot at Annie, but we'll see what happens at the trial."

Annie concentrated on the titles. She wanted a Christie, a book that would enfold her in warmth and laughter, an out-of-the-ordinary imaginative tale. Perhaps *Cat Among the Pigeons.* Or *Secret Adversary.* She knelt and her hand moved to *The Man in the Brown Suit.*

Hurried steps slapped up the aisle. A pair of scuffed brown loafers stood unmoving by her knee. Marian Kenyon's raspy voice sounded as morose as a foghorn. "Story of the year and I can't use it. My God, they could have their fifteen minutes of fame."

Annie picked out the book and stood. "What story?"

"A feel-good story." Marian's dark eyes looked like a spaniel deprived of a favorite toy. "Everybody disses newspapers, says why do we have to print bad stuff all the time. They don't know how much we love sweetie-pie stories, the blind dog who finds his way to safety across miles of ice in Alaska, the chicken who clucks and wakes the family when the house is on fire, the cat who sleeps with a canary. And I track one down and will anybody talk? Hell no. So I'm going to tell you. I kind of have a feeling you're the reason it happened."

"Would a great big cappuccino with whipped cream and a cherry help?"

"Better than nada." Marian scuffed morosely down the center aisle.

Annie worked coffee magic behind the counter, brought two mugs to a table, slid into a chair opposite Marian. "So what did I do?"

Marian dunked the cherry in the whipped cream, took a bite. "You got Billy to send out Lou to talk to that distant cousin of Jane Corley's who was all upset in the receiving line at Jane's funeral. Well, people like to unload about this and that, especially at the Pink Parrot. An unnamed mutual friend was there one night and the talk got around to people with raw deals and he said it was sure a shame how Jane Corley died before she could help out a nice woman who really needed help. Long and short of it, word got back to Frankie Ford. She talked to Tom Edmonds. They checked around, found out the deal, and damned if Tom isn't going to relinquish his share in Jane's estate to Margaret Randall. All he's keeping are his own artworks and the contents of the studio. In fact, he rented a U-Haul and he and Frankie have already left the island for Atlanta. This means Margaret Randall can get the bone marrow treatment for her husband and besides that she'll be as rich as can be and everybody says she's a wonderful person and the family is rock solid. Her husband had a garage until he got too sick to work. One son is a sergeant in the army, a daughter is a nurse in Cleveland, and another son is a small farmer over near Bluffton. Now, can't you see what a great story I could have written? It would have been picked up by AP. But none of them want any publicity. Don't they understand how much those kinds of stories mean to people?"

Annie reached out and gave Marian a quick hug. "I'm sorry you didn't get your coast-to-coast story but you've made me happy. Maybe that counts for something."

Despite the Closed sign hanging in the door of Death on Demand, light spilled cheerfully across the coffee area. Max Darling made the rounds, depositing hot fresh coffee of choice: mocha cream for Annie, cappuccino for Laurel, raspberry-flavored latte for Henny, double espresso for Emma. He took a seat next to Annie, holding a mug of Colombian juiced with an ounce of Baileys Irish whiskey and topped with whipped cream. He maneuvered his chair until his knee pressed against Annie's.

Her smile was quick, her eyes held a promise.

"So strong." Laurel gave Annie a swift glance as she strummed a chord on her guitar. "What an arm you must have." In a husky voice she began to sing a Johnny Cash song.

Annie said lightly, "I'm the Popeye of booksellers."

Henny Brawley smiled. "You never thought when you pitched on the plains that a well-aimed throw would disable a woman ready to shoot."

Max tilted his chair back, looked expansive. "Annie beaned a bad guy once when I thought I was going to be blown away. It's not her first good pitch. The motto: Never trifle with a Sandie." Max's tone was light, but his glance at her held remembered horror when the cell phone rang and she didn't answer it.

Three faces looked puzzled.

"Sandie?" Laurel repeated.

Death at the Door

Annie laughed. "The Amarillo High School Golden Sandstorms. Or the Sandies."

Emma downed half the espresso. "I'll have to remember softball the next time Marigold saves the inspector." Then she frowned, sighed. "Actually I don't think Marigold could toss a beanbag much less a pool ball. But, all is not lost."

Everyone looked at her attentively.

"Lost?" murmured Laurel. "I'd say nothing was lost. Our dear Annie is safe. Frankie is free. She and Tom will someday make a match. I understand they've already left the island. Of course, much is lost for Madeleine Corley. I fear she glimpsed her husband on the terrace that day. She carries a great burden even though she did hurry to Sherry, possibly to warn her. I imagine the psychic toll was enormous and that's why she took refuge in her bed, terrified that she might be accused, not knowing which way to turn, and frozen by the fear that he might realize she was afraid of him and kill her, too."

Emma cleared her throat.

Obediently, they all looked at her.

"When I say *lost*, I meant that Marigold may not heave a baseball—rather unsubtle, in any event—but definitely she can look for the man who thought too far ahead. David Corley planned every move, outwitted everyone, but in the end that was what brought him down—he created an alibi when no one knew an alibi would be needed."

Henny lifted her mug in a toast. "To Annie, who in true Texas fashion kept on keeping on and uncovered a trail that led to a killer."

Mugs rose.

"Hear, hear," cried Laurel.

"And further, here's to Emma, who chose this month's watercolors." Henny's smile wasn't quite patronizing. "Of course, I've pinned them down. *All Sales Fatal* by Laura DiSilverio, *Spice 'N Deadly* by Gail Oust, *A Killing at Cotton Hill* by Terry Shames, *Bones of a Feather* by Carolyn Haines, and *Dog in the Manger* by Mike Resnick."

Emma attempted a gracious smile.

FROM *NEW YORK TIMES* BESTSELLING AUTHOR

CAROLYN HART

Don't Go Home

Annie Darling, owner of the Death on Demand mystery bookstore, is hosting a party to celebrate successful Southern literary icon Alex Griffith and his bestselling novel, *Don't Go Home.* But not everyone in town is ready to give him a glowing review.

As Annie attempts damage control, her friend Marian Kenyon gets in a heated argument with Griffith. It's a fight Annie won't soon forget—especially after the author turns up dead. Despite an array of suspects to match Griffith's cast of characters, Annie's not about to let the police throw the book at her friend when the real killer remains at large…

**"Hart's work is both utterly reliable
and utterly unpredictable."**

**—Charlaine Harris, #1 *New York Times*
bestselling author**

carolynhart.com
facebook.com/AuthorCarolynHart
penguin.com

FROM *NEW YORK TIMES* BESTSELLING AUTHOR

CAROLYN HART

DEATH ON DEMAND MYSTERIES

Death on Demand

Design for Murder

Something Wicked

Honeymoon with Murder

A Little Class on Murder

Deadly Valentine

The Christie Caper

Southern Ghost

Mint Julep Murder

Yankee Doodle Dead

White Elephant Dead

Sugarplum Dead

April Fool Dead

Engaged to Die

Murder Walks the Plank

Death of the Party

Dead Days of Summer

Death Walked In

Dare to Die

Laughed 'til He Died

Dead by Midnight

Death Comes Silently

Dead, White, and Blue

Death at the Door

Don't Go Home

BAILEY RUTH GHOST MYSTERIES

Ghost Gone Wild

Ghost Wanted

Ghost to the Rescue

Ghost Times Two

Ghost at Work

Ghost in Trouble

carolynhart.com

Penguin Random House

M1323AS0715